A NORMA AND BELLY BOOK

APPLE OF 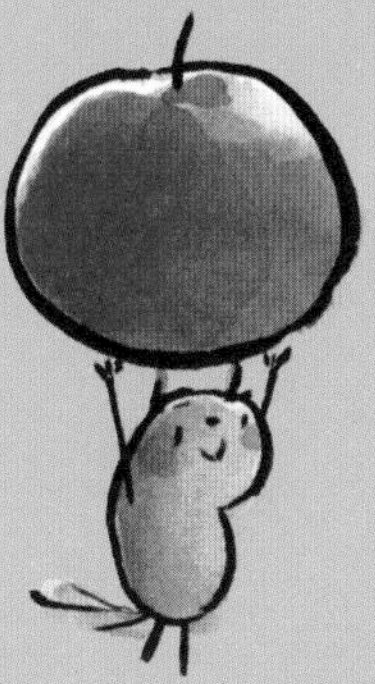 MY PIE

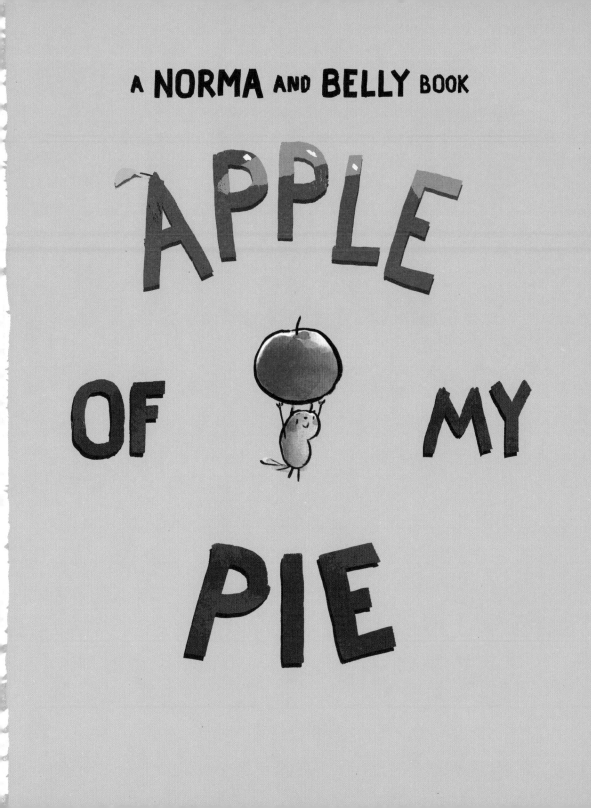

This book was drawn with pencils, sumi brushes, sumi ink, and watercolors on watercolor paper.

Text, cover art, and interior illustrations copyright © 2021 by Mika Song

All rights reserved. Published in the United States by RH Graphic, an imprint of Random House Children's Books, a division of Penguin Random House LLC, New York.

RH Graphic with the book design is a trademark of Penguin Random House LLC.

Visit us on the web and sign up for our newsletter! RHKidsGraphic.com • @RHKidsGraphic

Educators and librarians, for a variety of teaching tools, visit us at RHTeachersLibrarians.com

Library of Congress Cataloging-in-Publication Data is available upon request.
ISBN 978-1-9848-9585-1 (hc) — ISBN 978-0-593-12540-3 (lib. bdg.) — ISBN 978-1-9848-9586-8 (ebk)

Designed by Patrick Crotty

MANUFACTURED IN CHINA
10 9 8 7 6 5 4 3 2 1
First Edition

RH GRAPHIC
A comic on every bookshelf.

A NORMA AND BELLY BOOK

APPLE OF 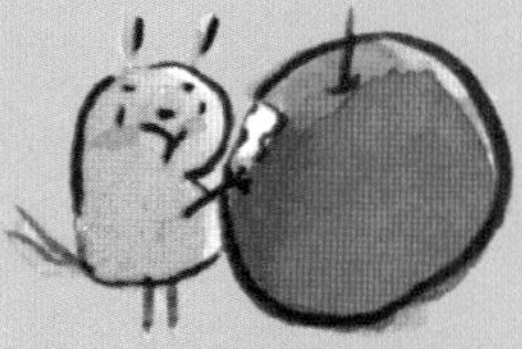 MY PIE

Mika Song

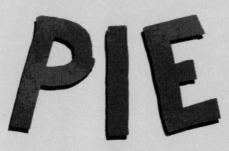

Also by Mika Song

———

Tea with Oliver
Picnic with Oliver
Donut Feed the Squirrels

To my grandparents

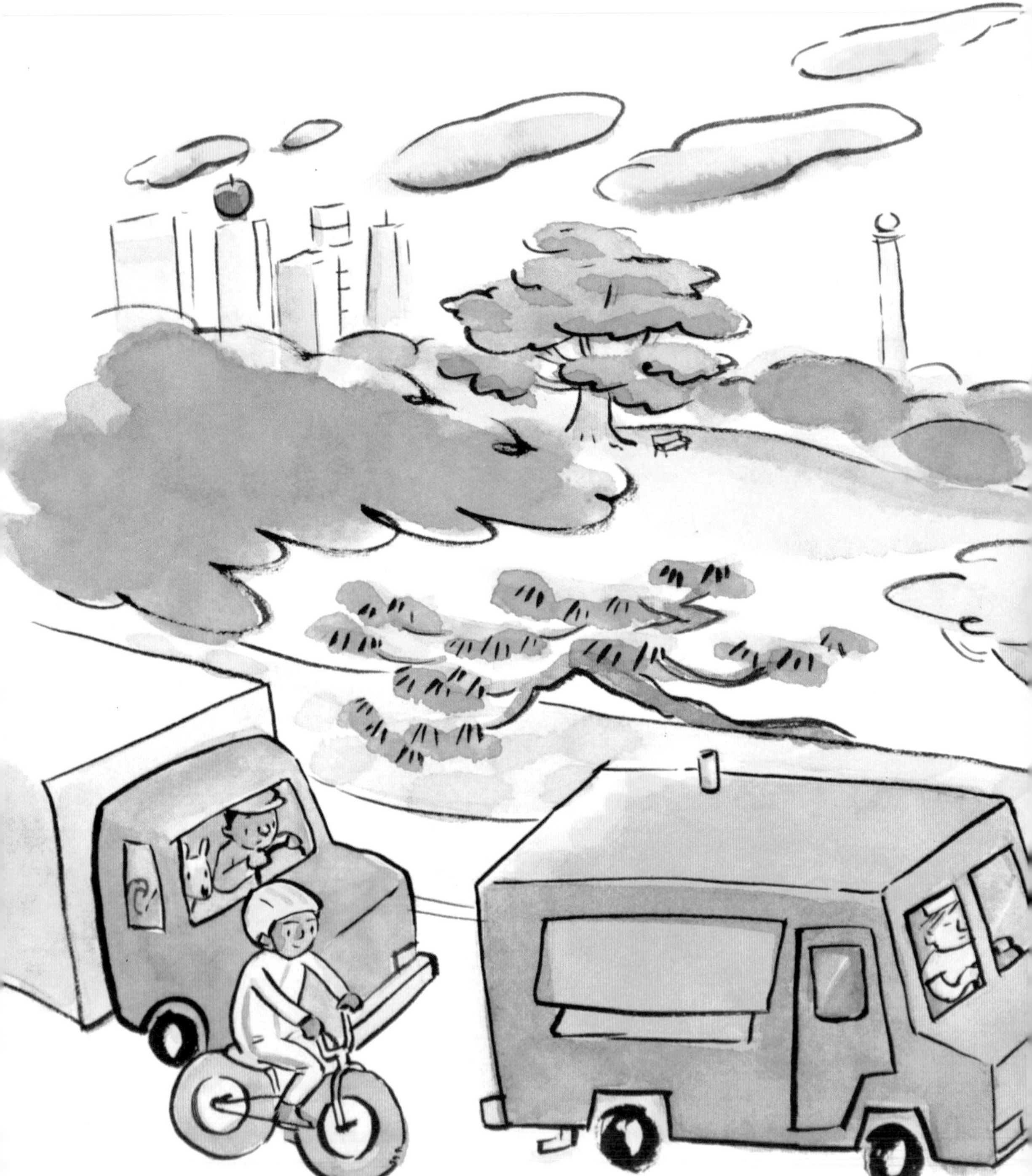

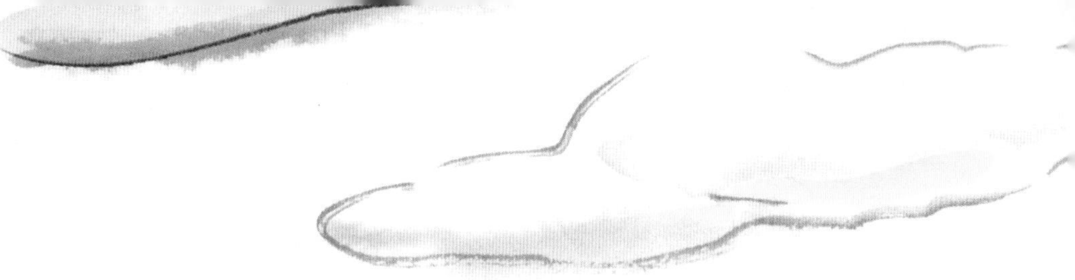

chapter 1

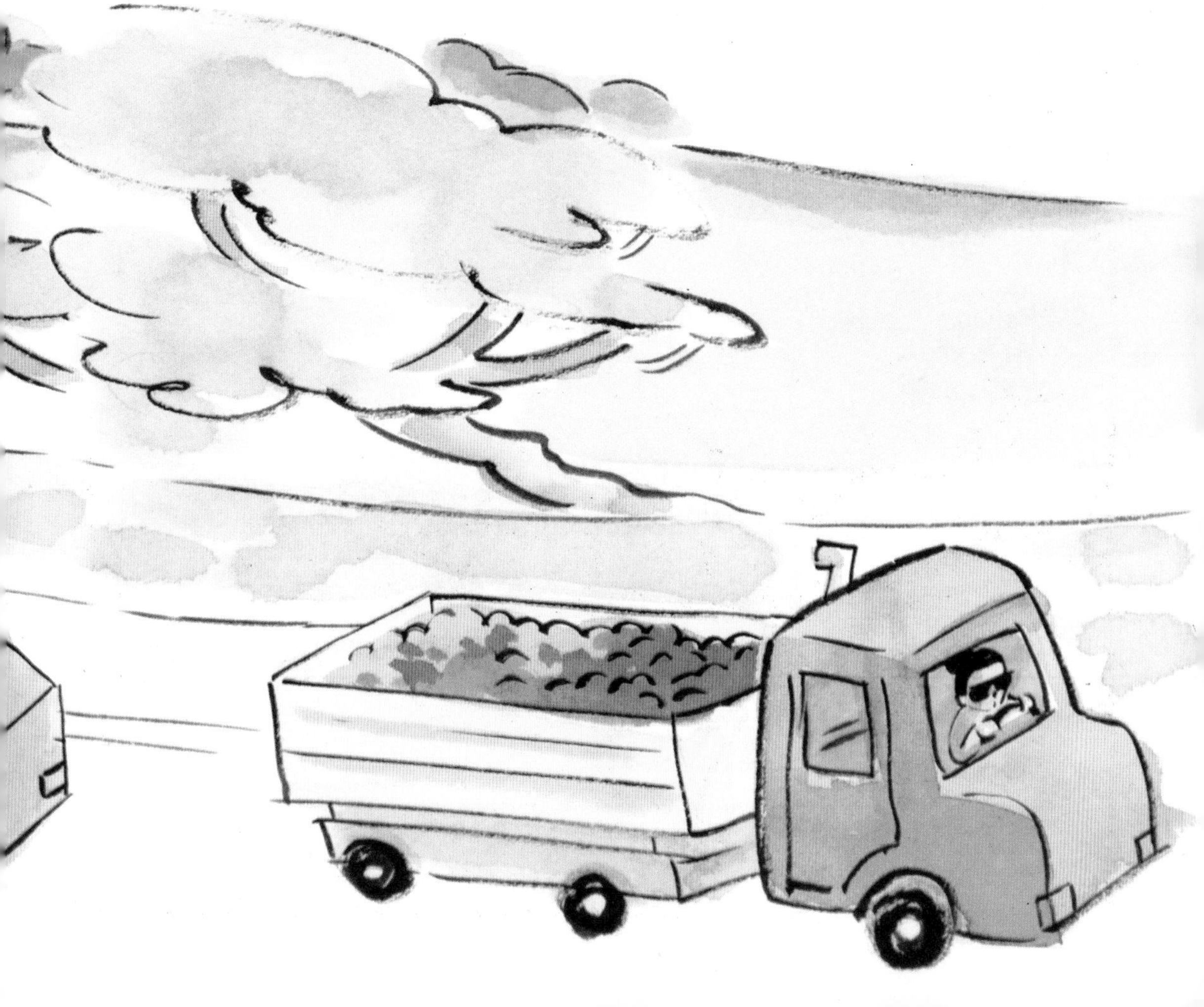

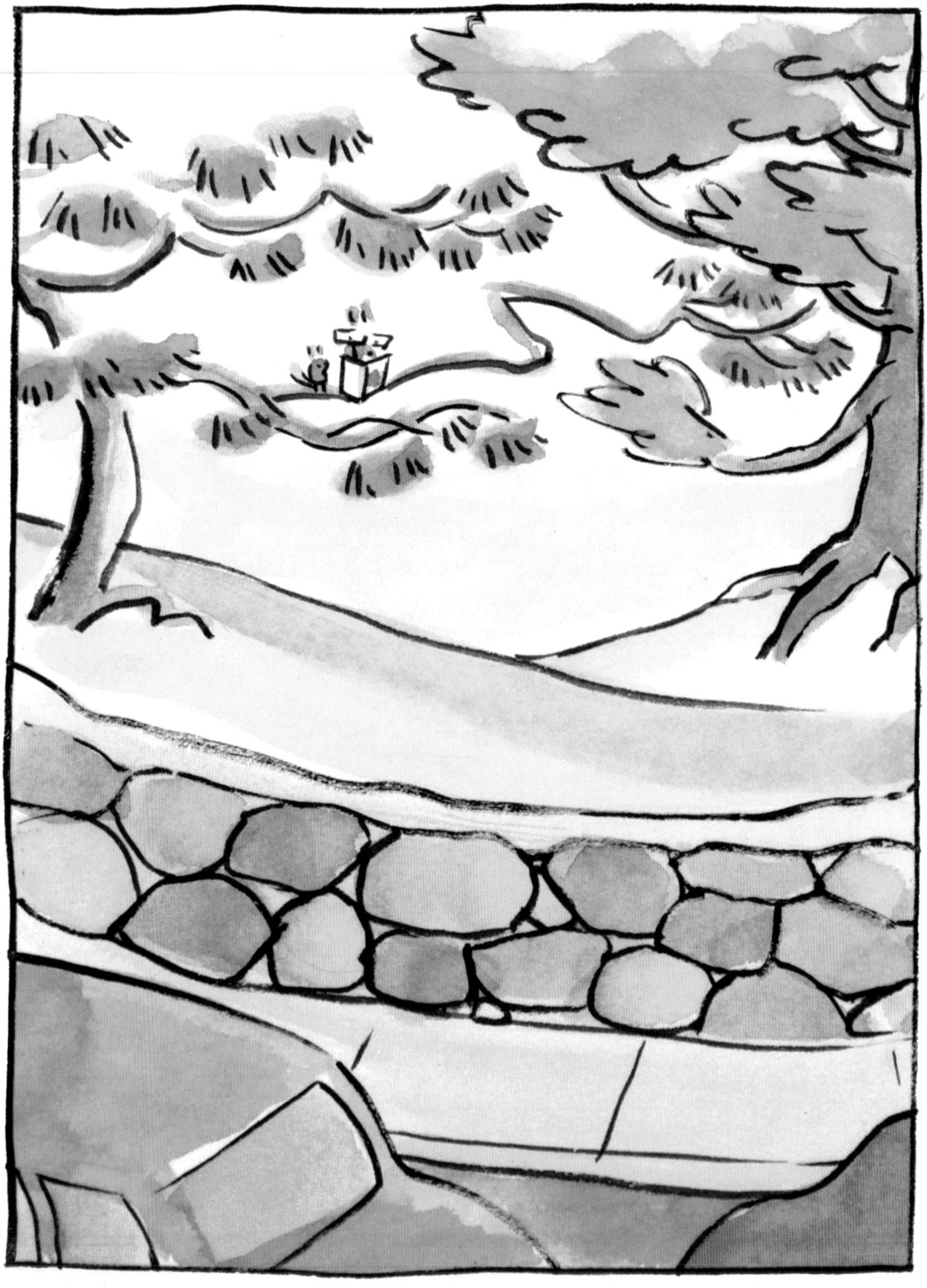

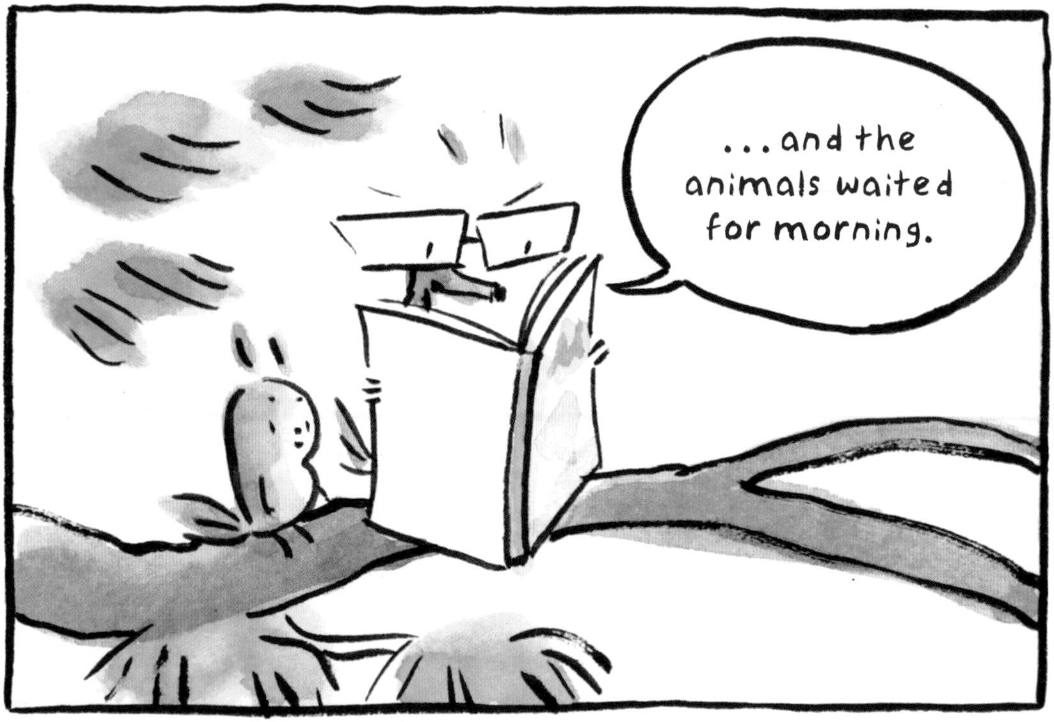
...and the animals waited for morning.

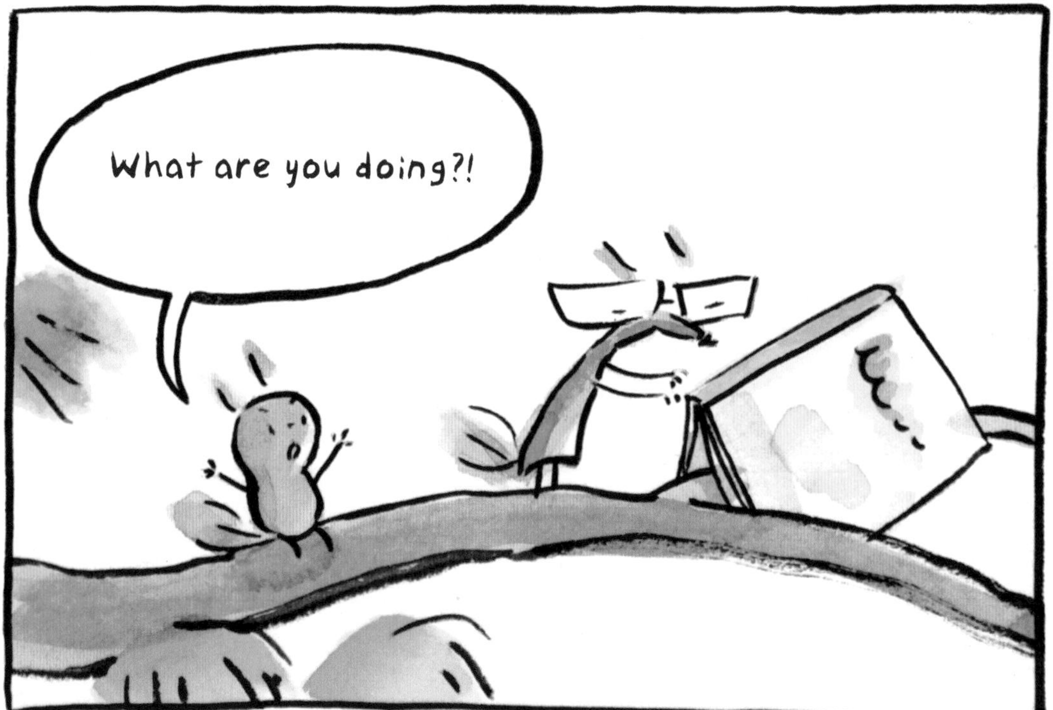
What are you doing?!

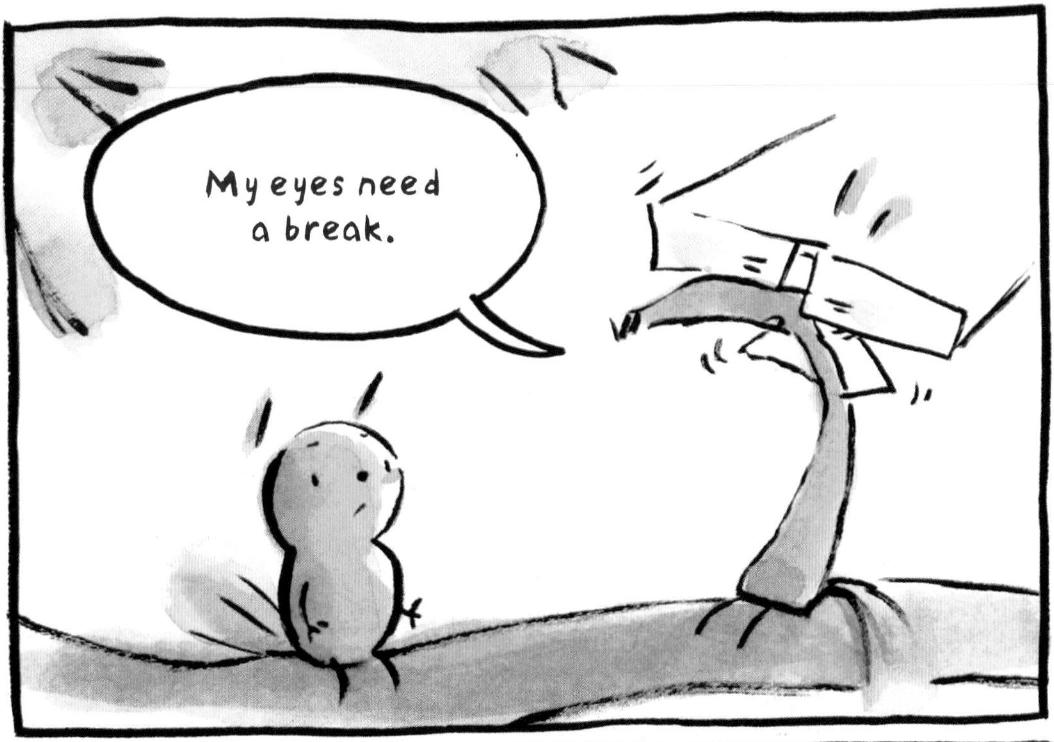
My eyes need a break.

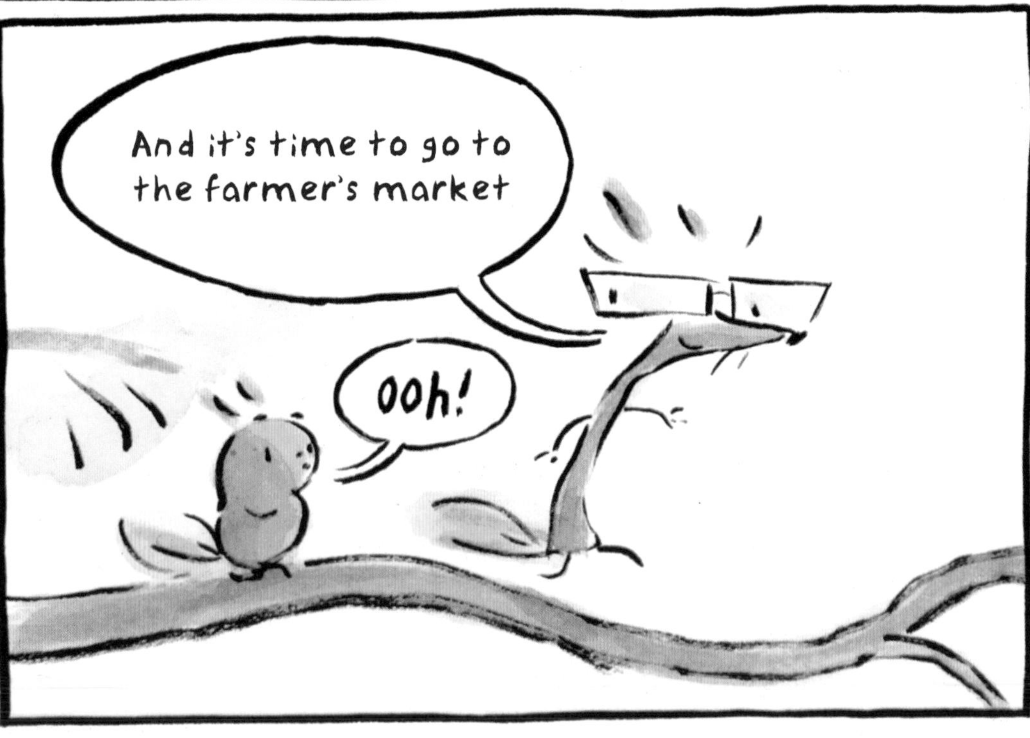
And it's time to go to the farmer's market
OOh!

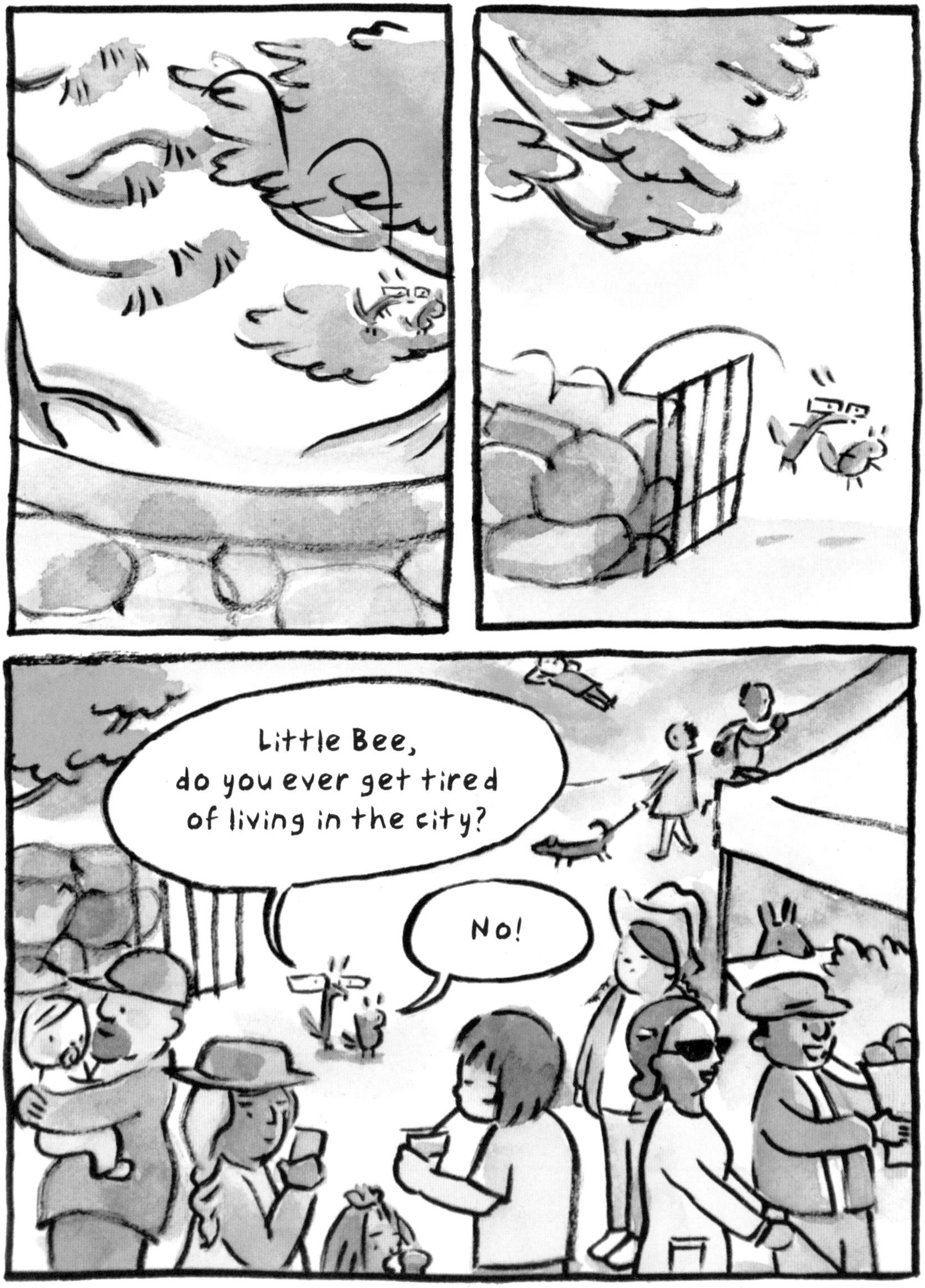
Little Bee,
do you ever get tired
of living in the city?
No!

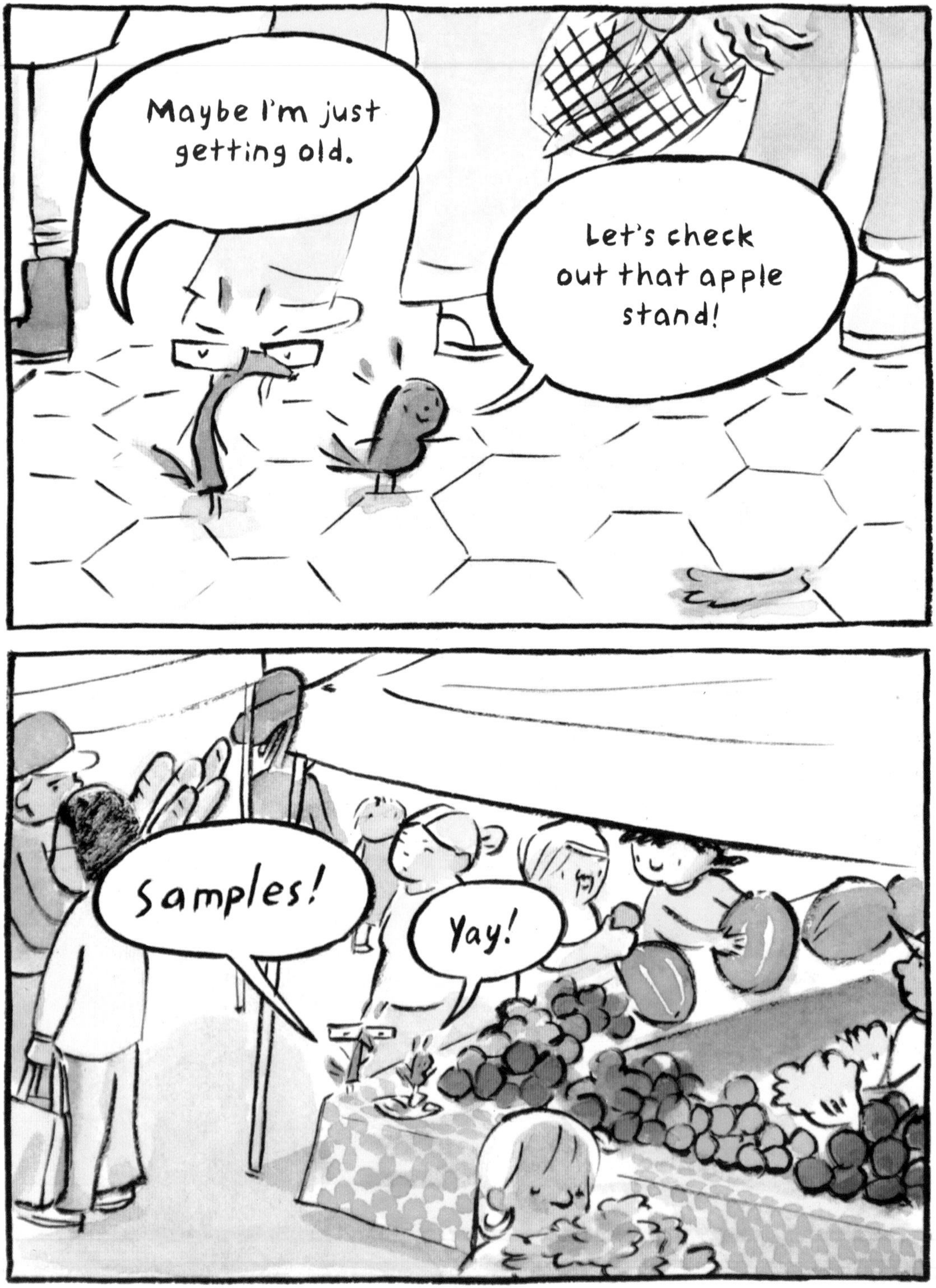

Maybe I'm just getting old.
Let's check out that apple stand!
Samples!
Yay!

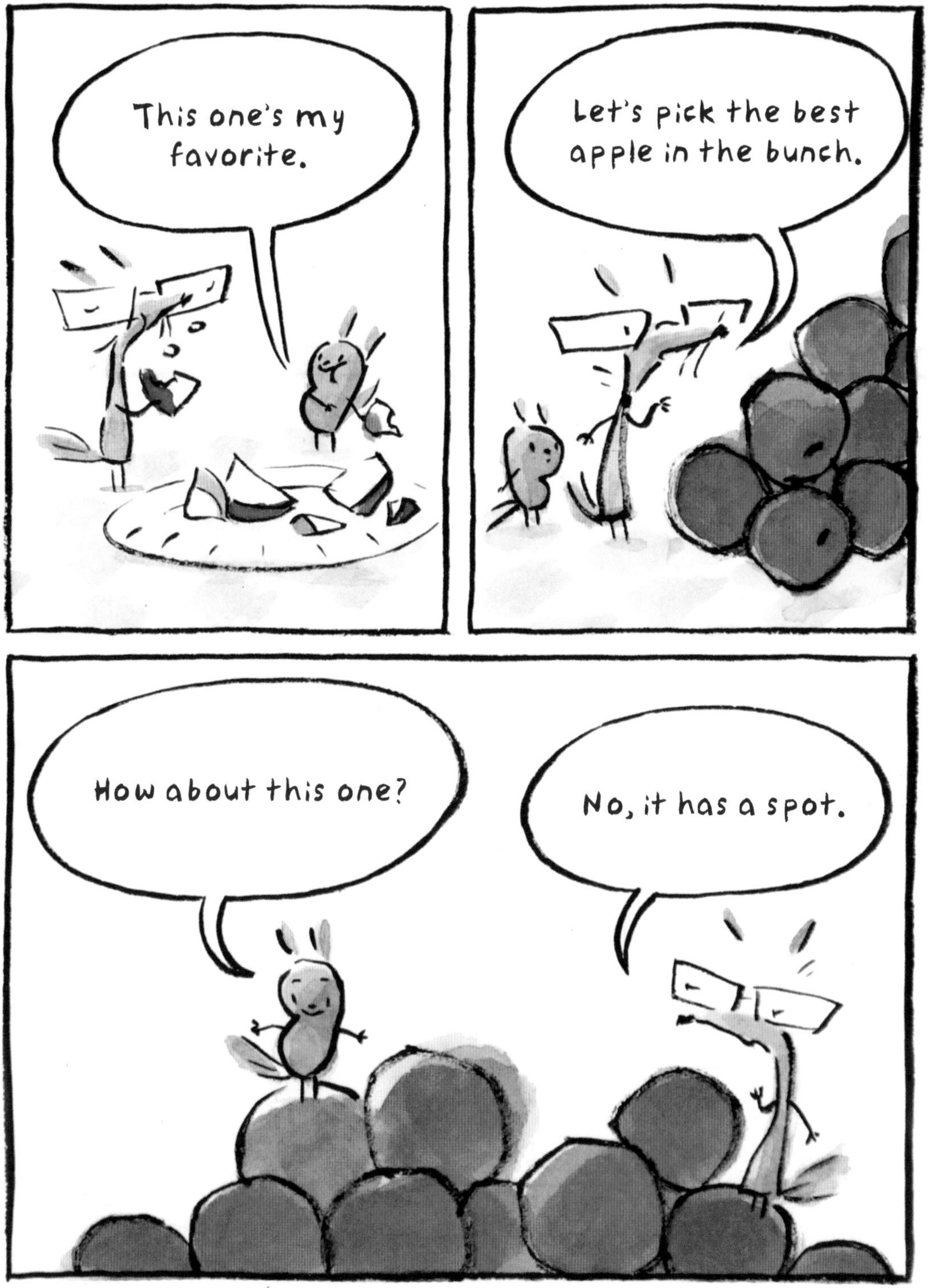
This one's my favorite.
Let's pick the best apple in the bunch.
How about this one?
No, it has a spot.

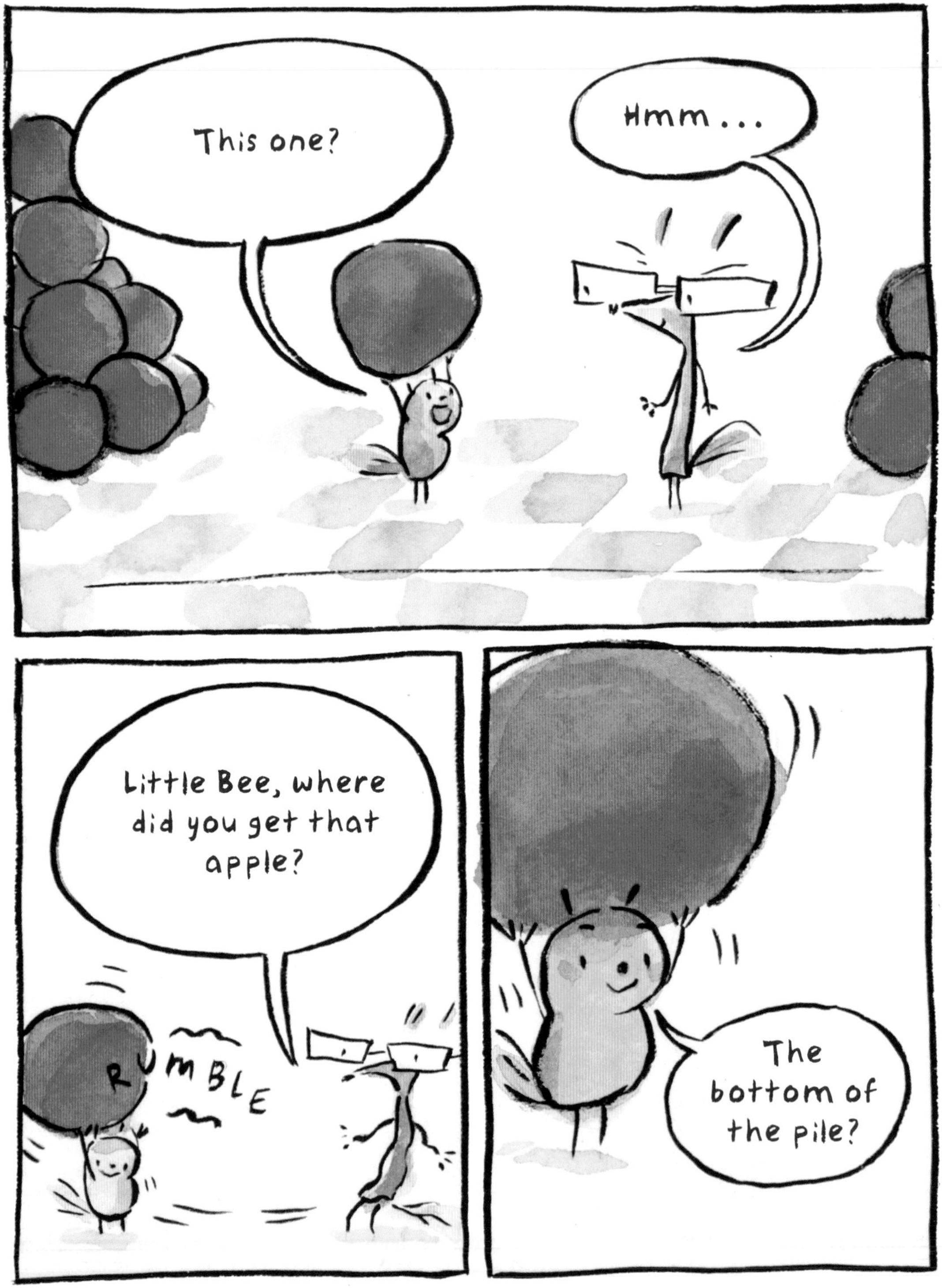
This one?
Hmm...
Little Bee, where did you get that apple?
RUMBLE
The bottom of the pile?

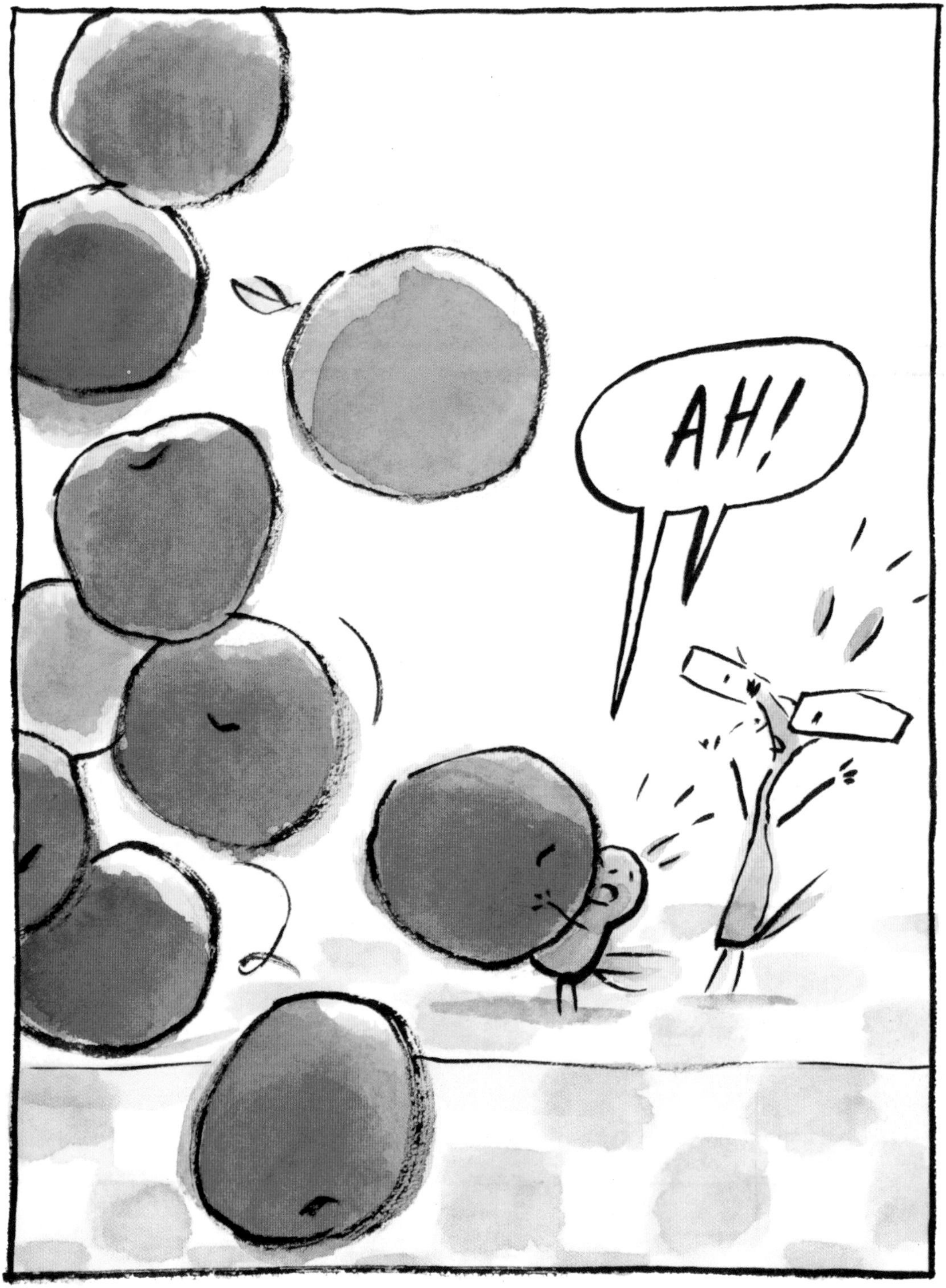
AH!

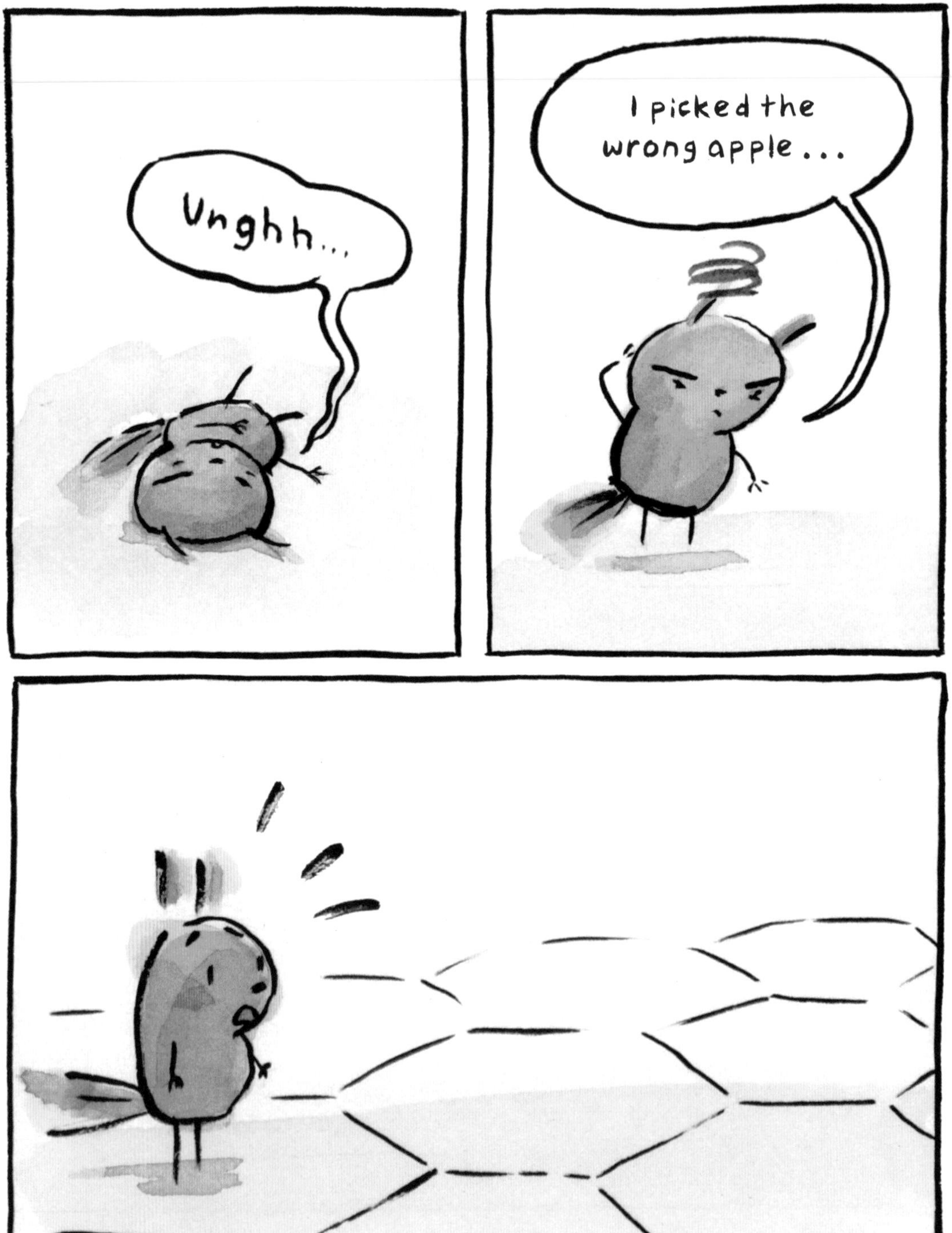
Unghh...
I picked the wrong apple...

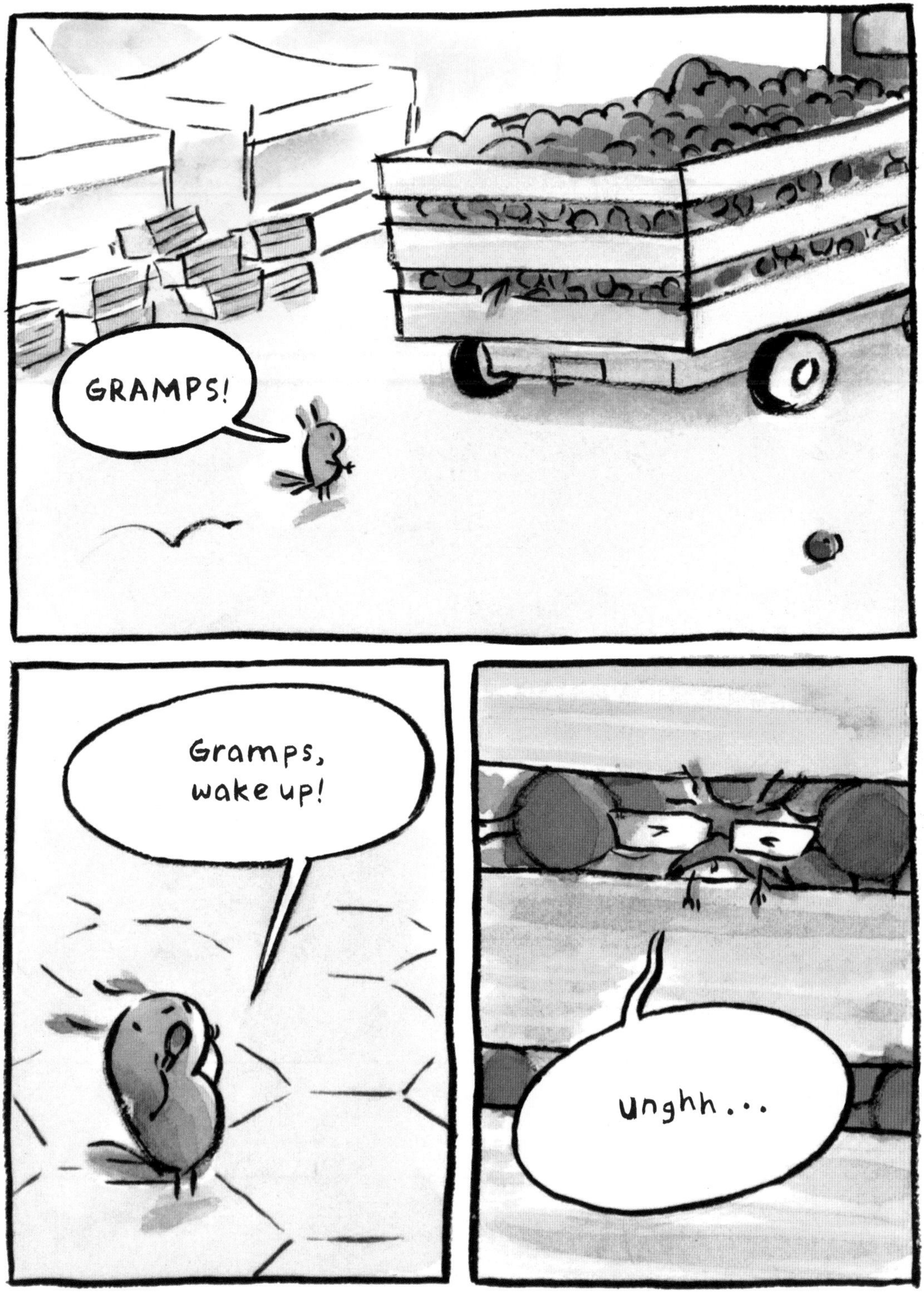
GRAMPS!
Gramps, wake up!
unghh...

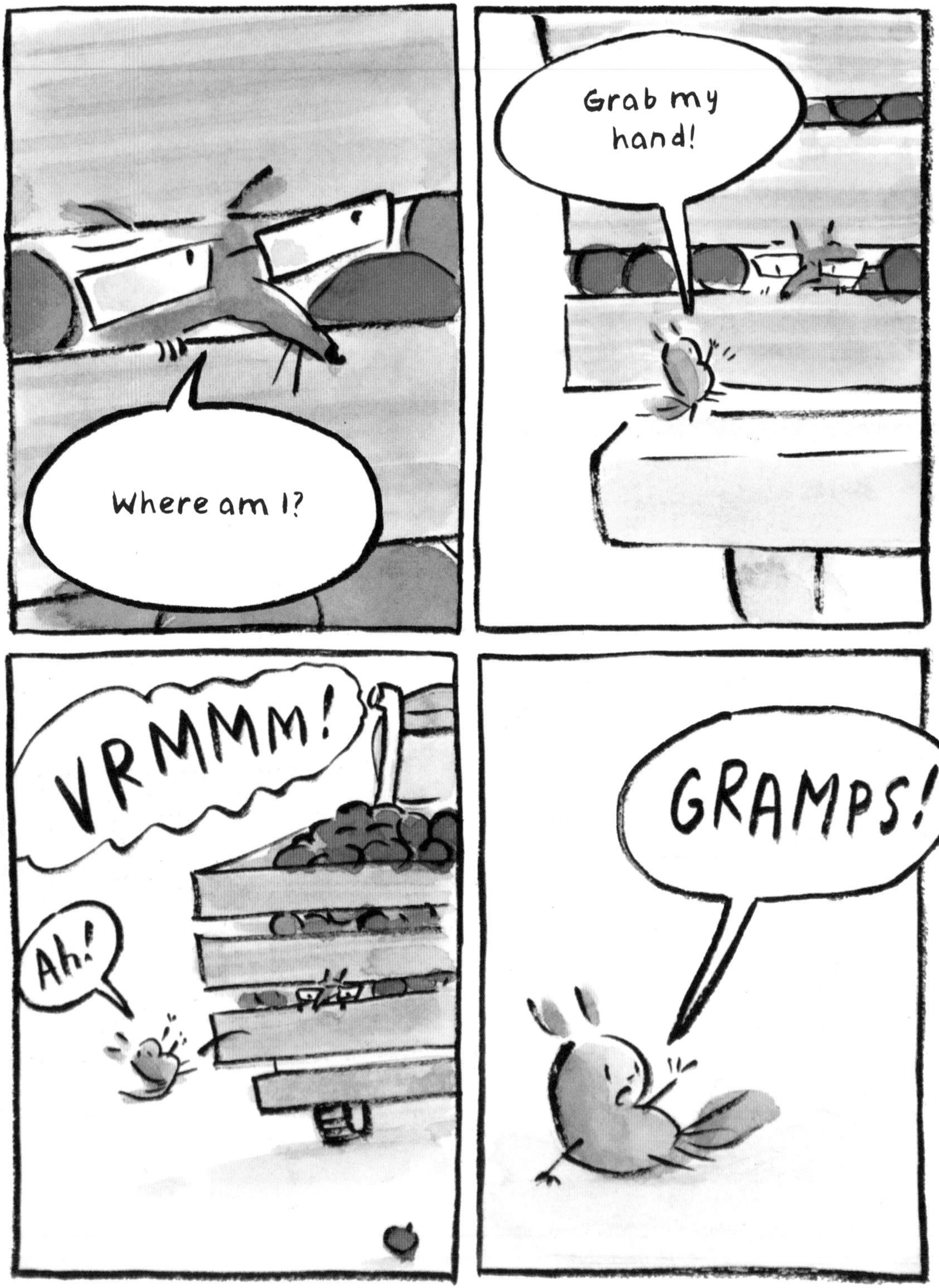
Where am I?
Grab my hand!
VRMMM!
Ah!
GRAMPS!

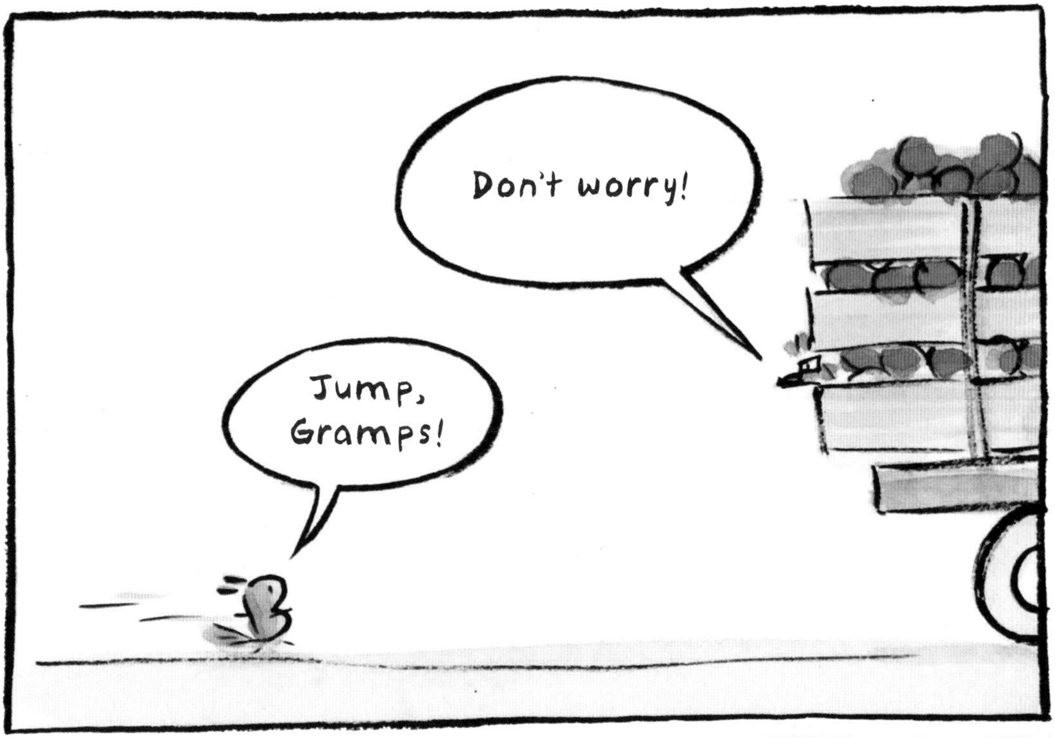
Don't worry!
Jump, Gramps!

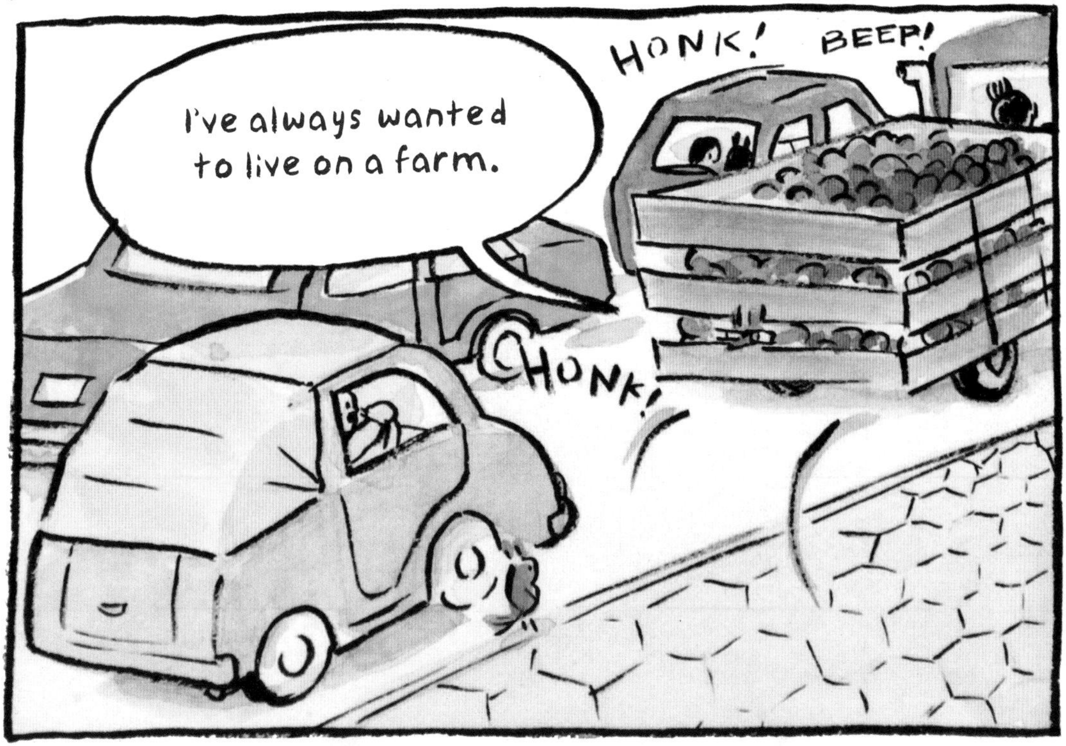
HONK! BEEP!
I've always wanted to live on a farm.
HONK!

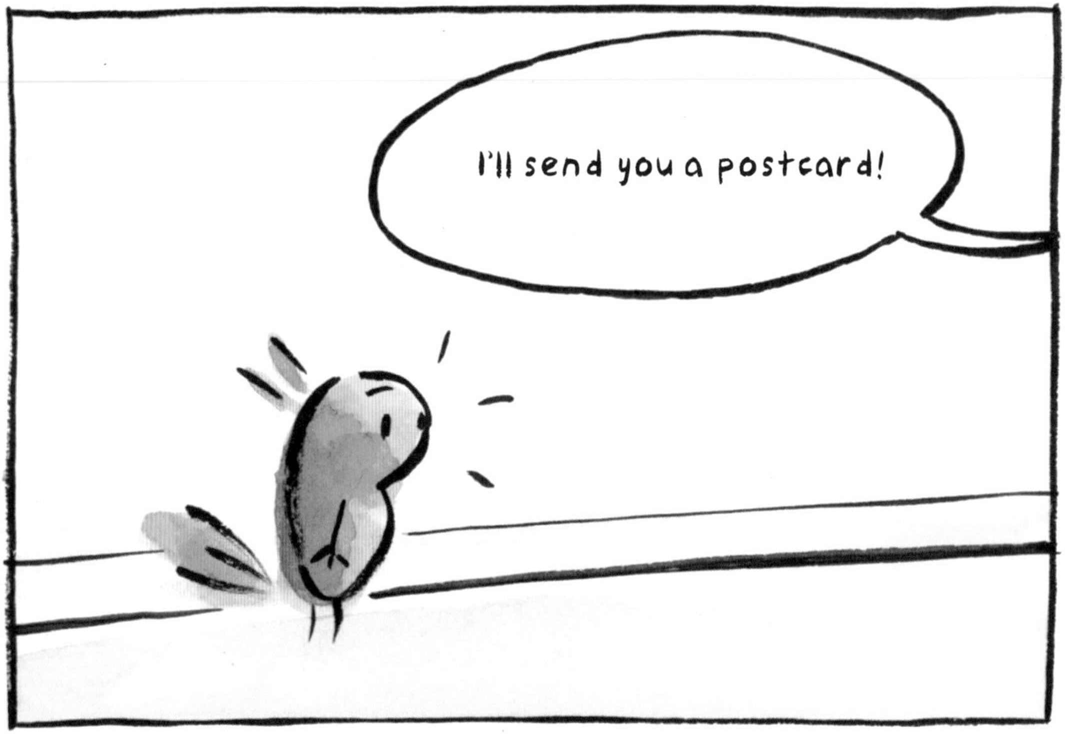
I'll send you a postcard!

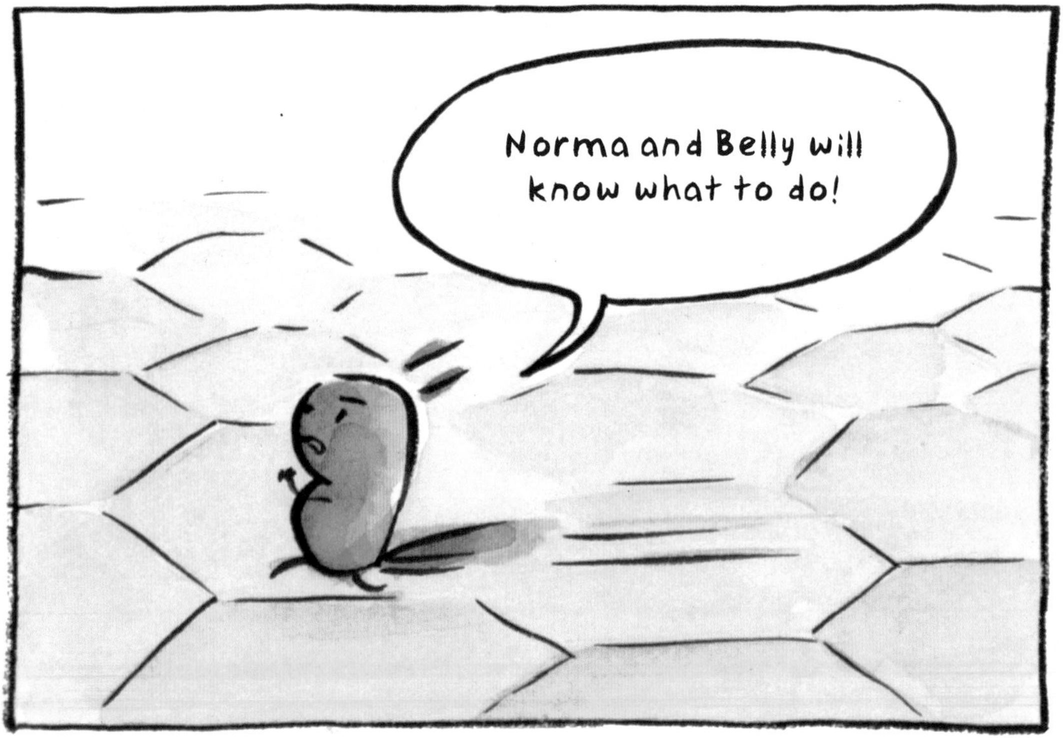
Norma and Belly will know what to do!

chapter 2

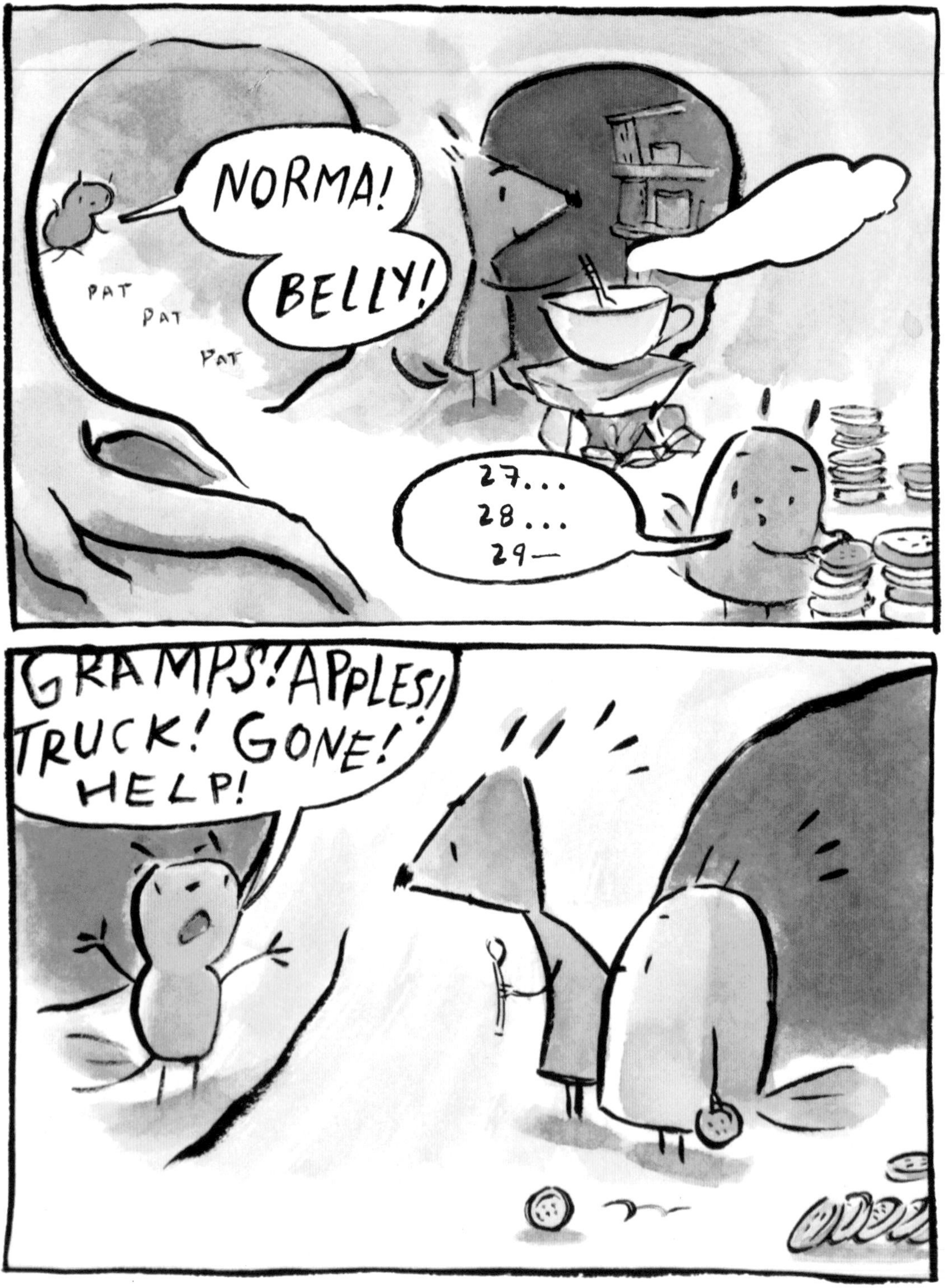
NORMA!
BELLY!
PAT PAT PAT
27...
28...
29—
GRAMPS! APPLES! TRUCK! GONE! HELP!

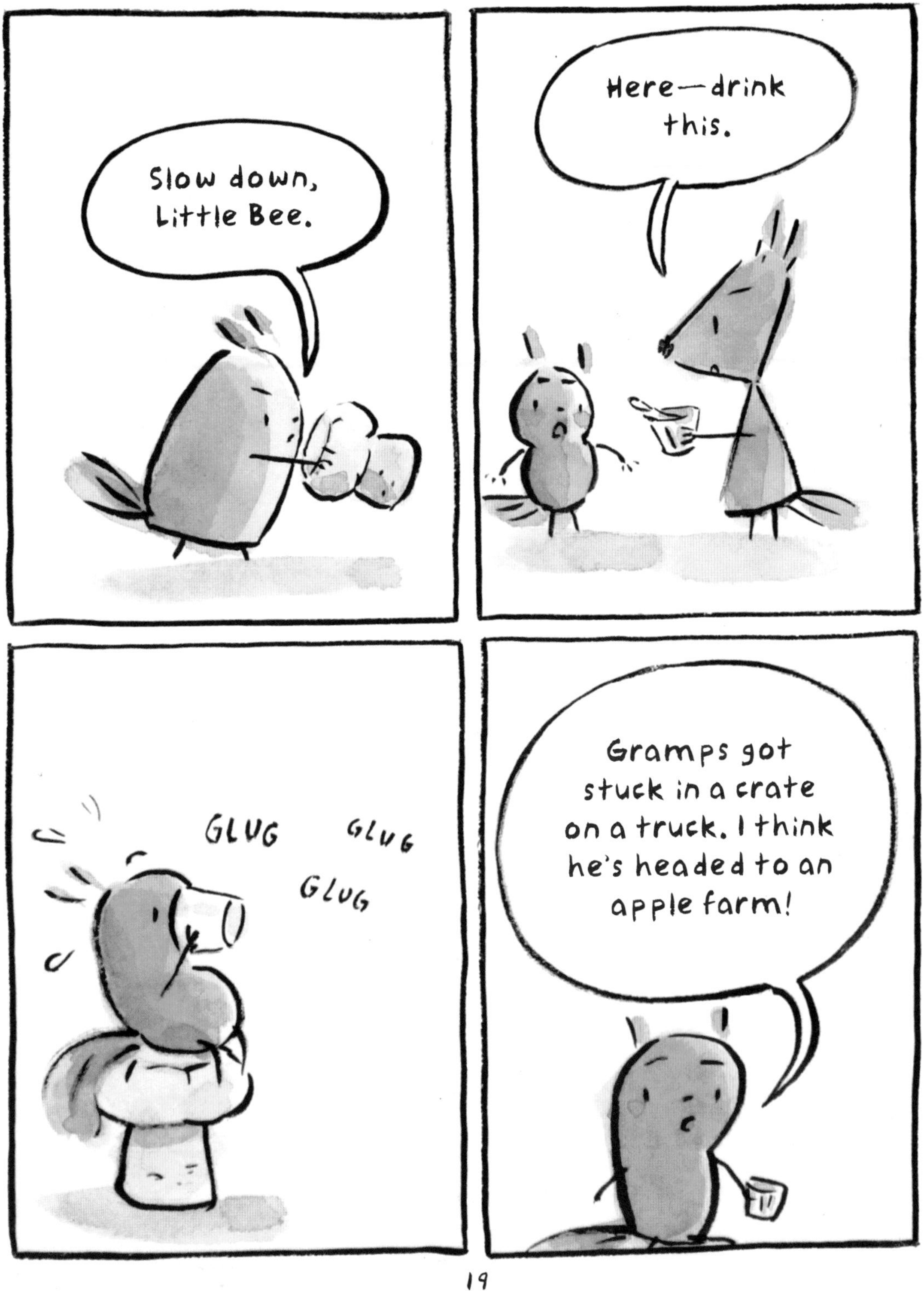

Slow down, Little Bee.
Here—drink this.
GLUG
GLUG
GLUG
Gramps got stuck in a crate on a truck. I think he's headed to an apple farm!

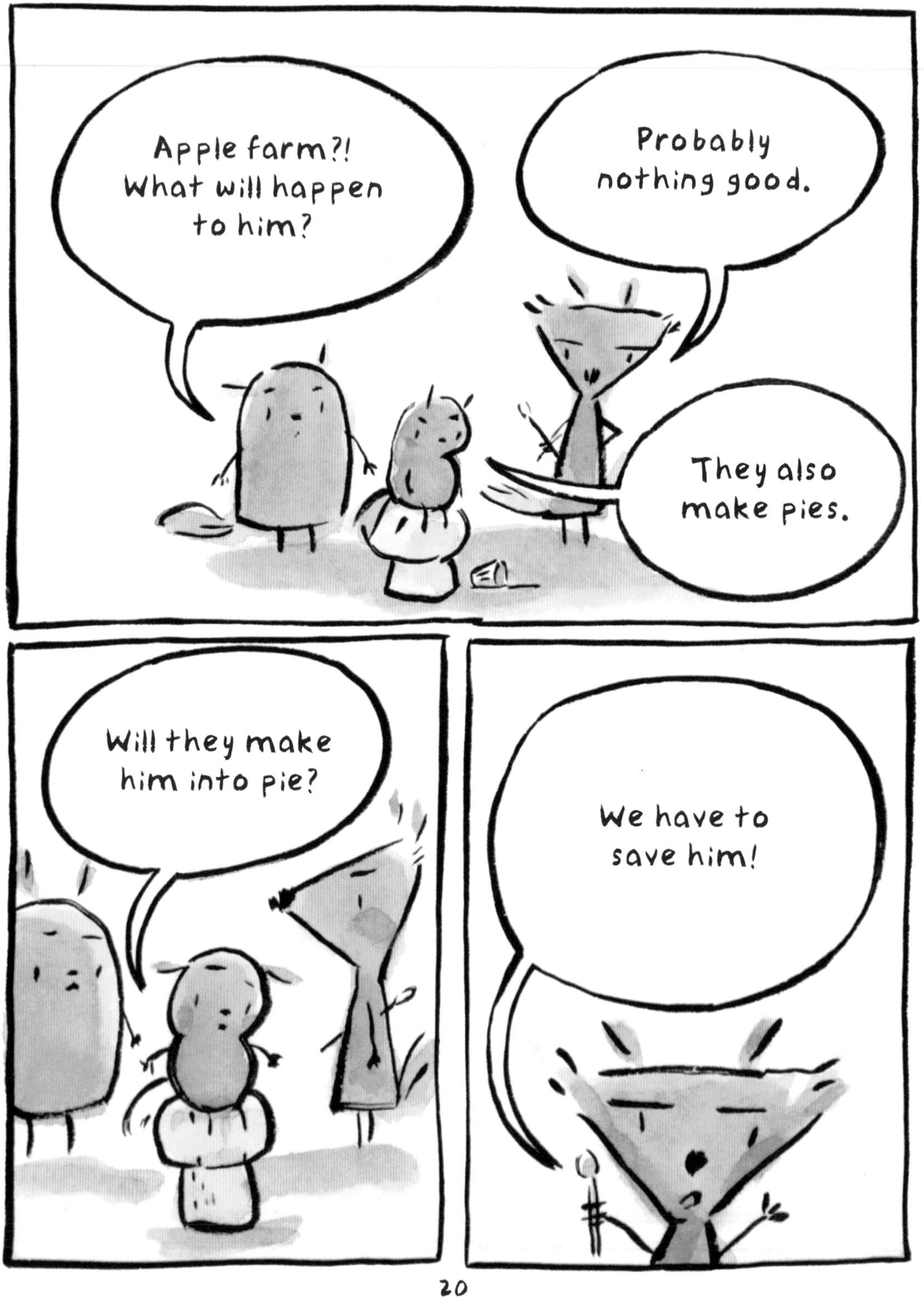
Apple farm?! What will happen to him?
Probably nothing good.
They also make pies.
Will they make him into pie?
We have to save him!

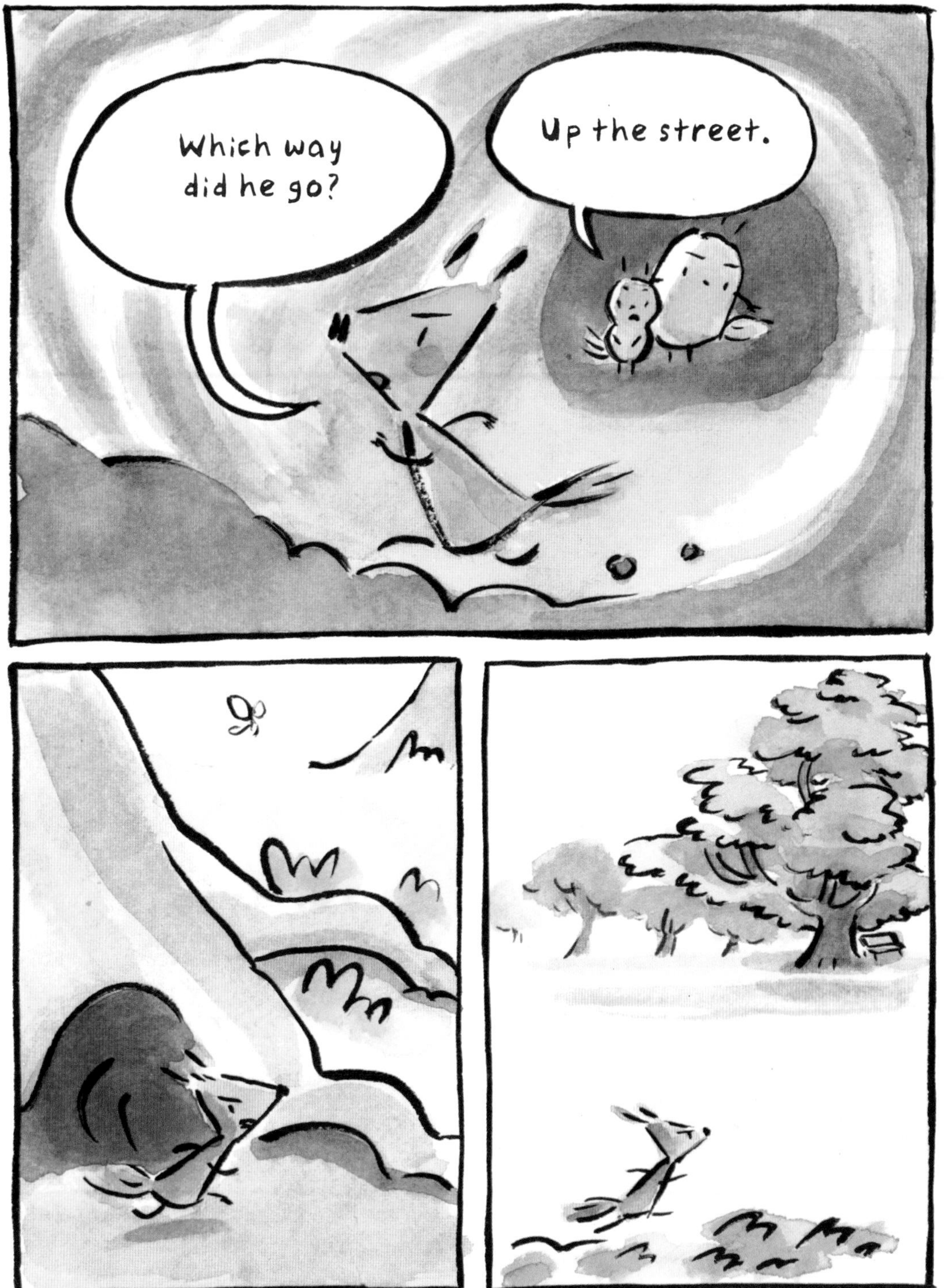
Which way did he go?
Up the street.

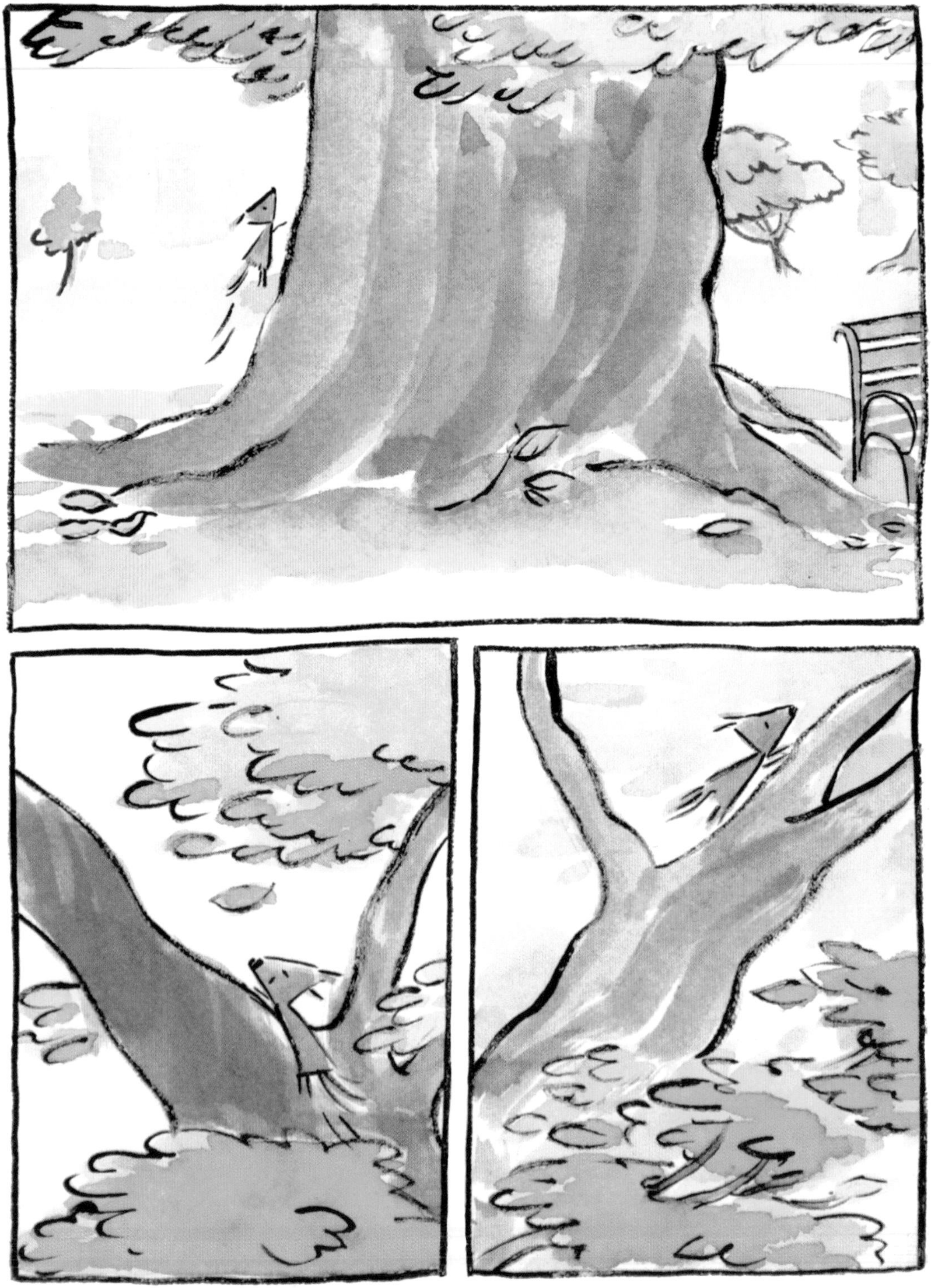

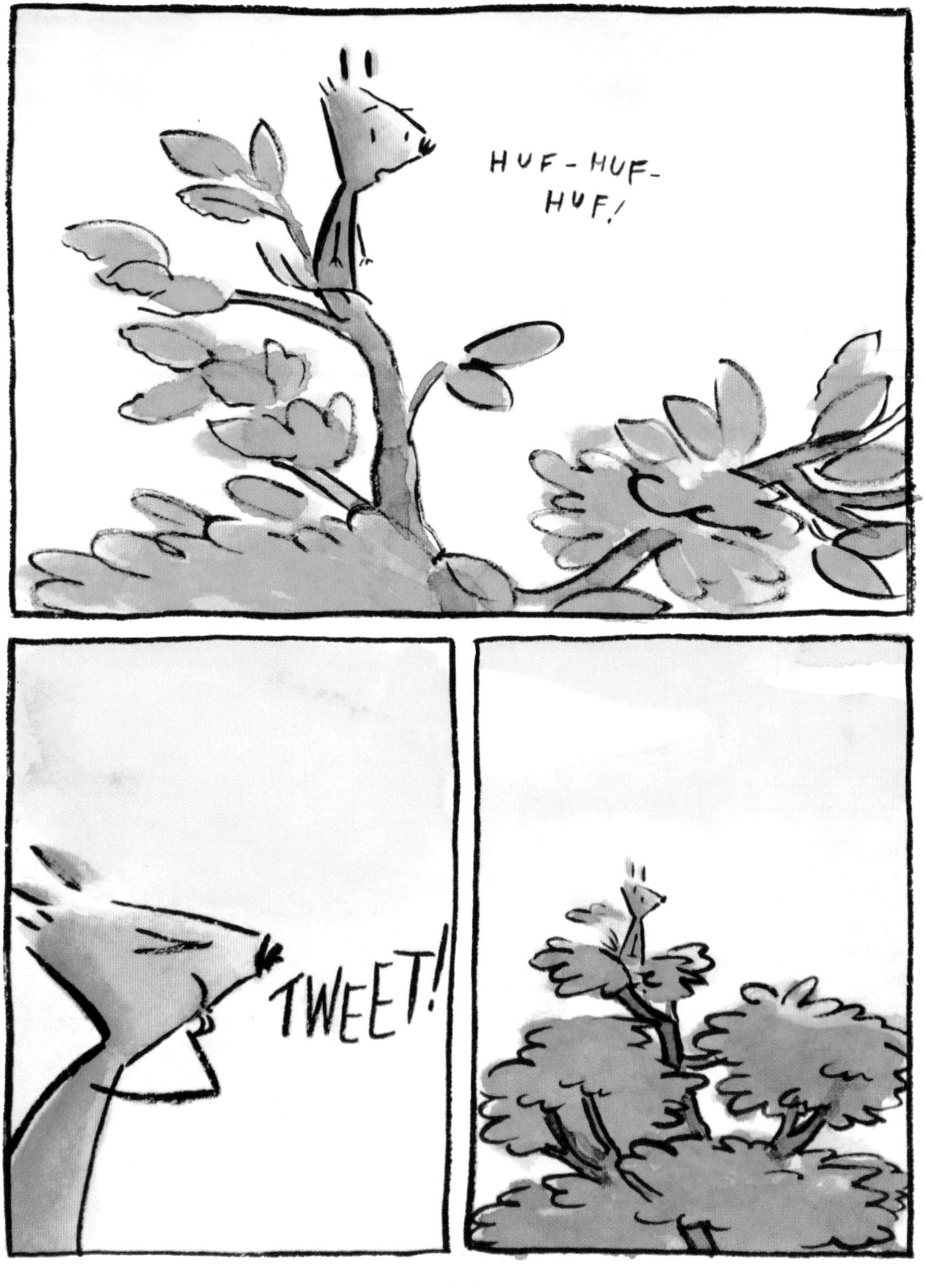
HUF-HUF-
HUF!
TWEET!

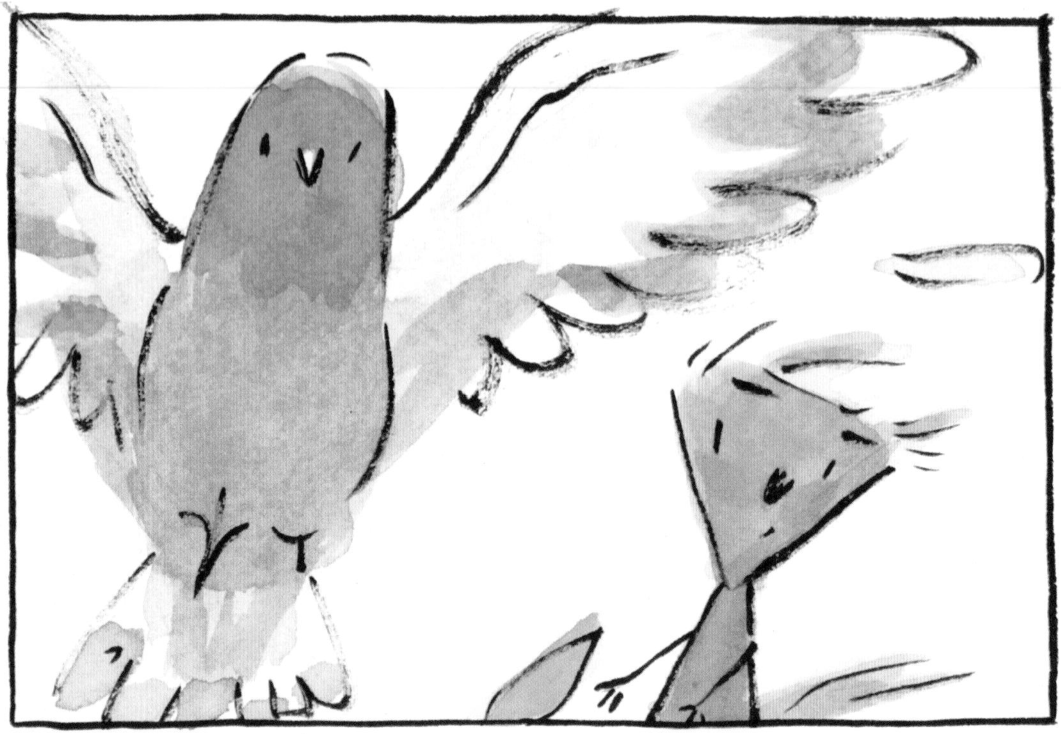

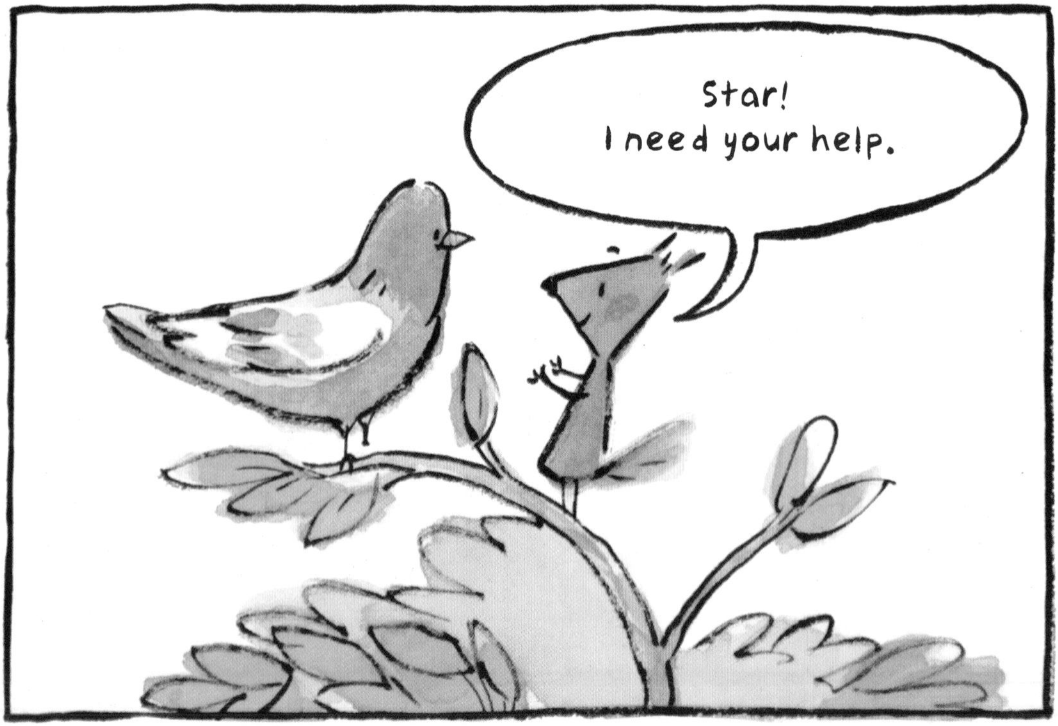
Star!
I need your help.

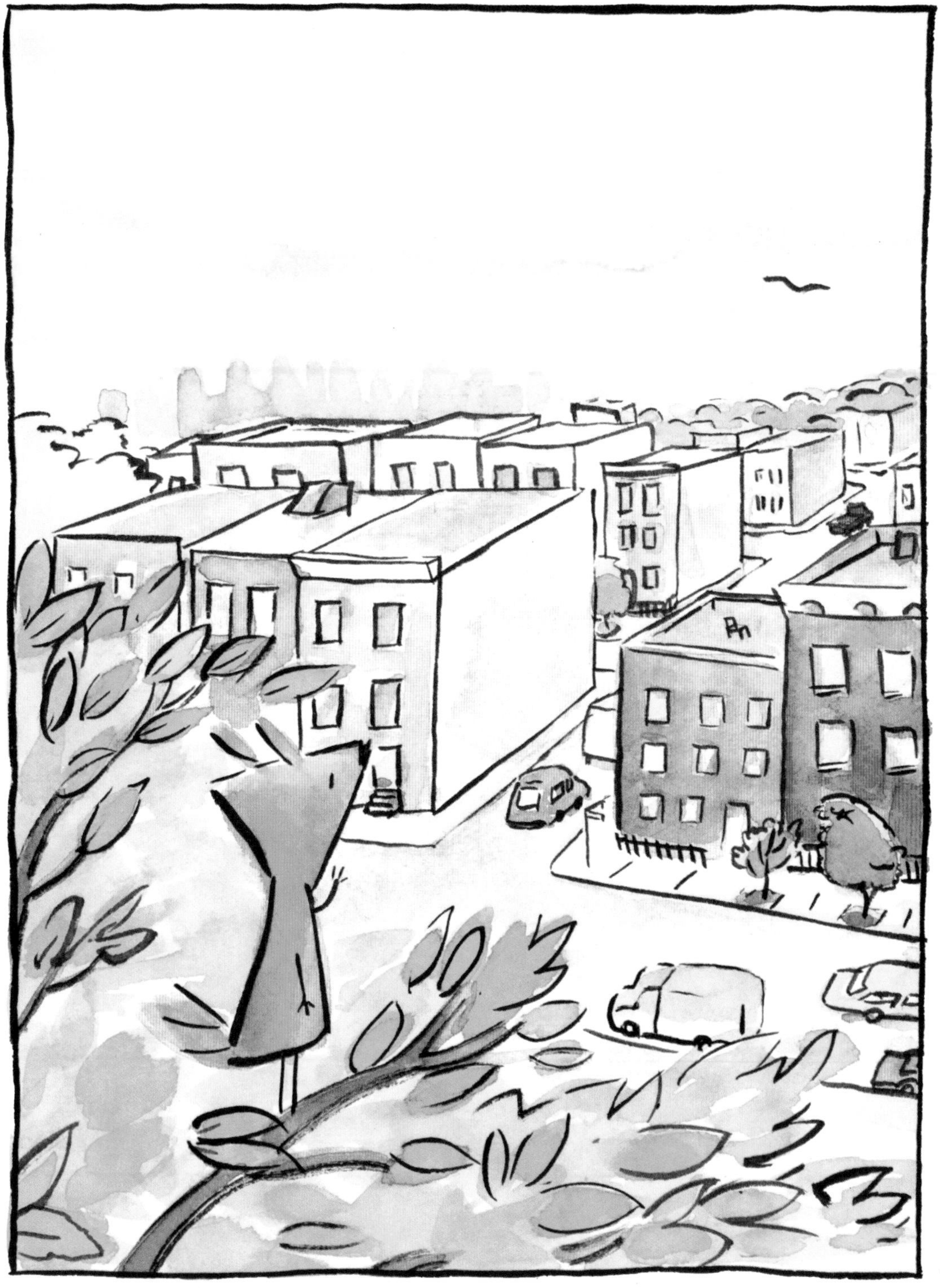

chapter 3

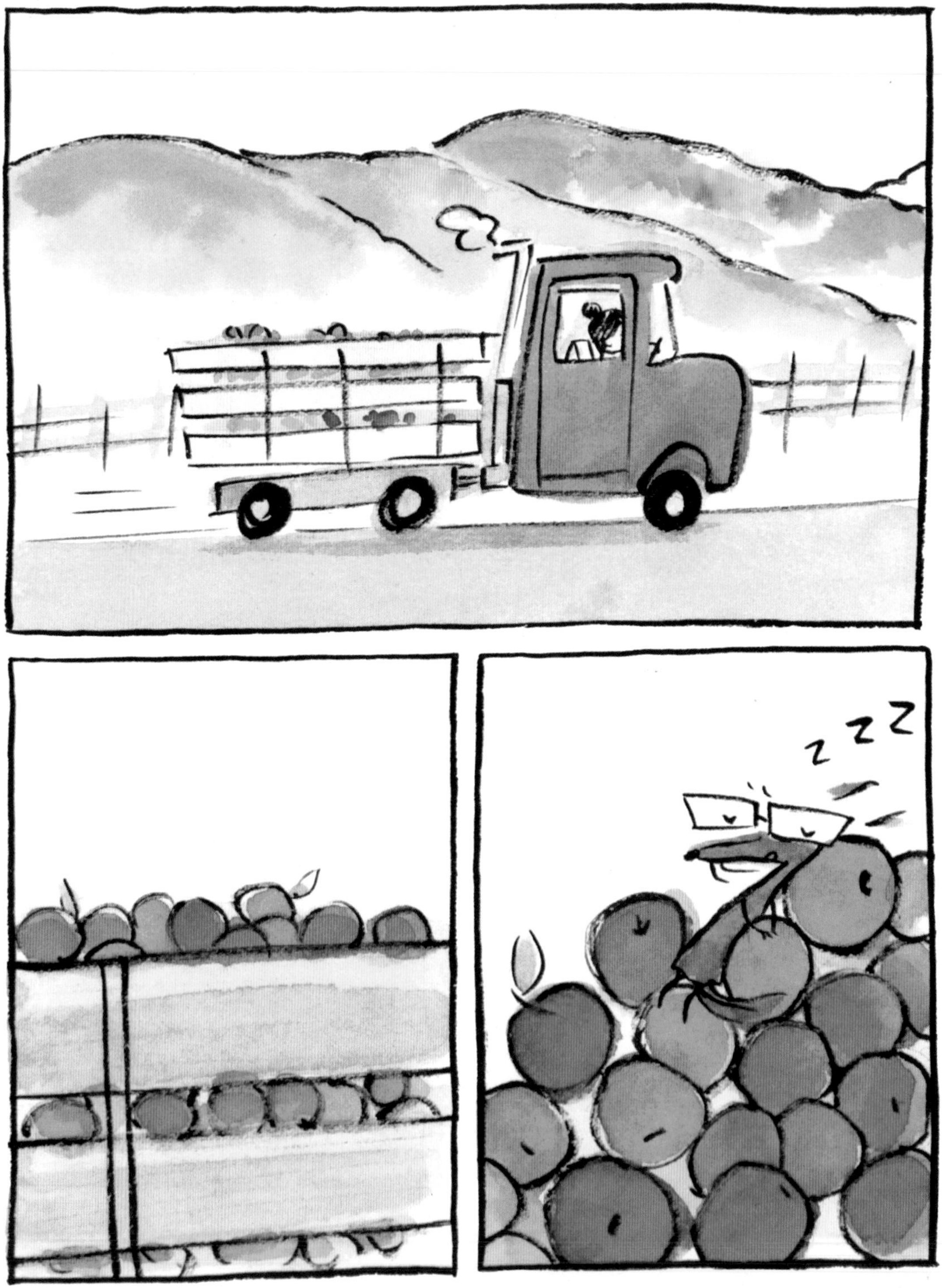
Z Z Z

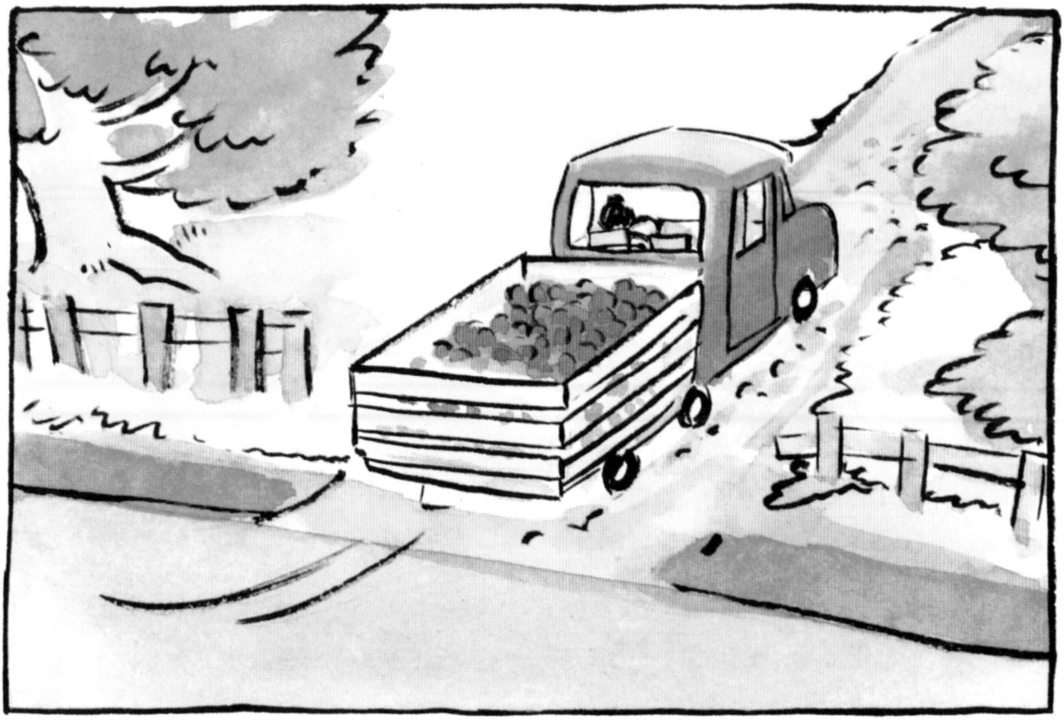

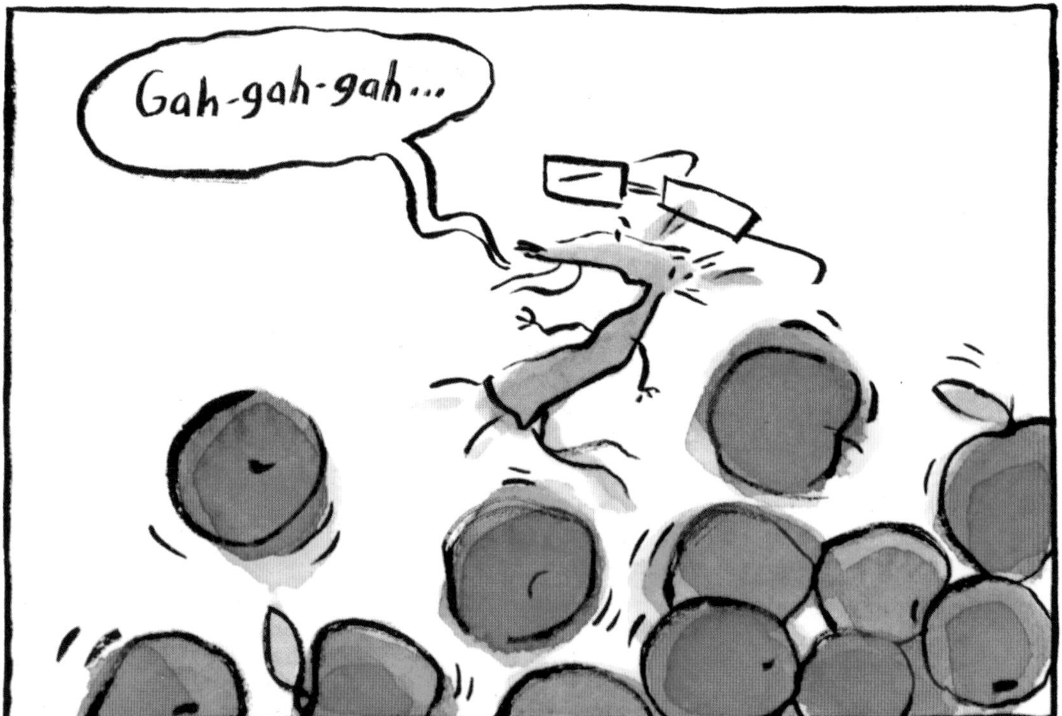
Gah-gah-gah...

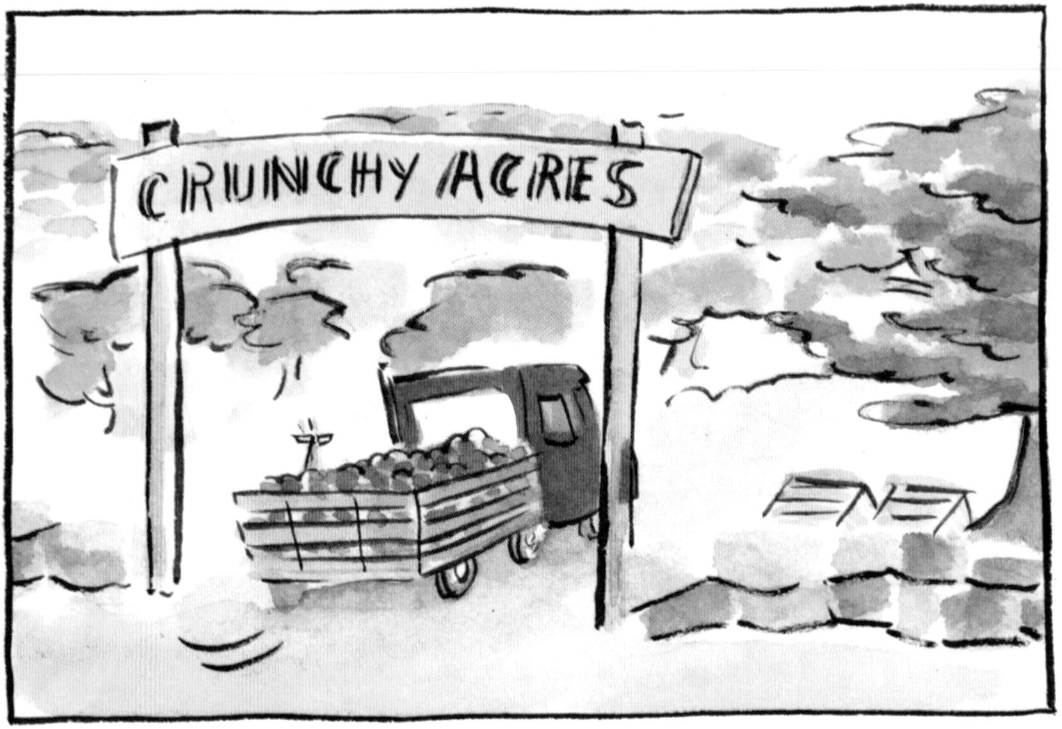
CRUNCHY ACRES

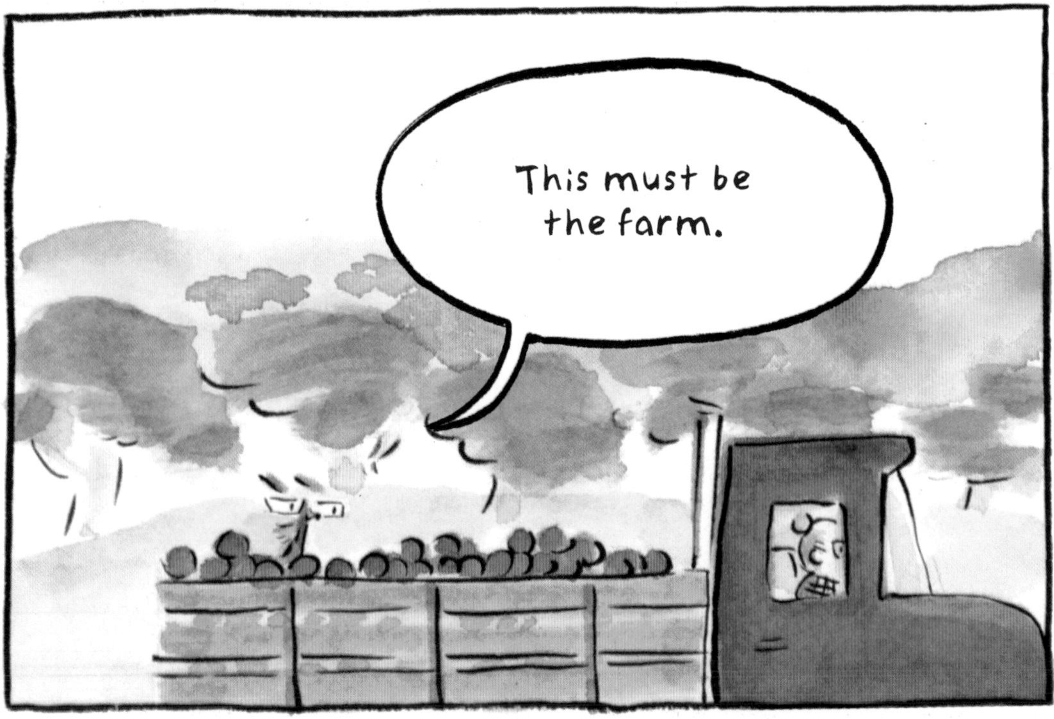
This must be the farm.

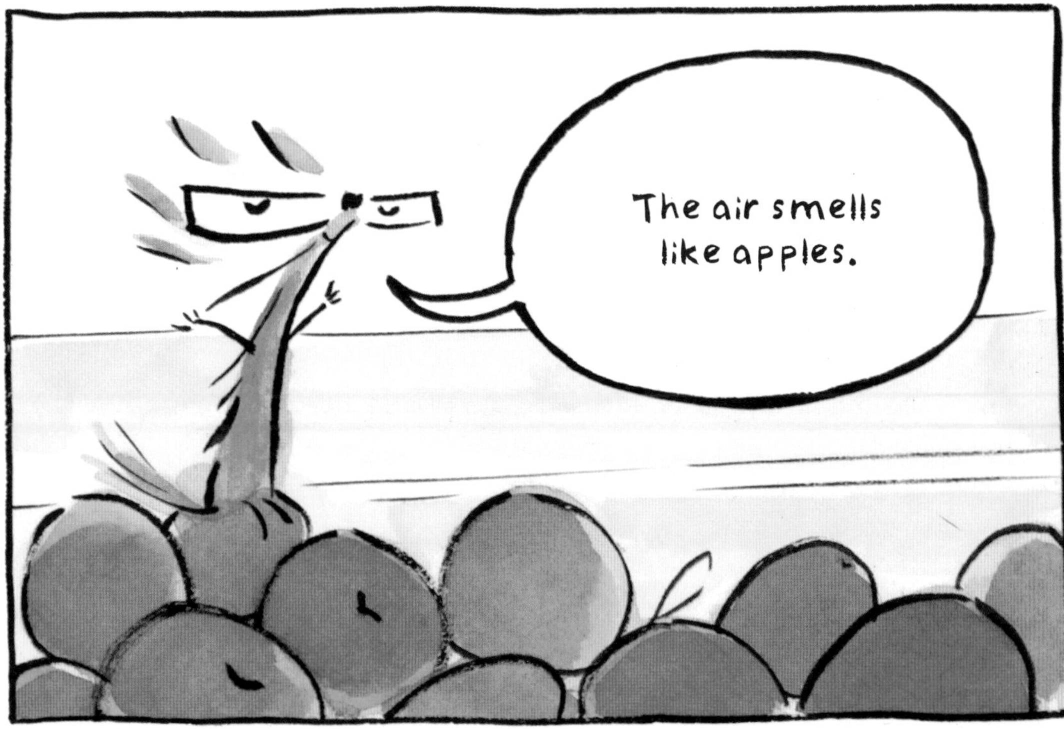
The air smells like apples.

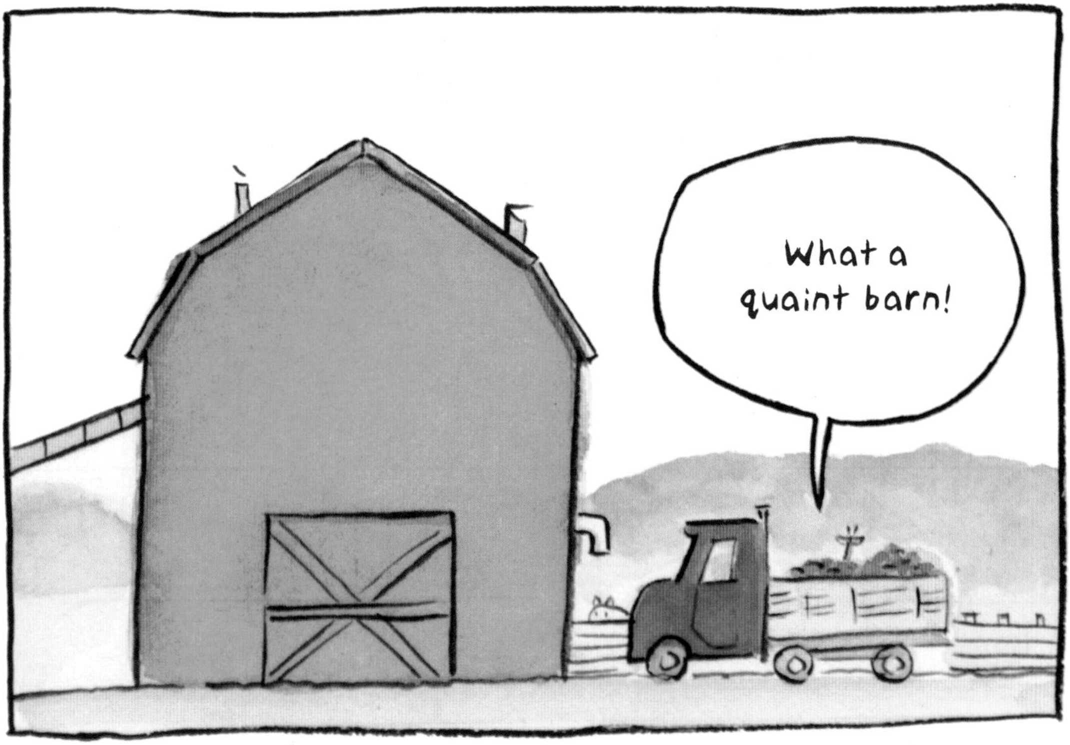
What a quaint barn!

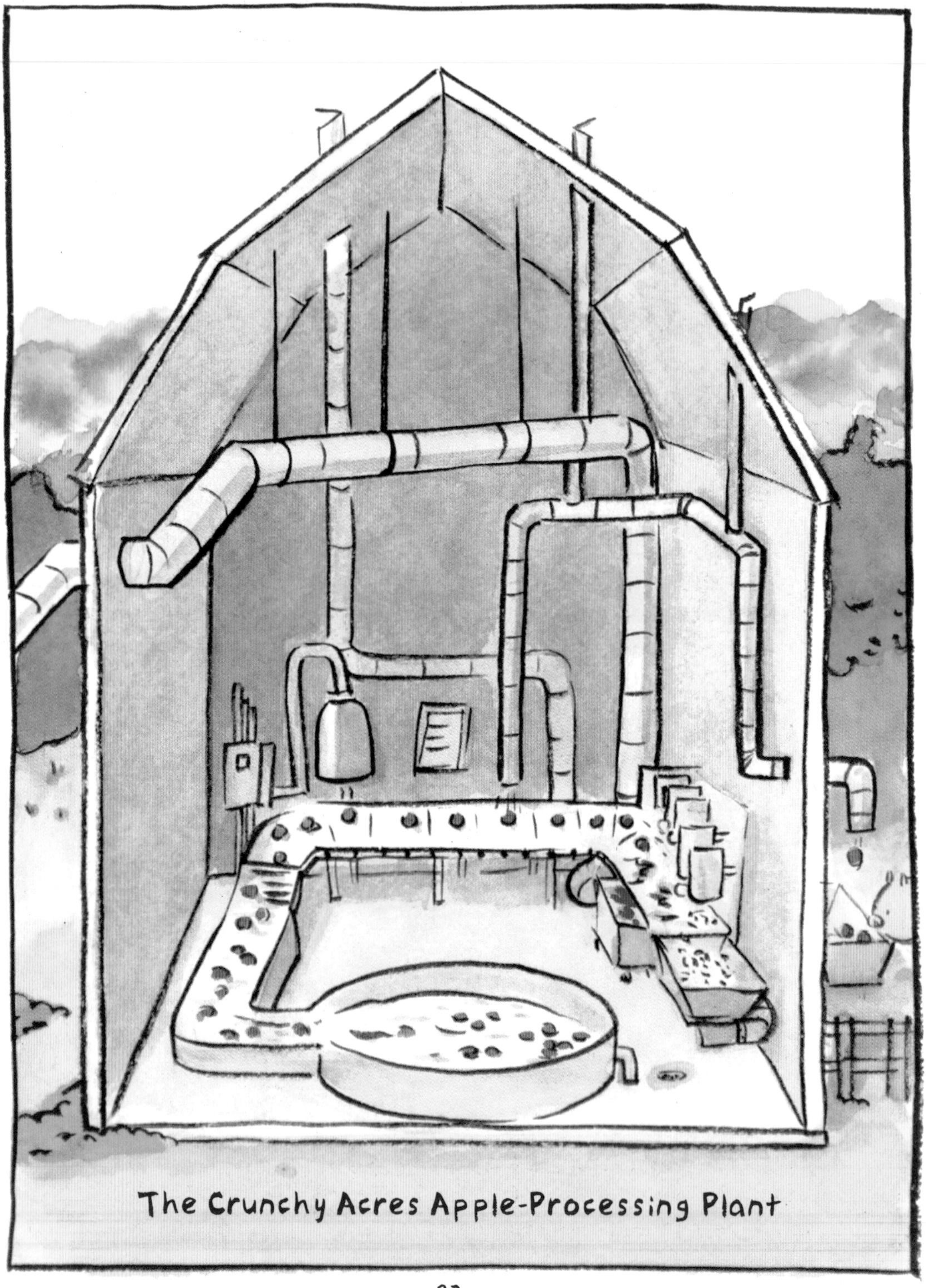

The Crunchy Acres Apple-Processing Plant

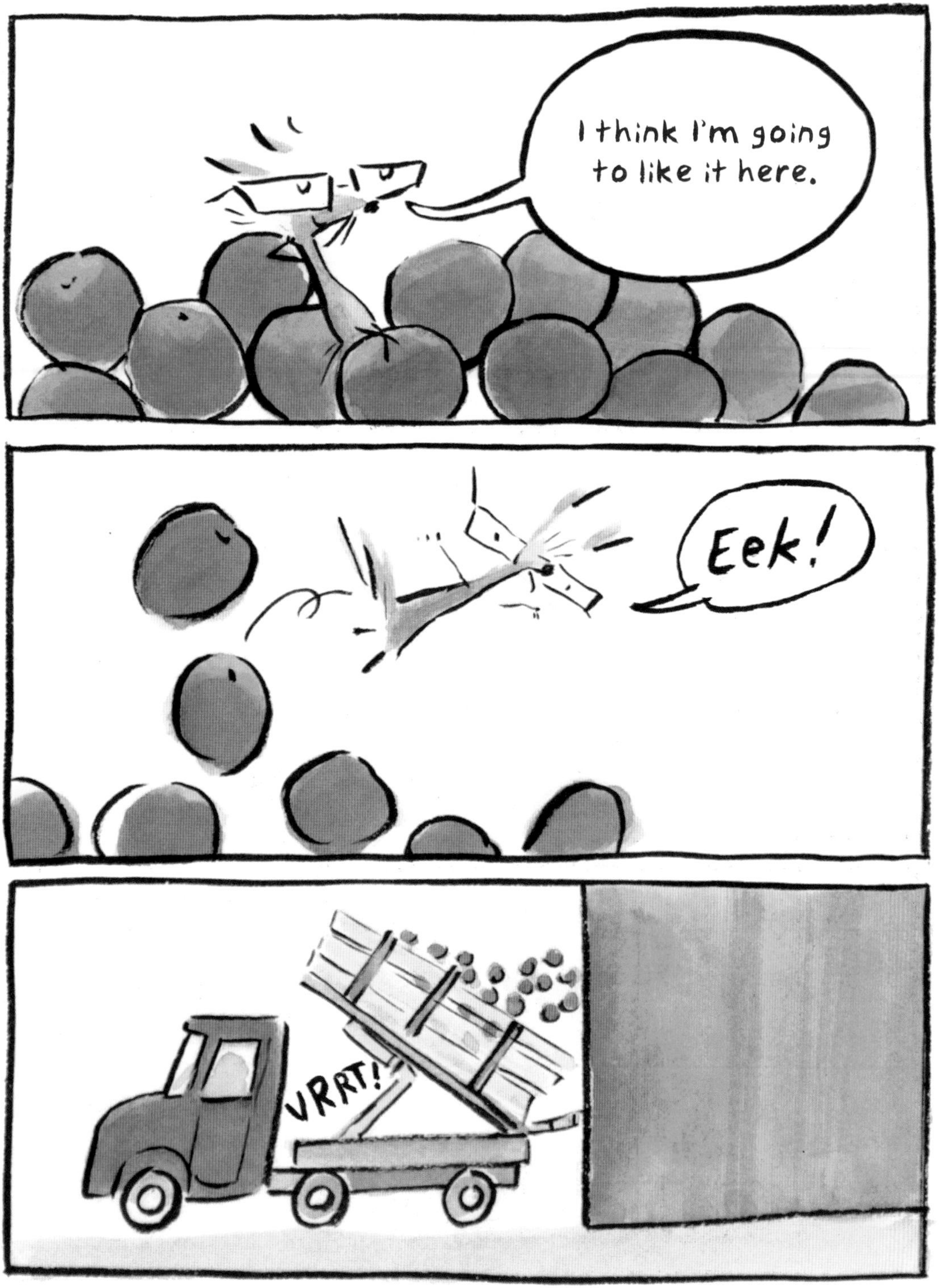
I think I'm going to like it here.
Eek!
VRRT!

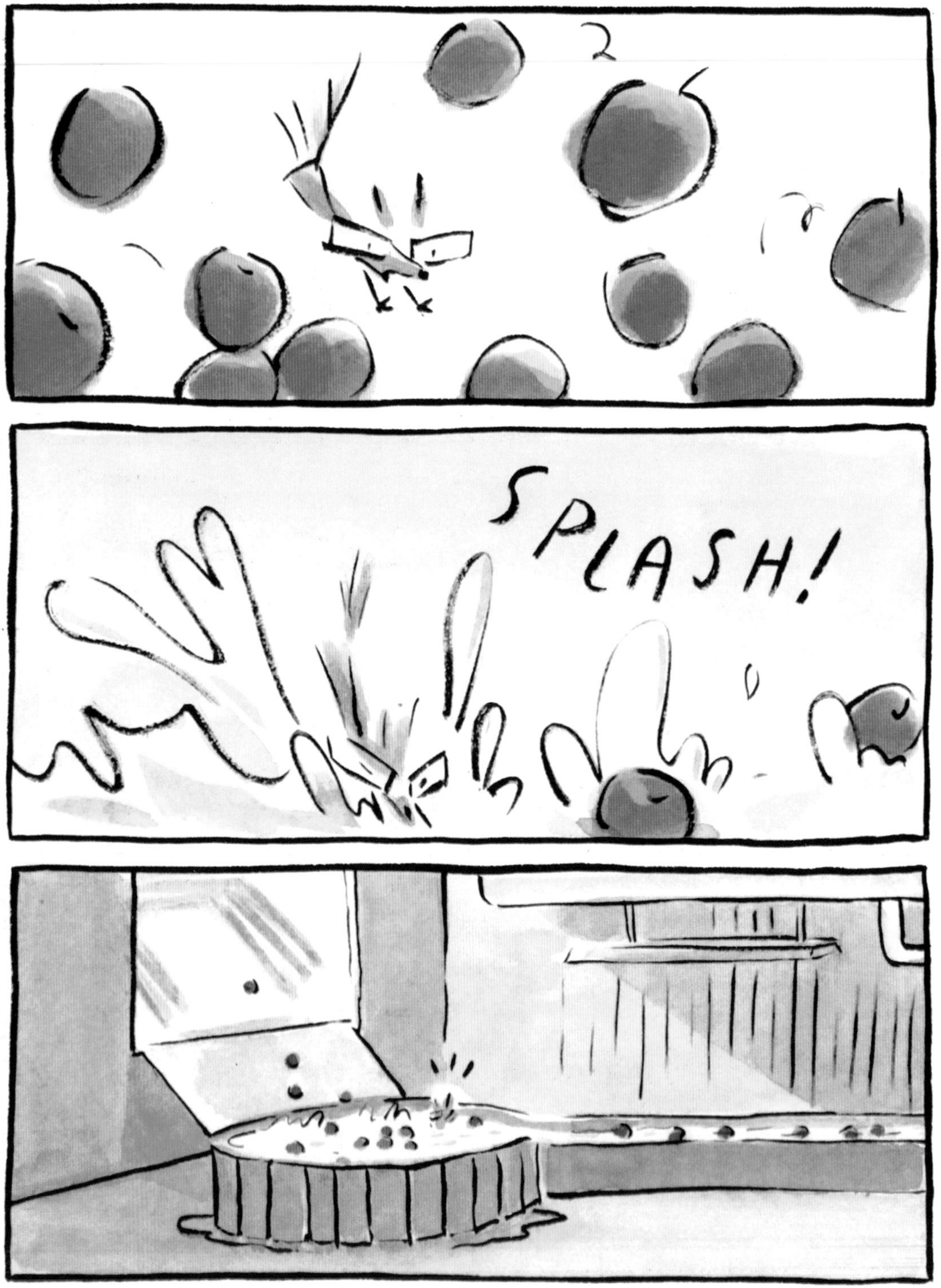
SPLASH!

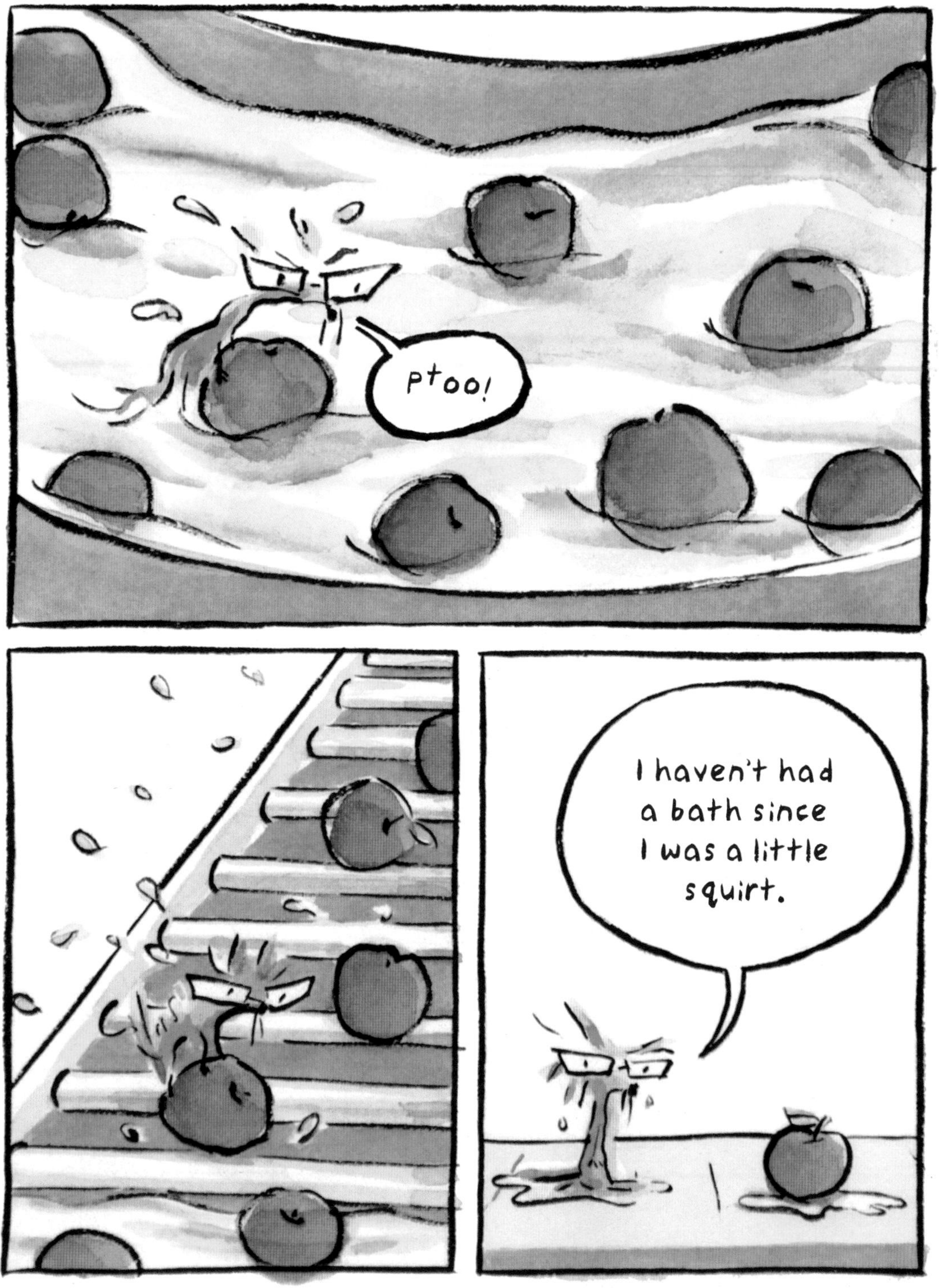
Ptoo!
I haven't had a bath since I was a little squirt.

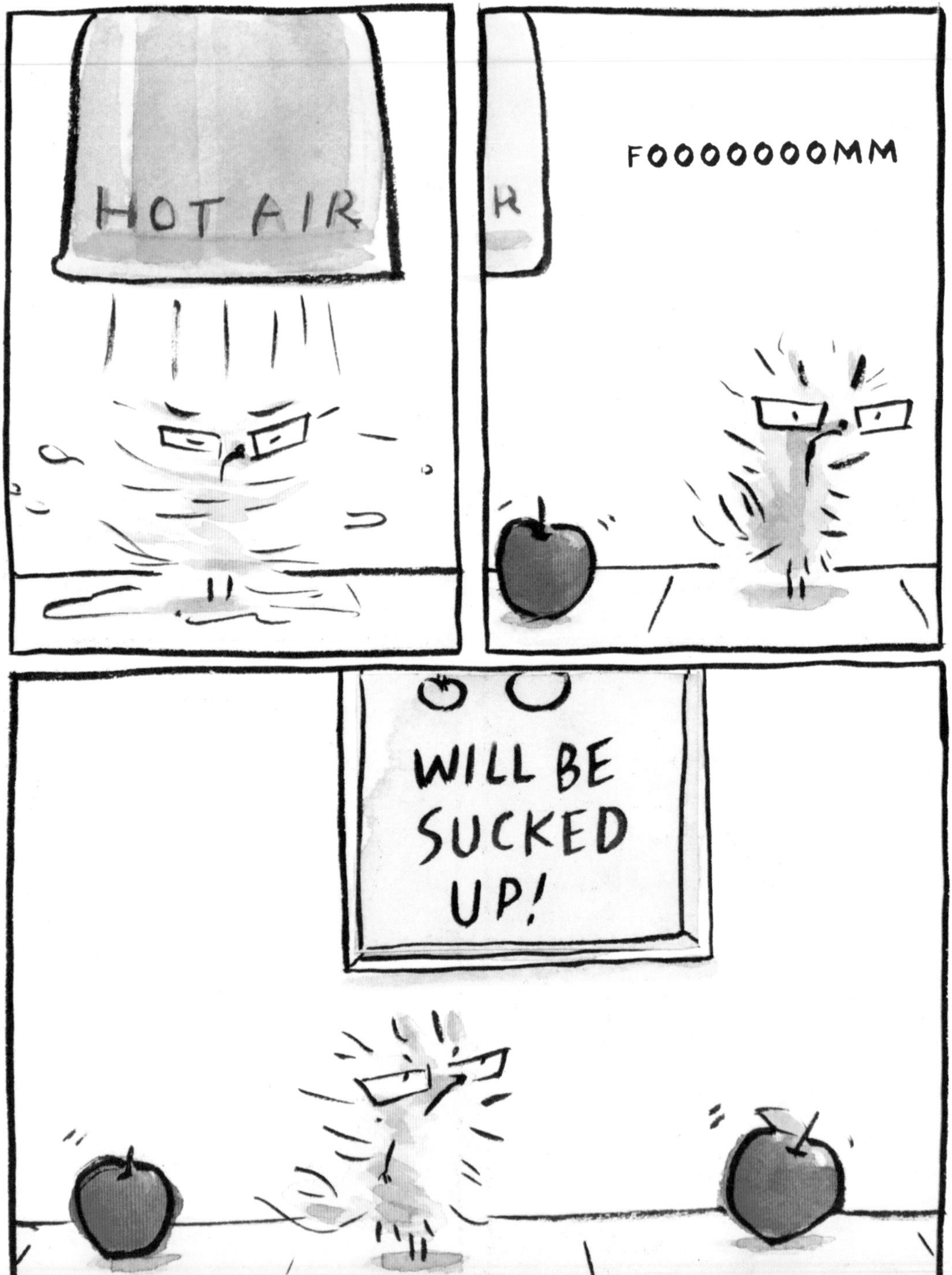
HOT AIR
R
FOOOOOOOMM
WILL BE SUCKED UP!

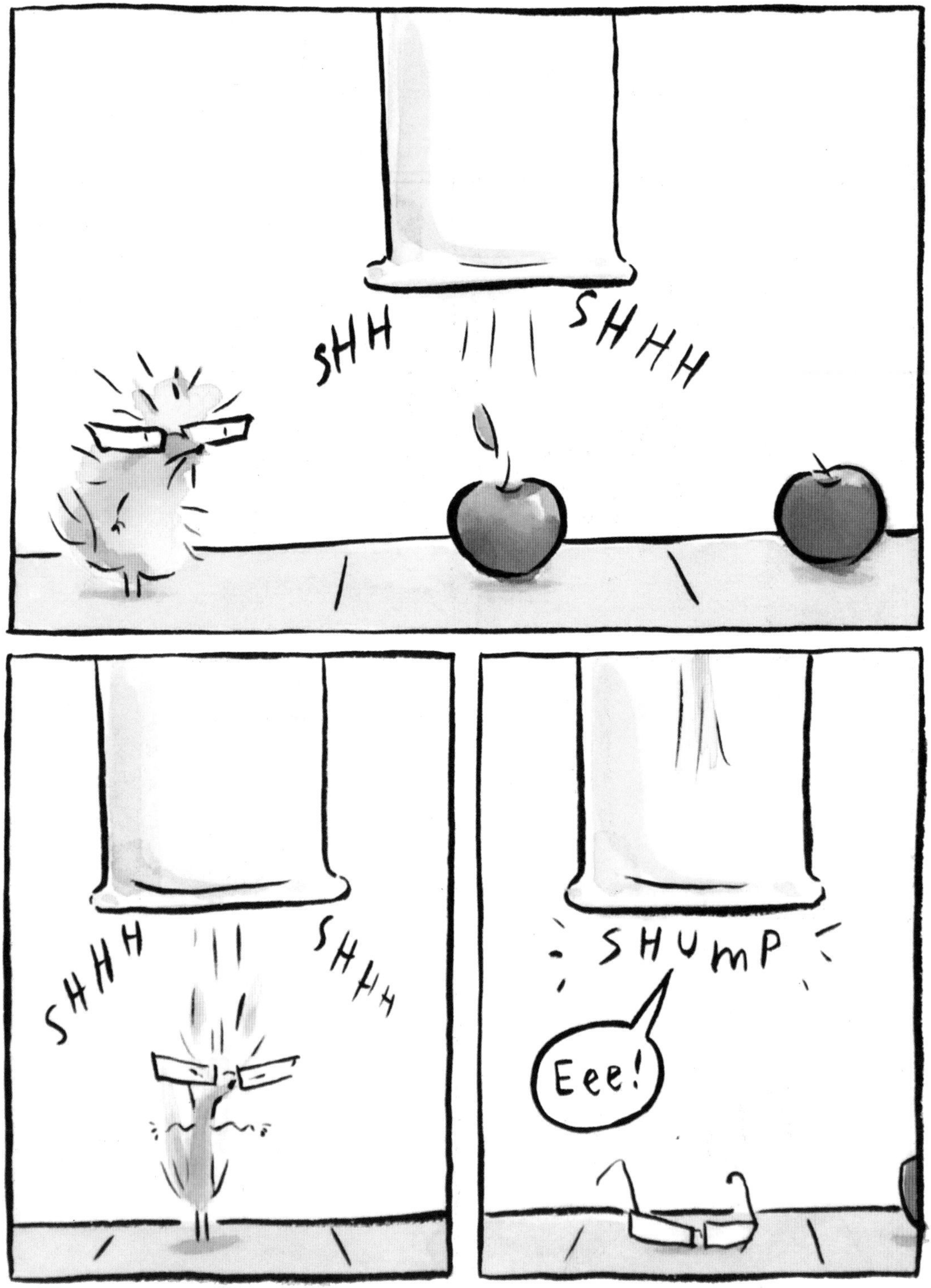
SHH
SHHH
SHHH
SHHH
SHUMP
Eee!

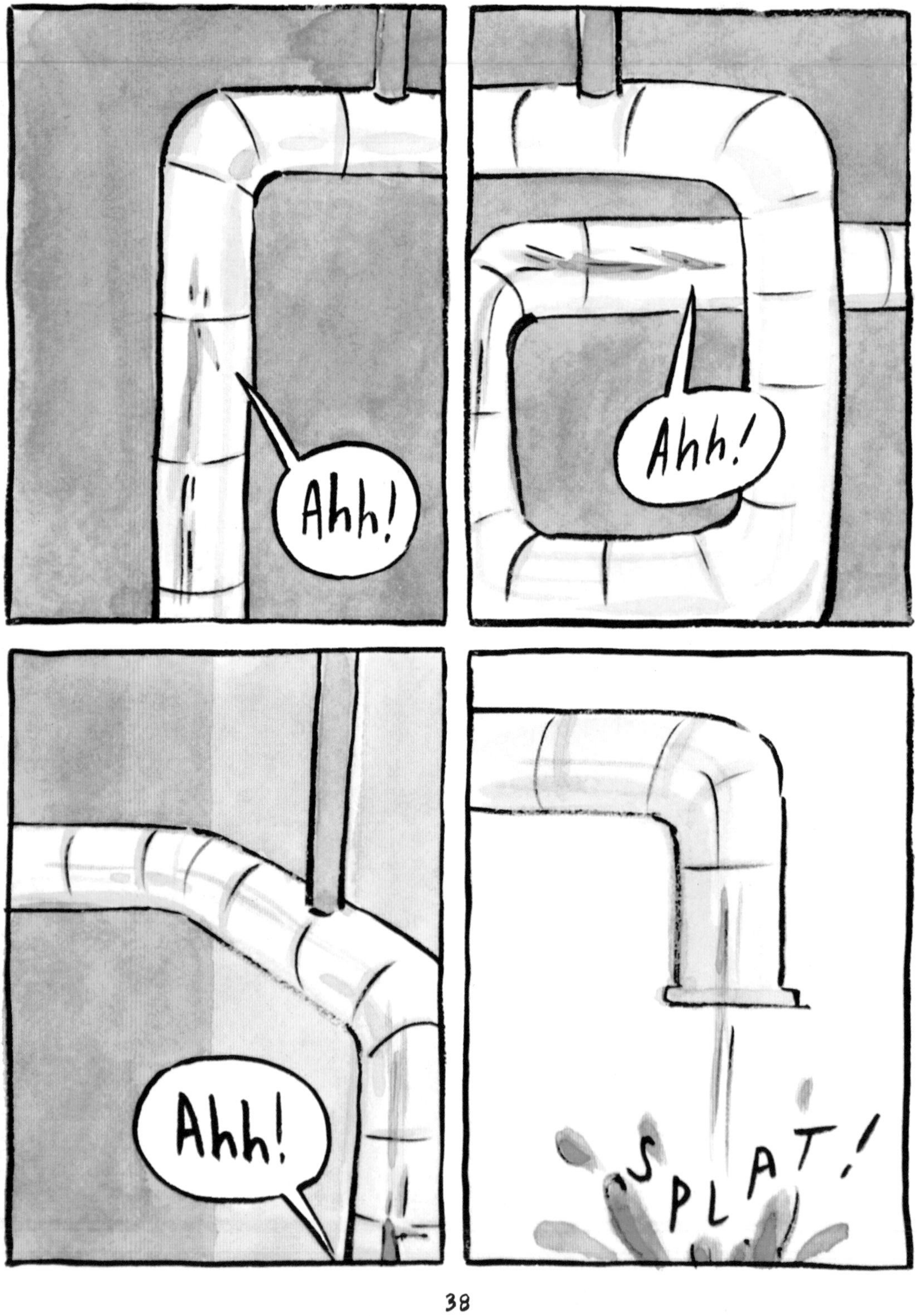
Ahh!
Ahh!
Ahh!
SPLAT!

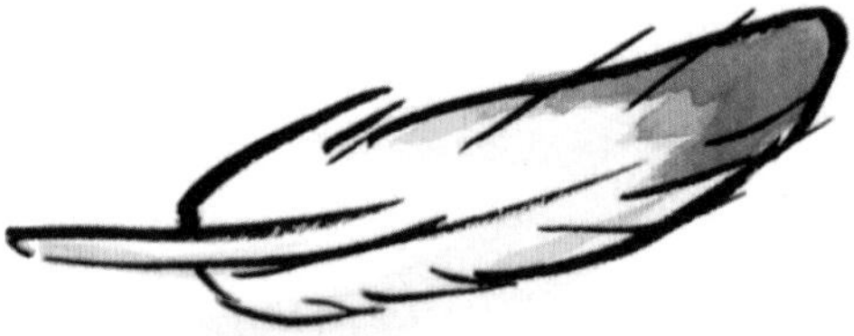

Chapter 4

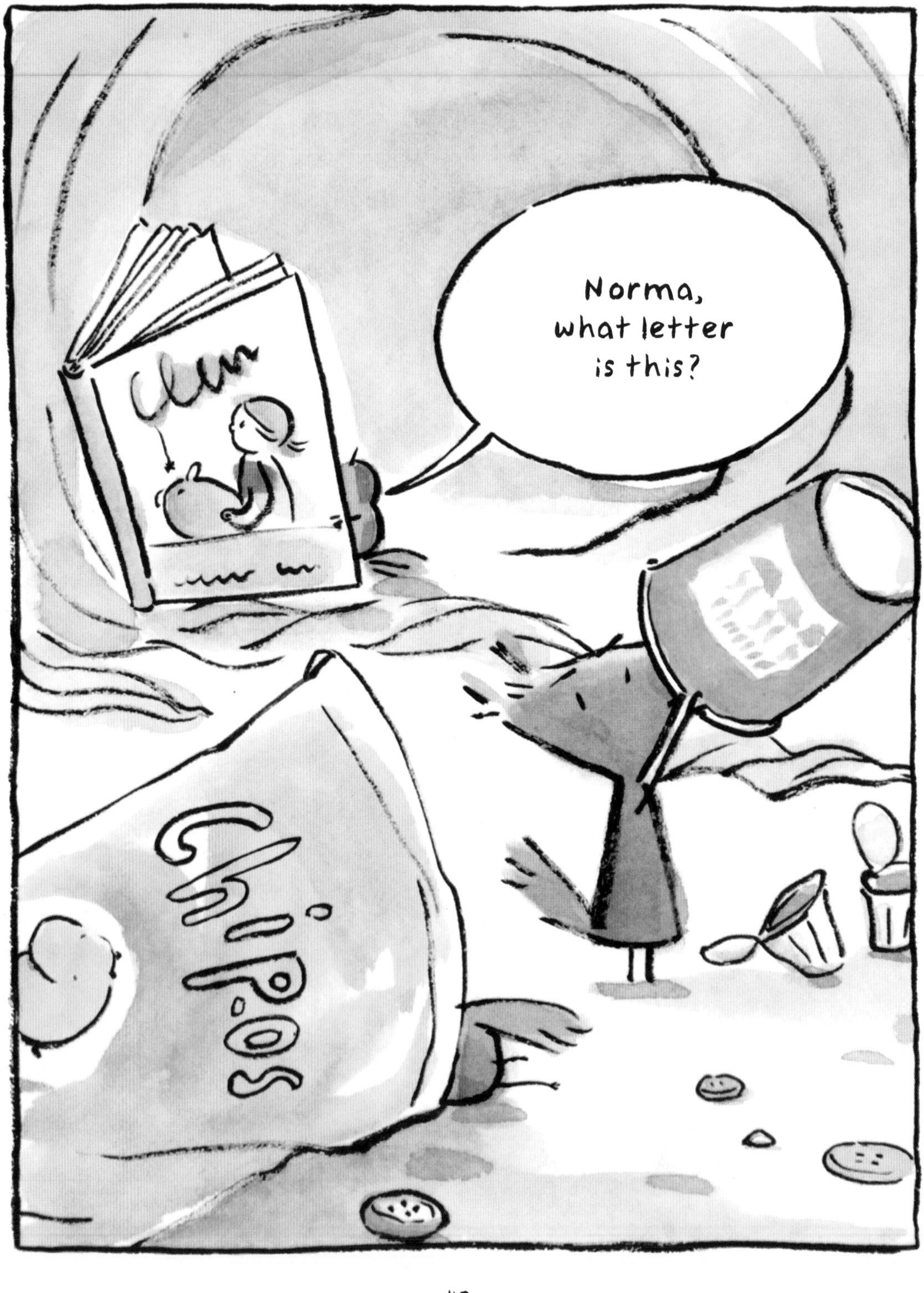
Norma, what letter is this?
Chipos

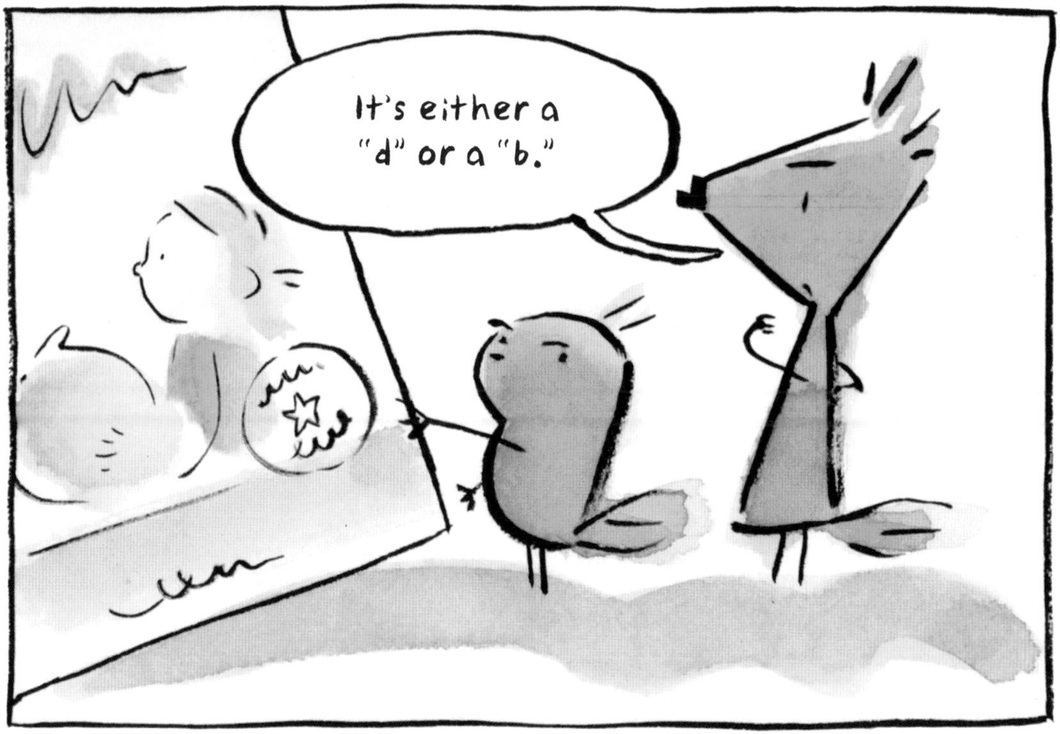
It's either a "d" or a "b."

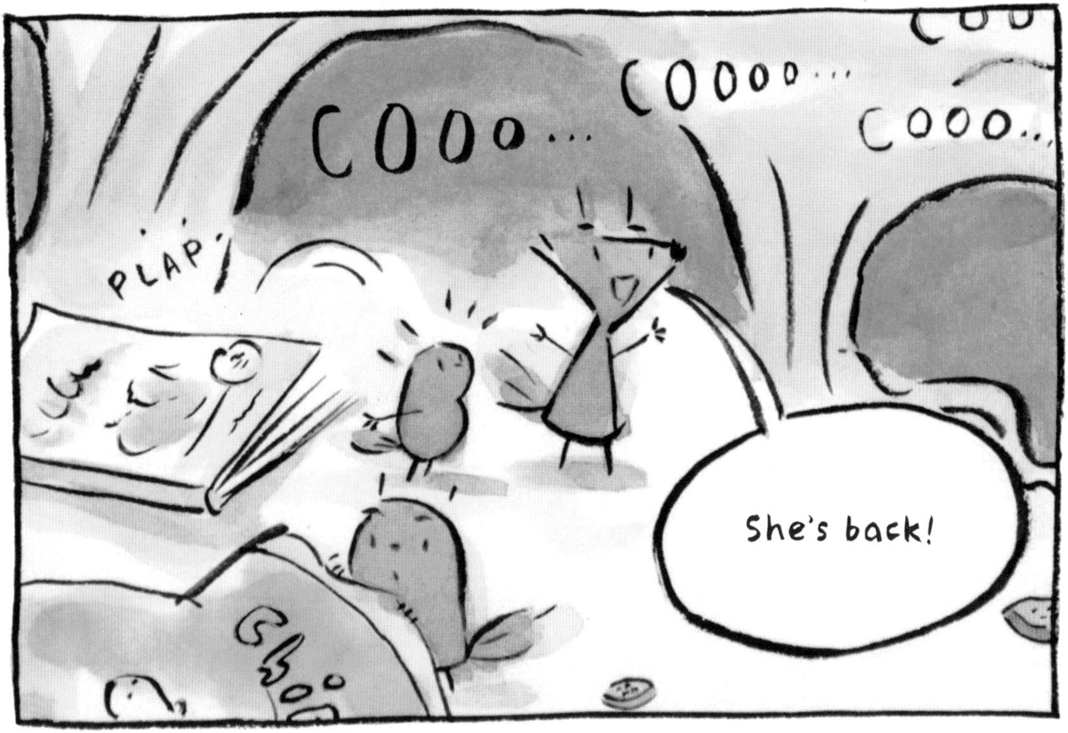
PLAP
COOO...
COOOO...
COOO...
She's back!

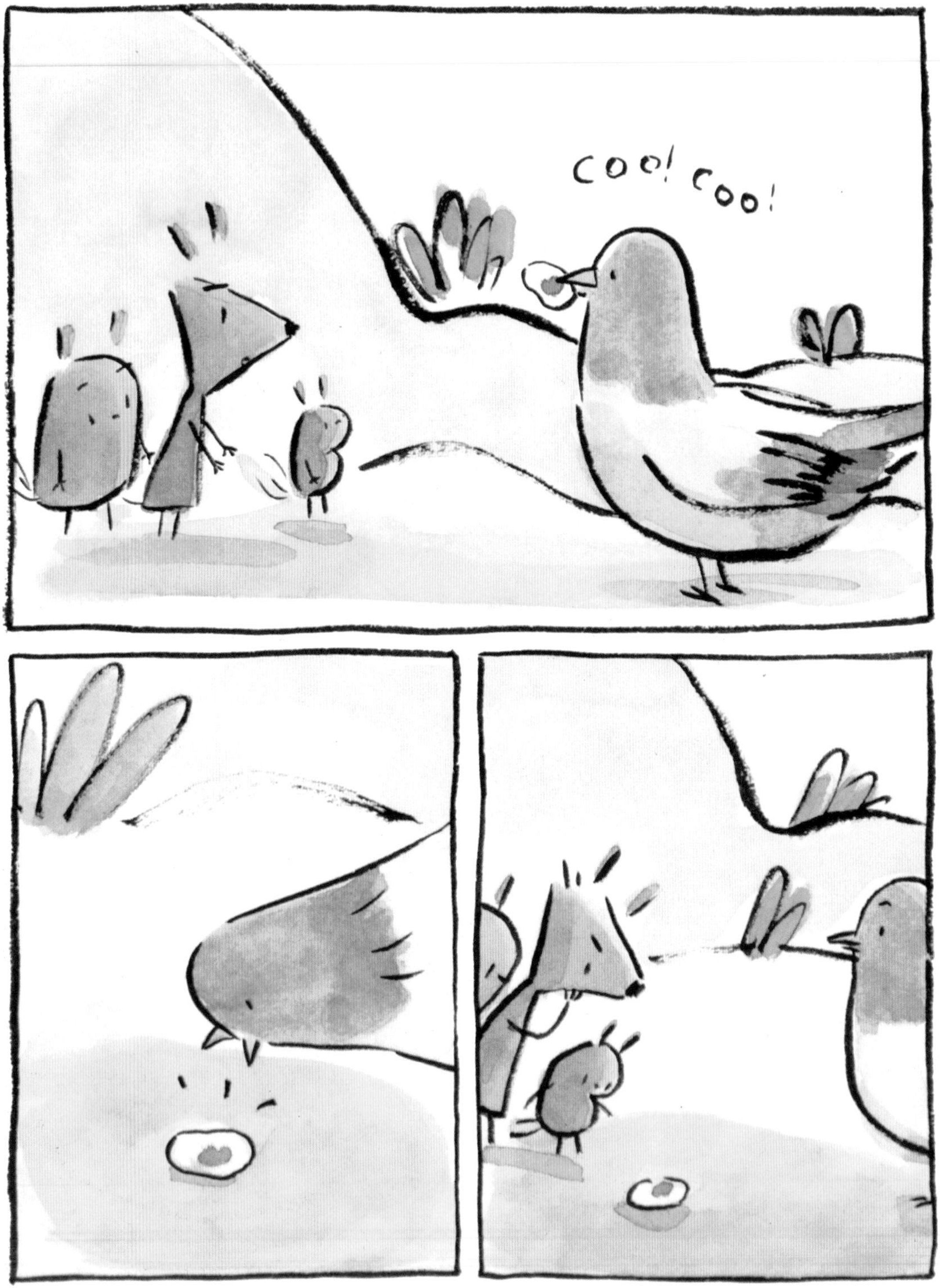
coo! coo!

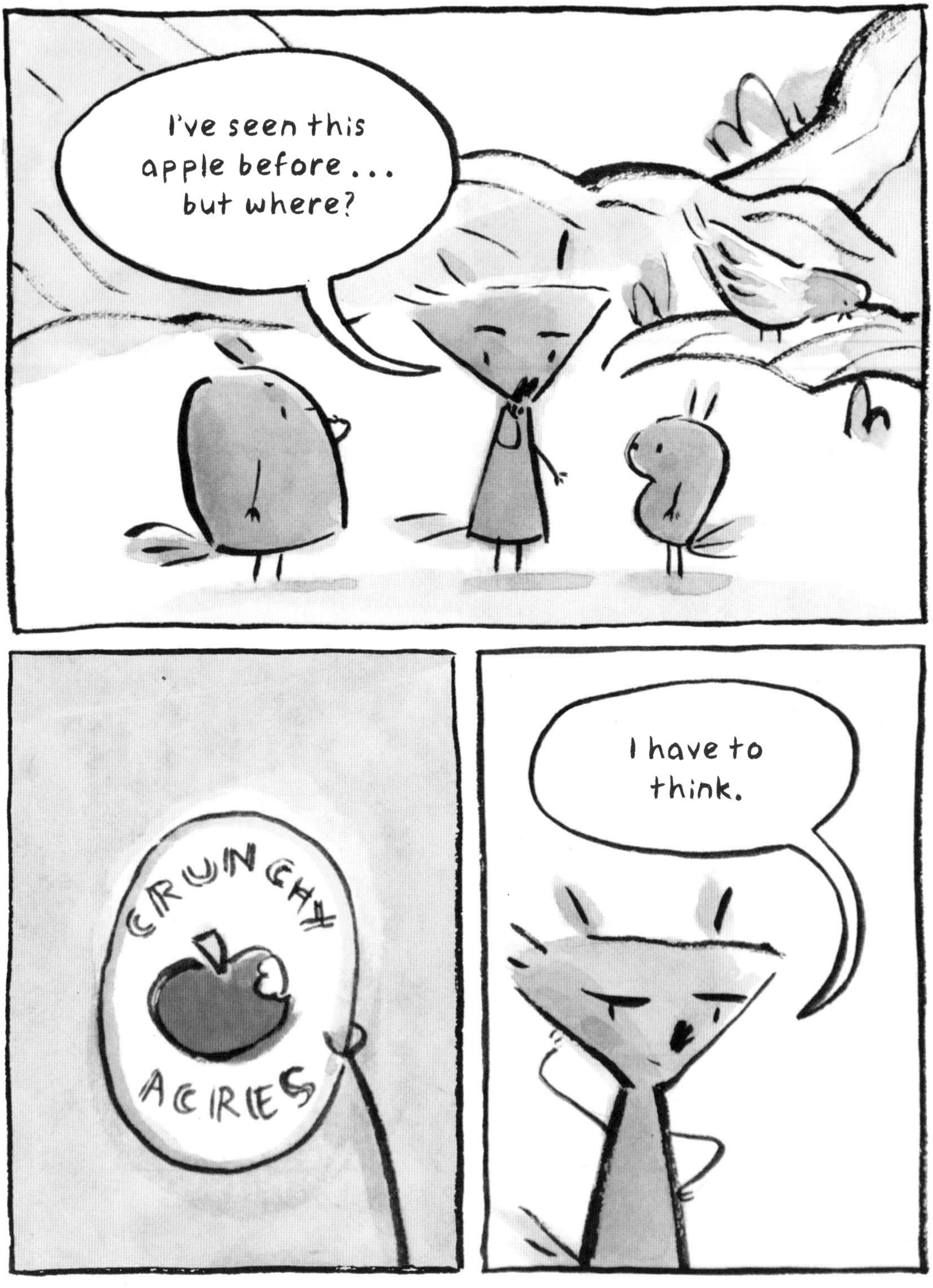
I've seen this apple before... but where?
CRUNCHY ACRES
I have to think.

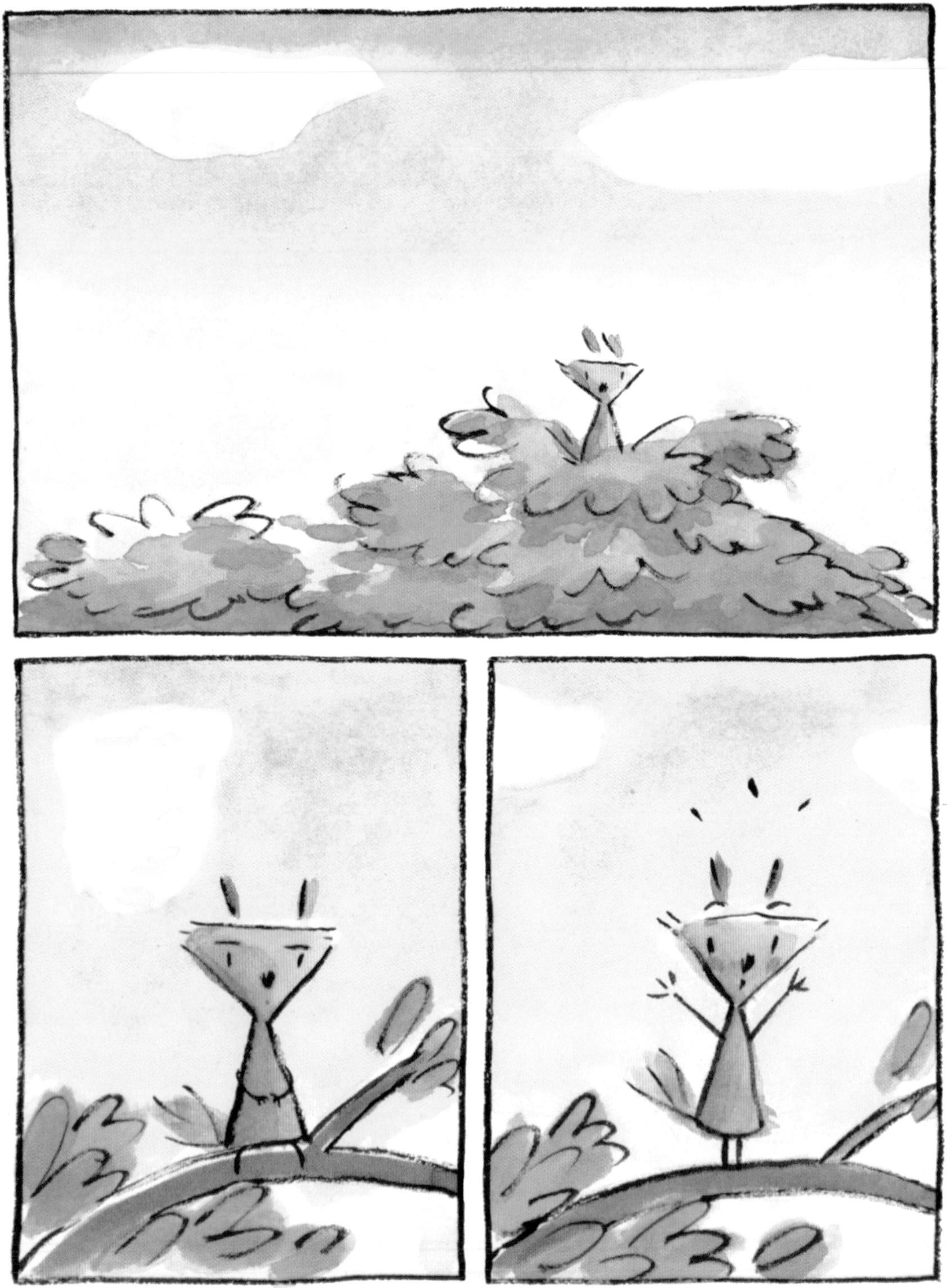

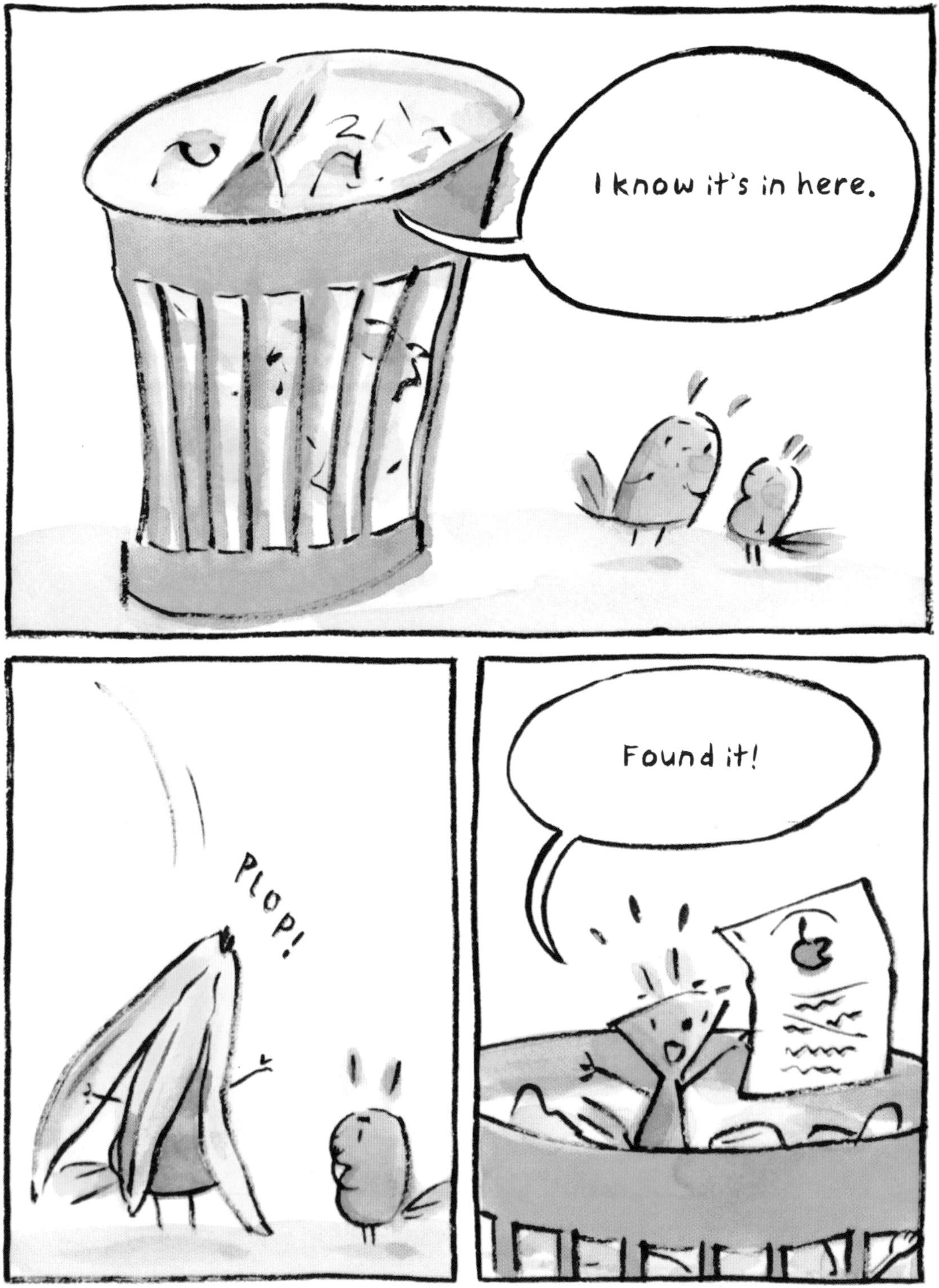
I know it's in here.
PLOP!
Found it!

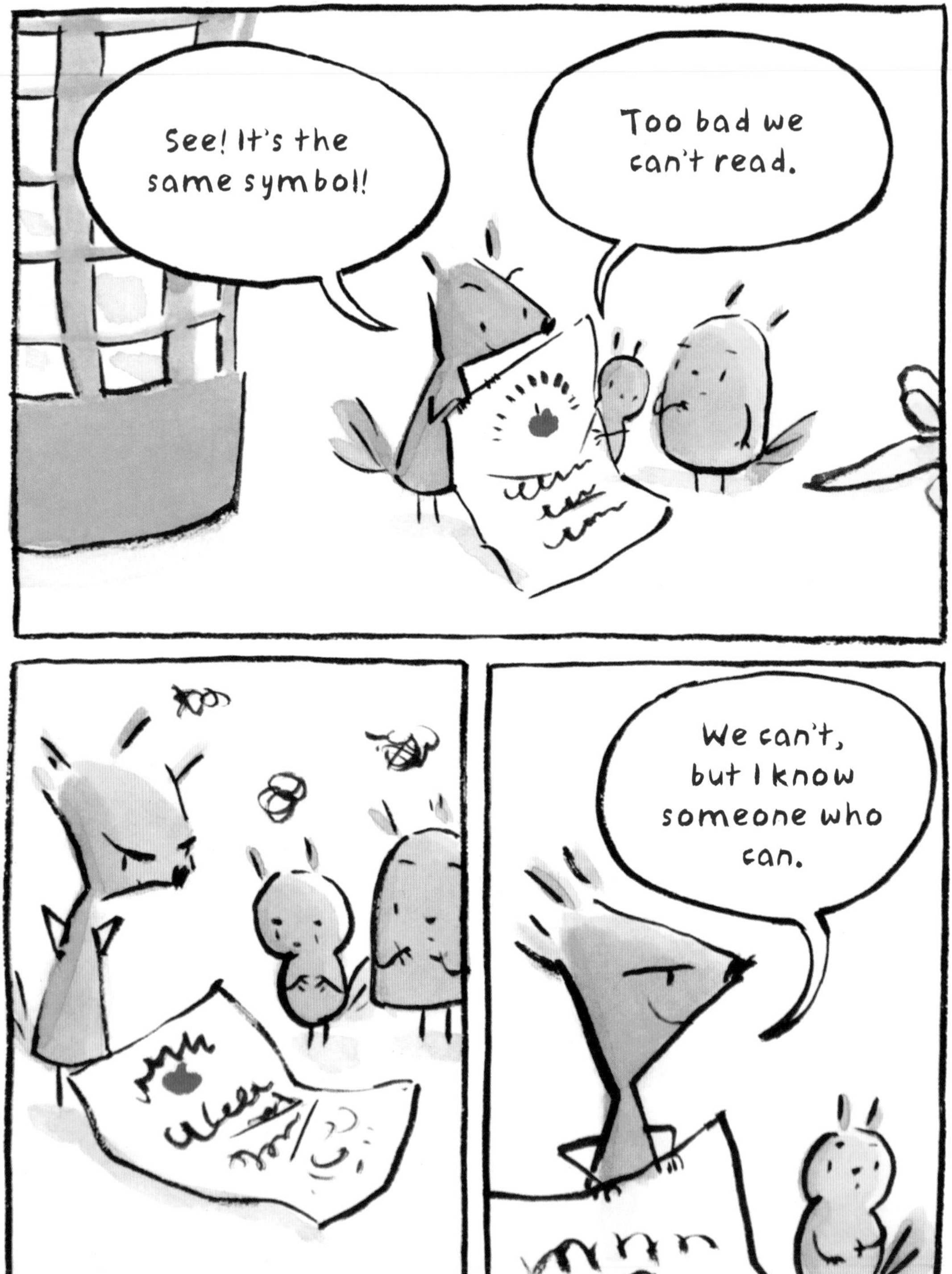
See! It's the same symbol!
Too bad we can't read.
We can't, but I know someone who can.

Chapter 5

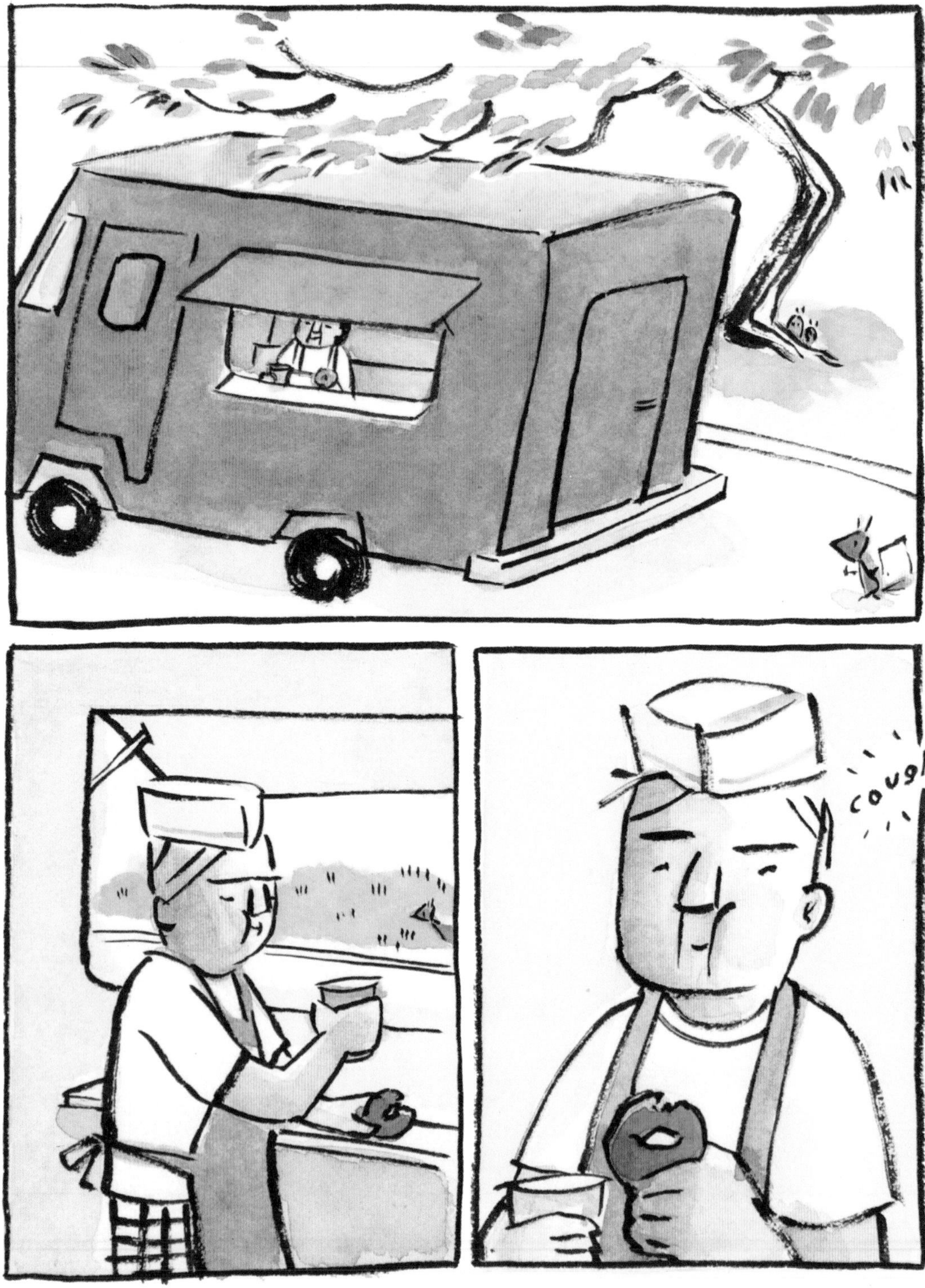
cough

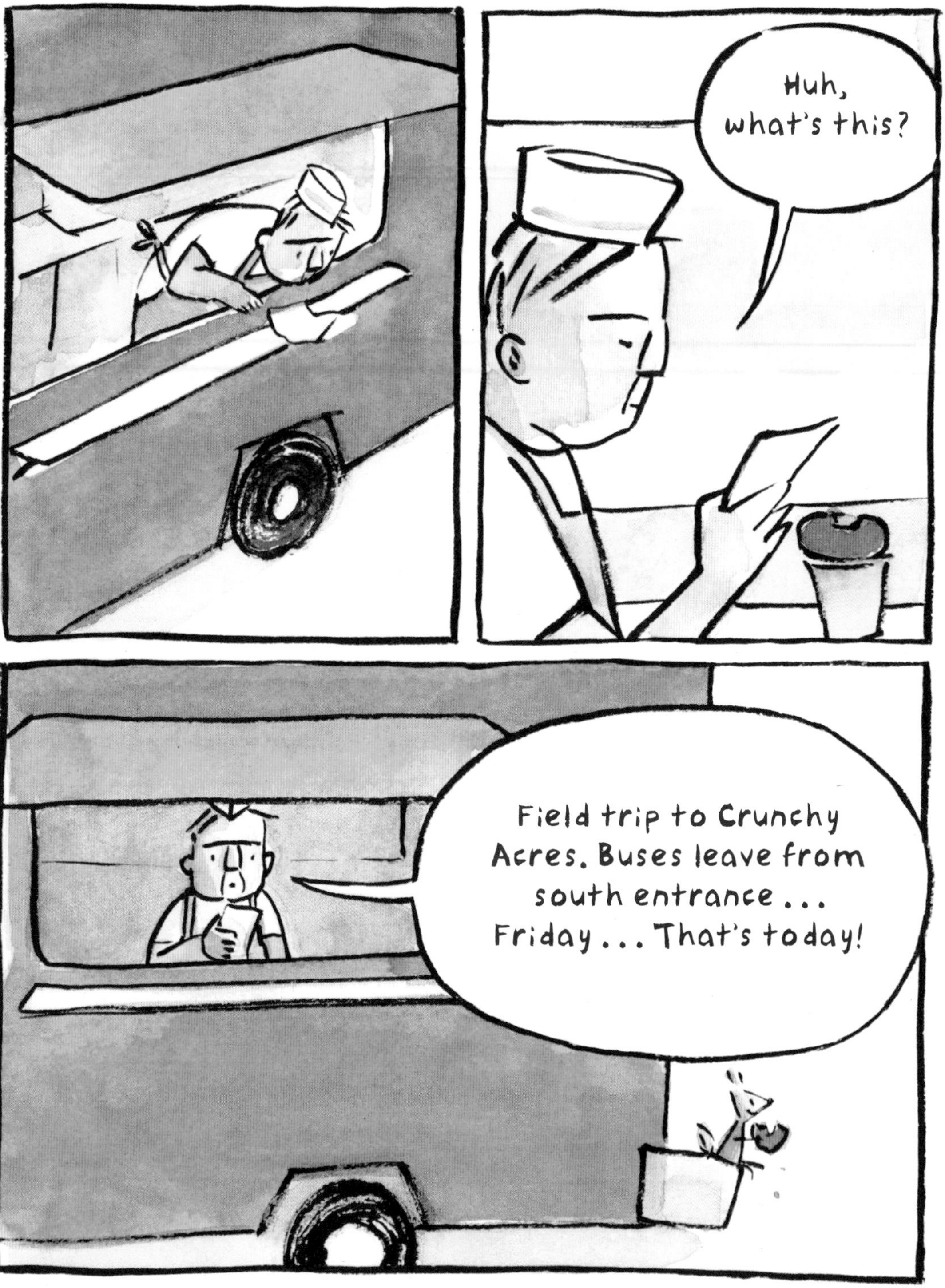
Huh, what's this?
Field trip to Crunchy Acres. Buses leave from south entrance . . . Friday . . . That's today!

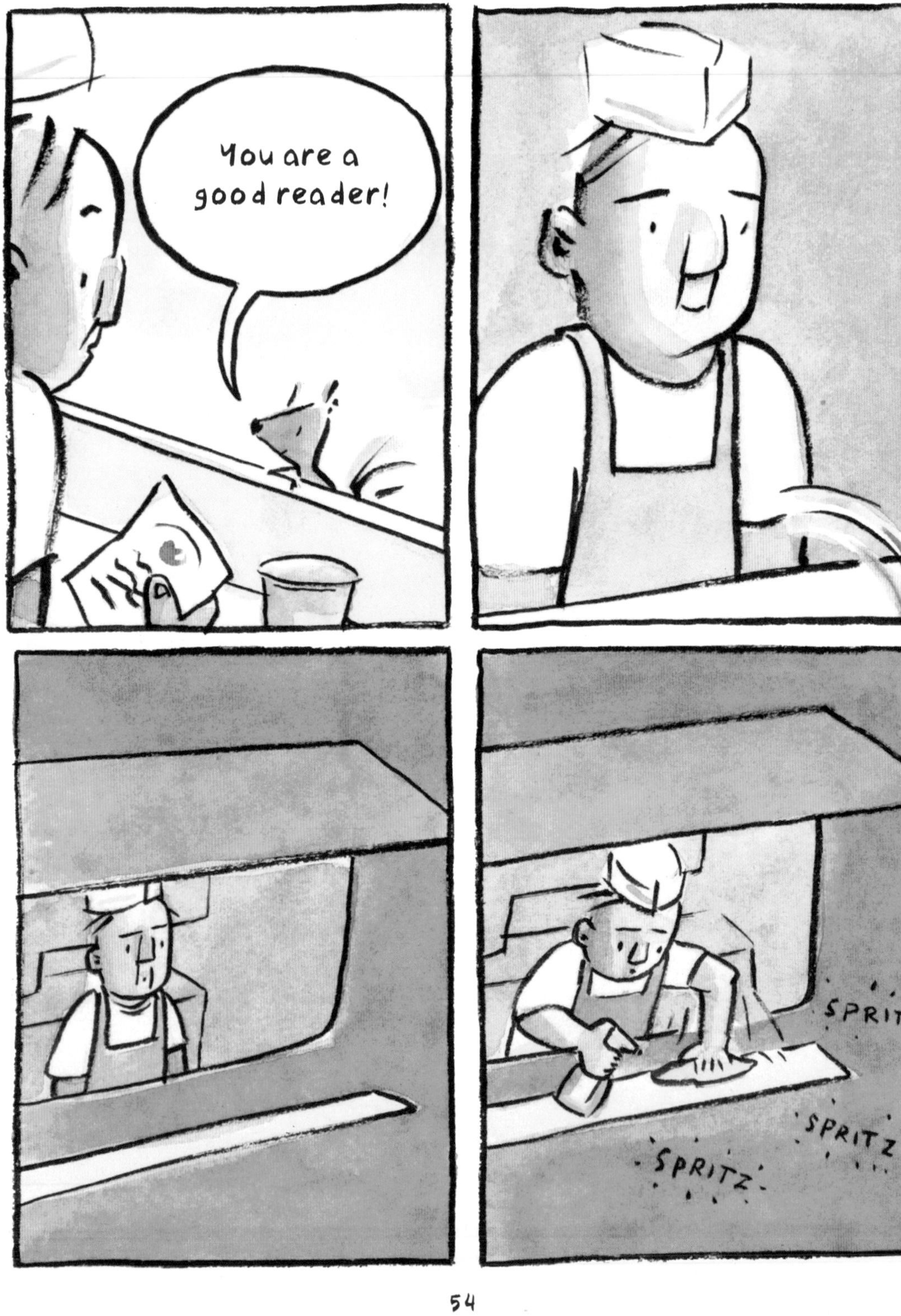
You are a good reader!
SPRITZ
SPRITZ
SPRITZ

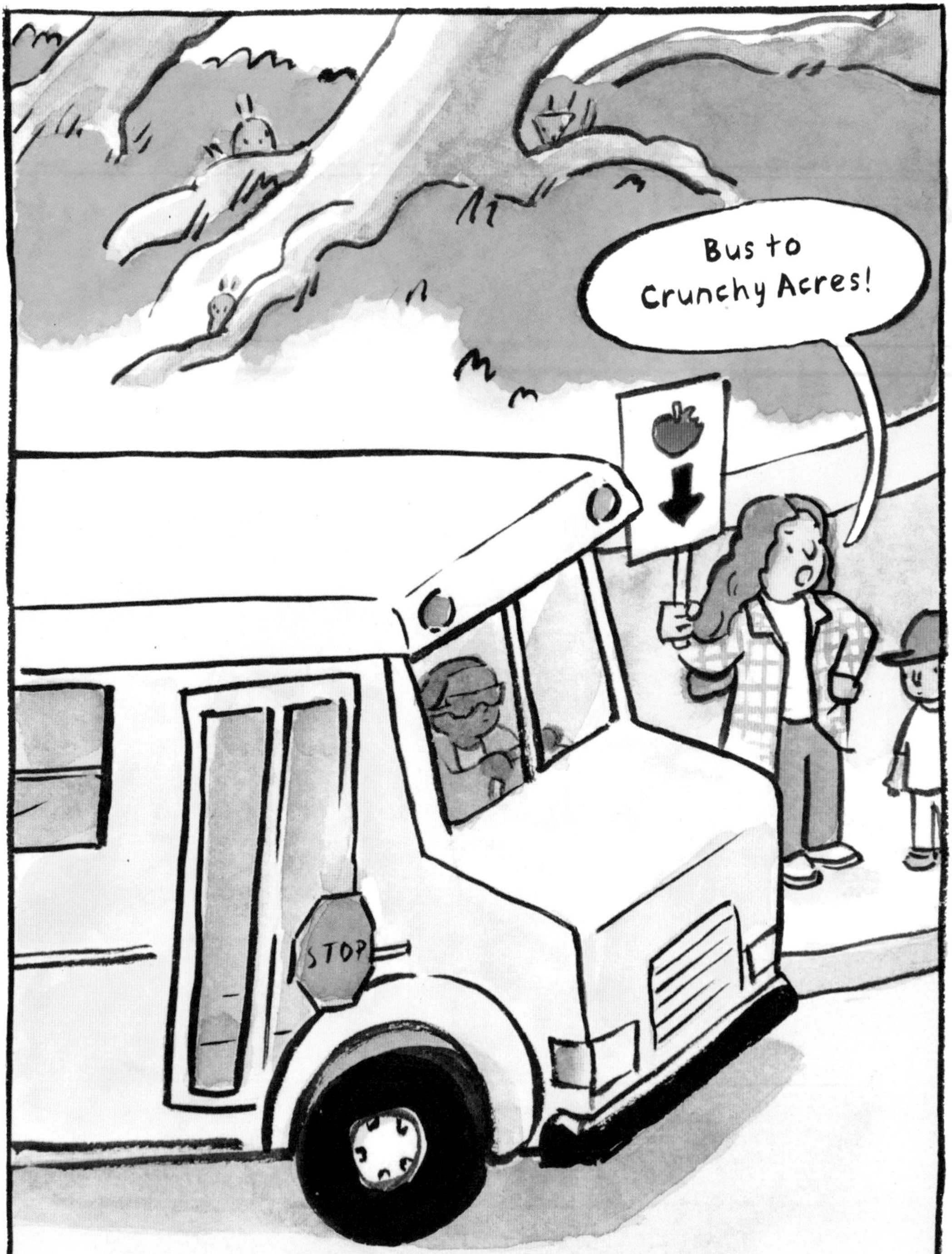
Bus to Crunchy Acres!
STOP

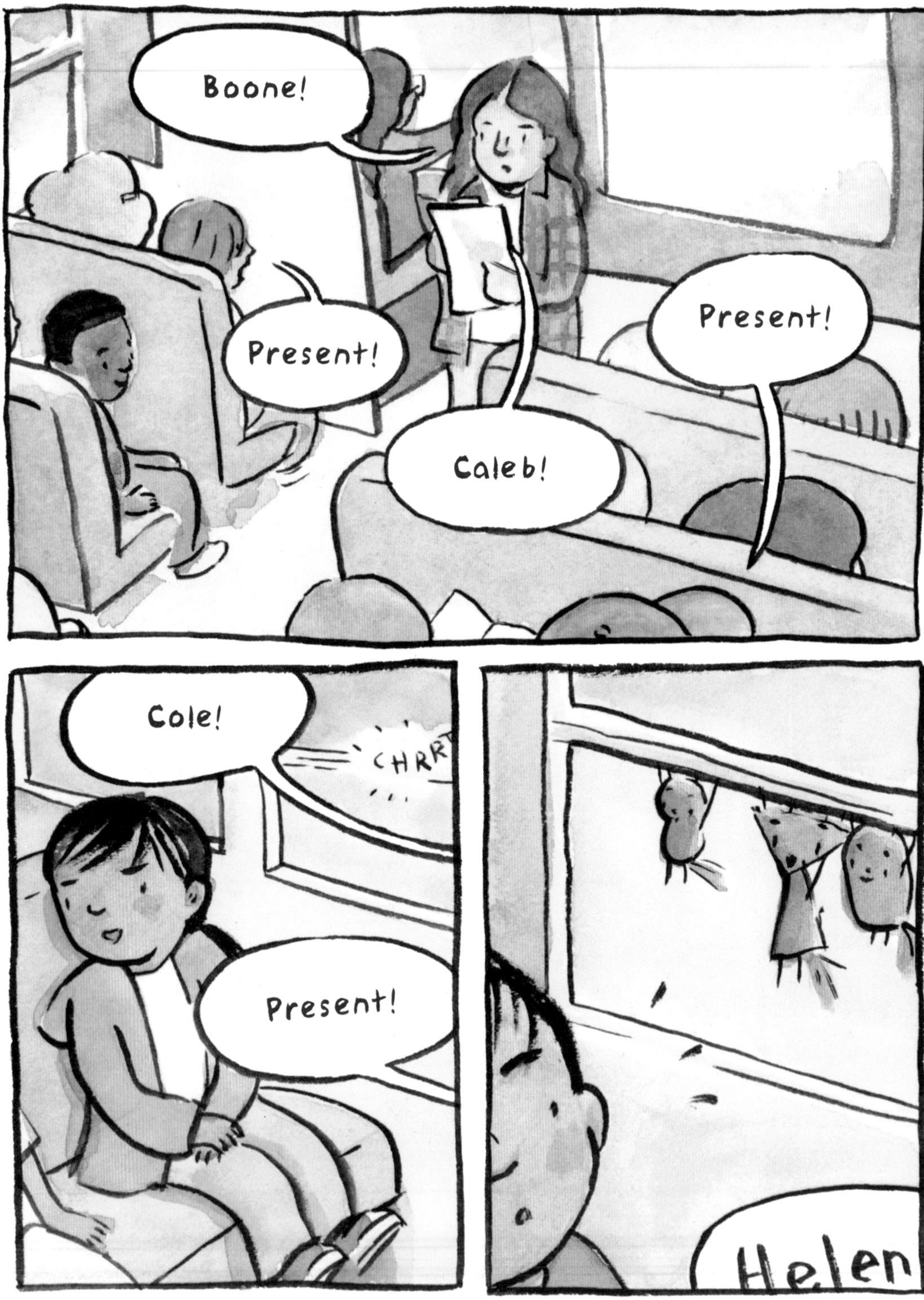
Boone!
Present!
Caleb!
Present!
Cole!
CHRR
Present!
Helen

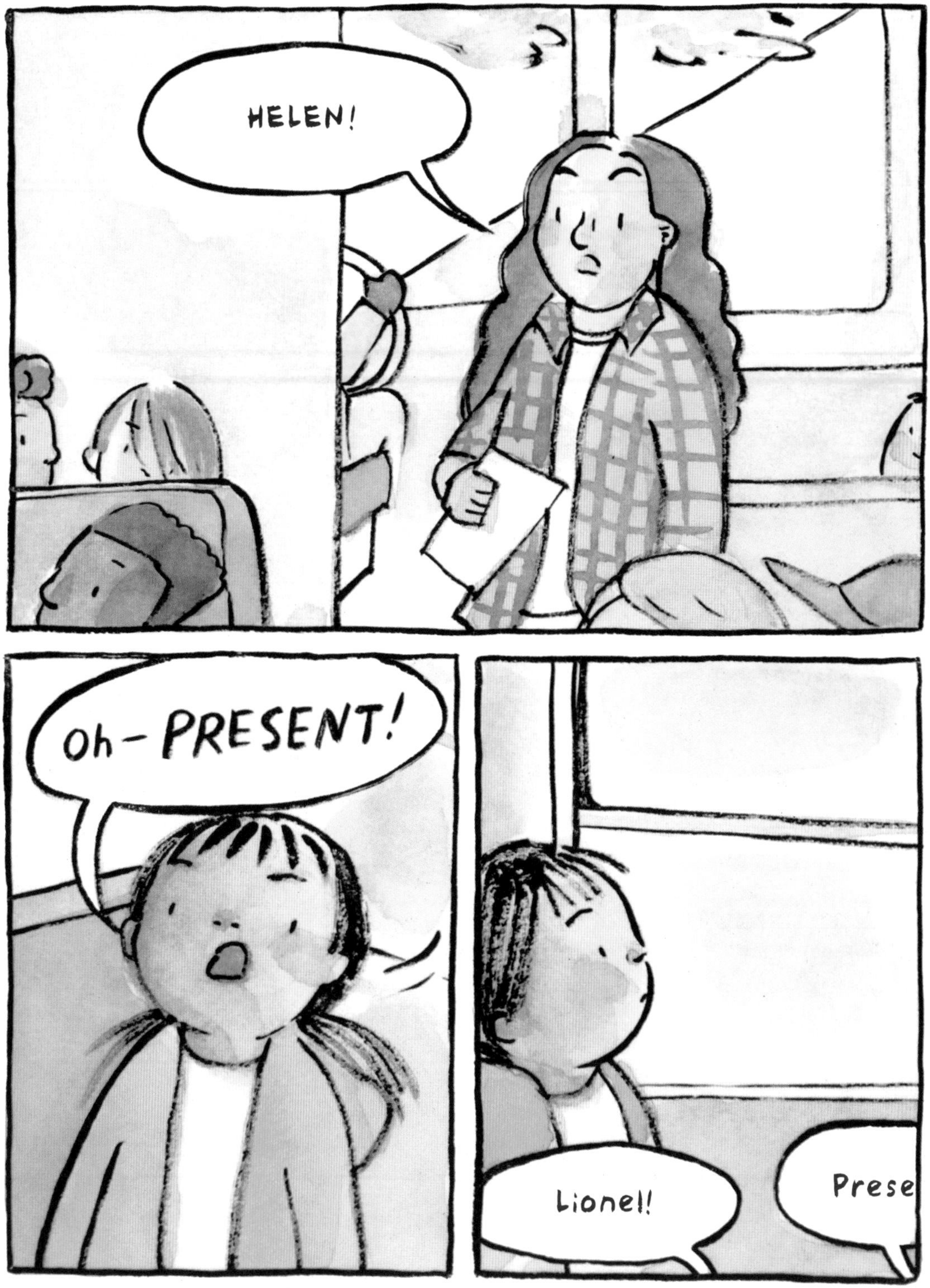
HELEN!
Oh- PRESENT!
Lionel!
Prese

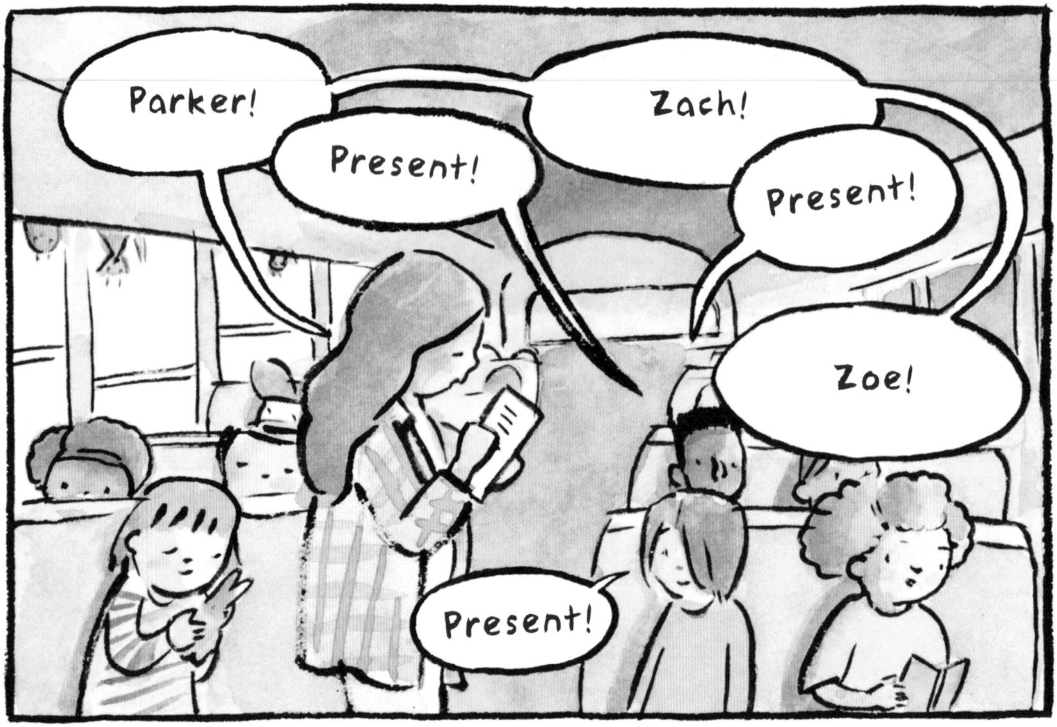
Parker!
Present!
Zach!
Present!
Zoe!
Present!

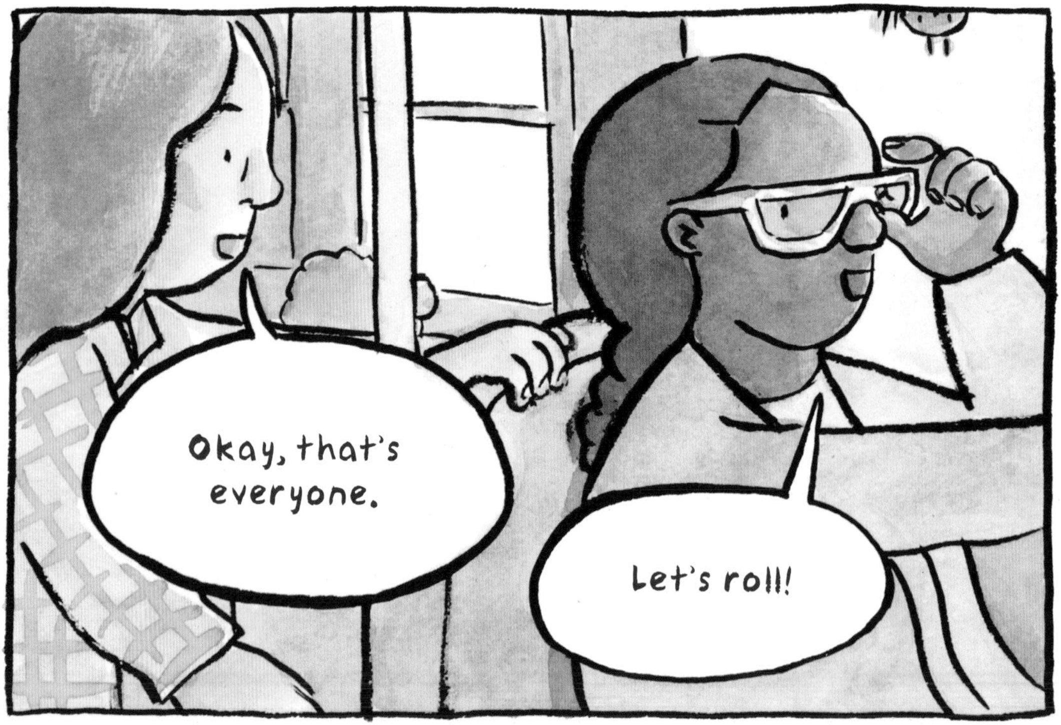
Okay, that's everyone.
Let's roll!

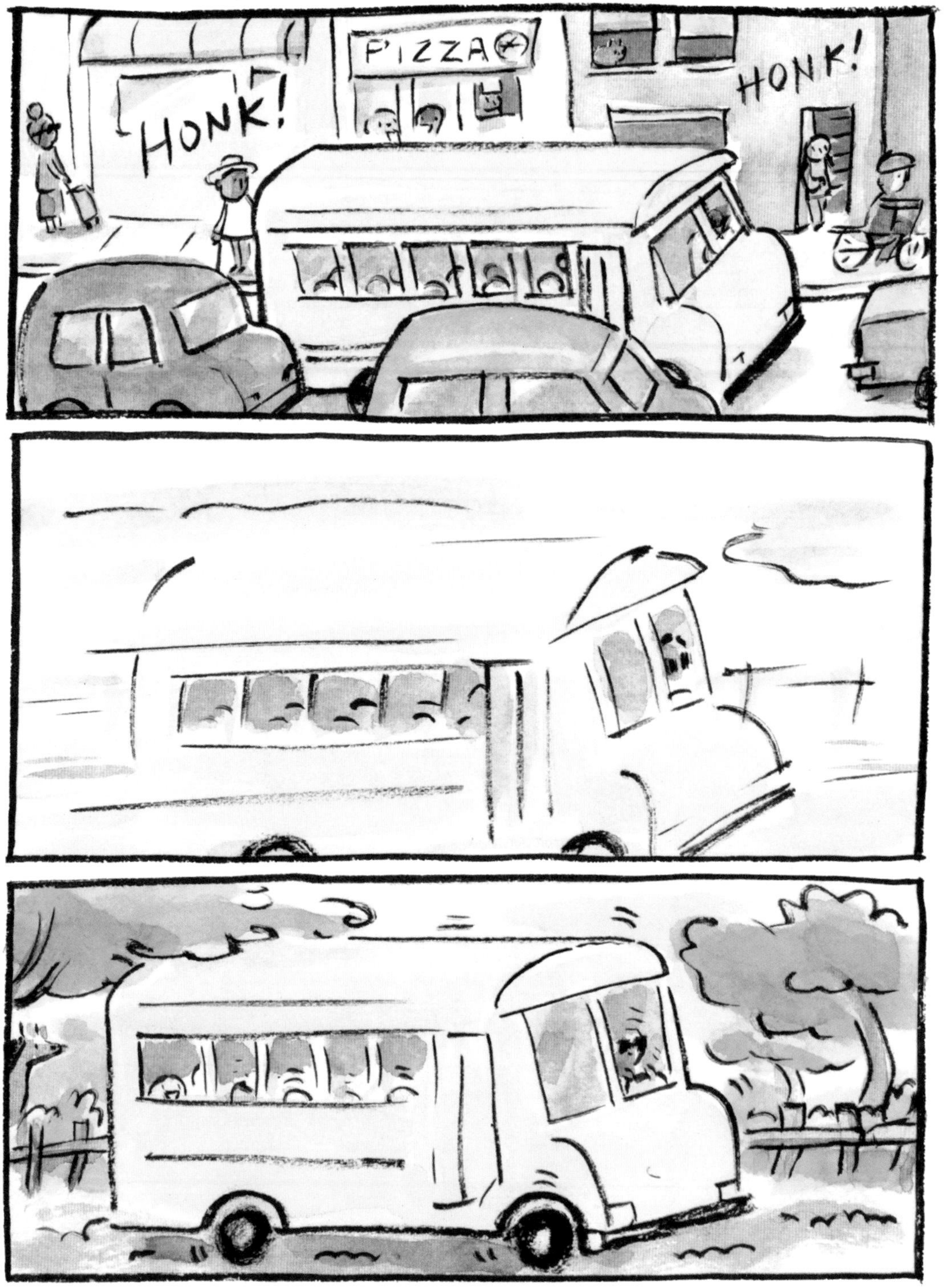
PIZZA
HONK!
HONK!

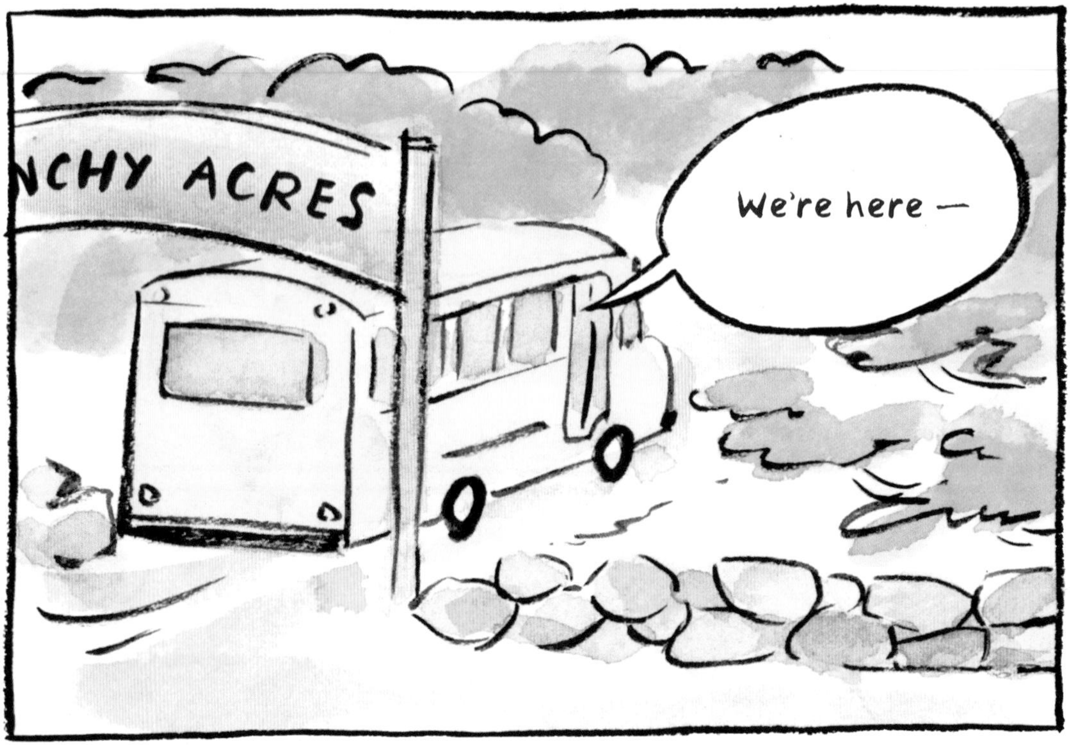
NCHY ACRES
We're here –

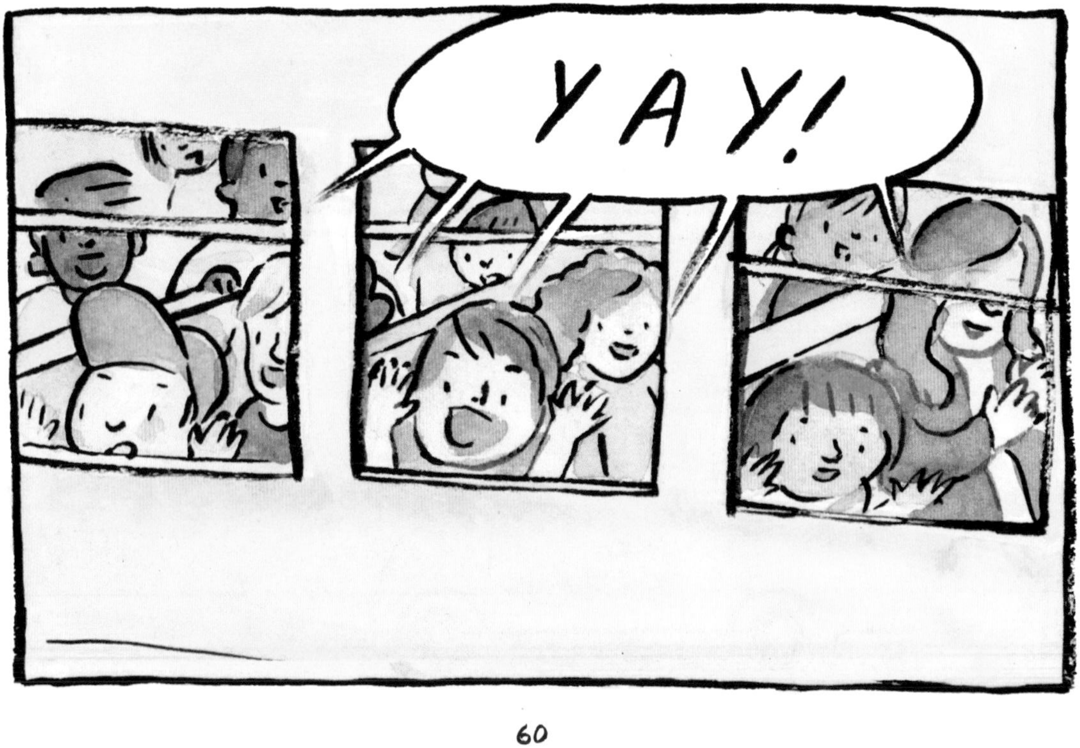
YAY!

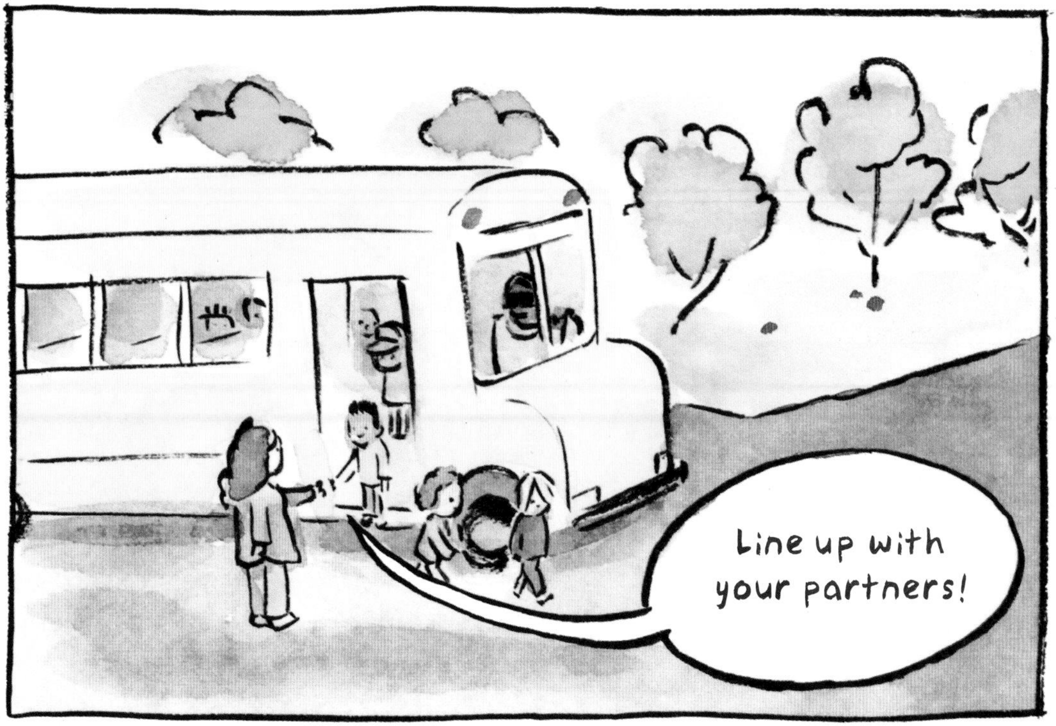
Line up with your partners!

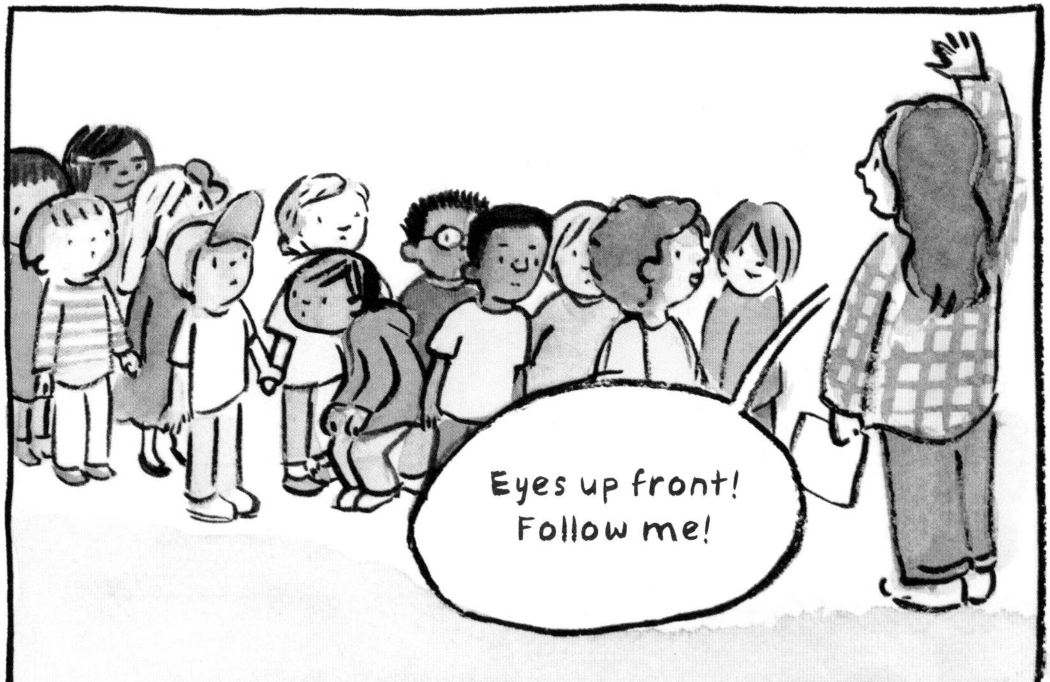
Eyes up front! Follow me!

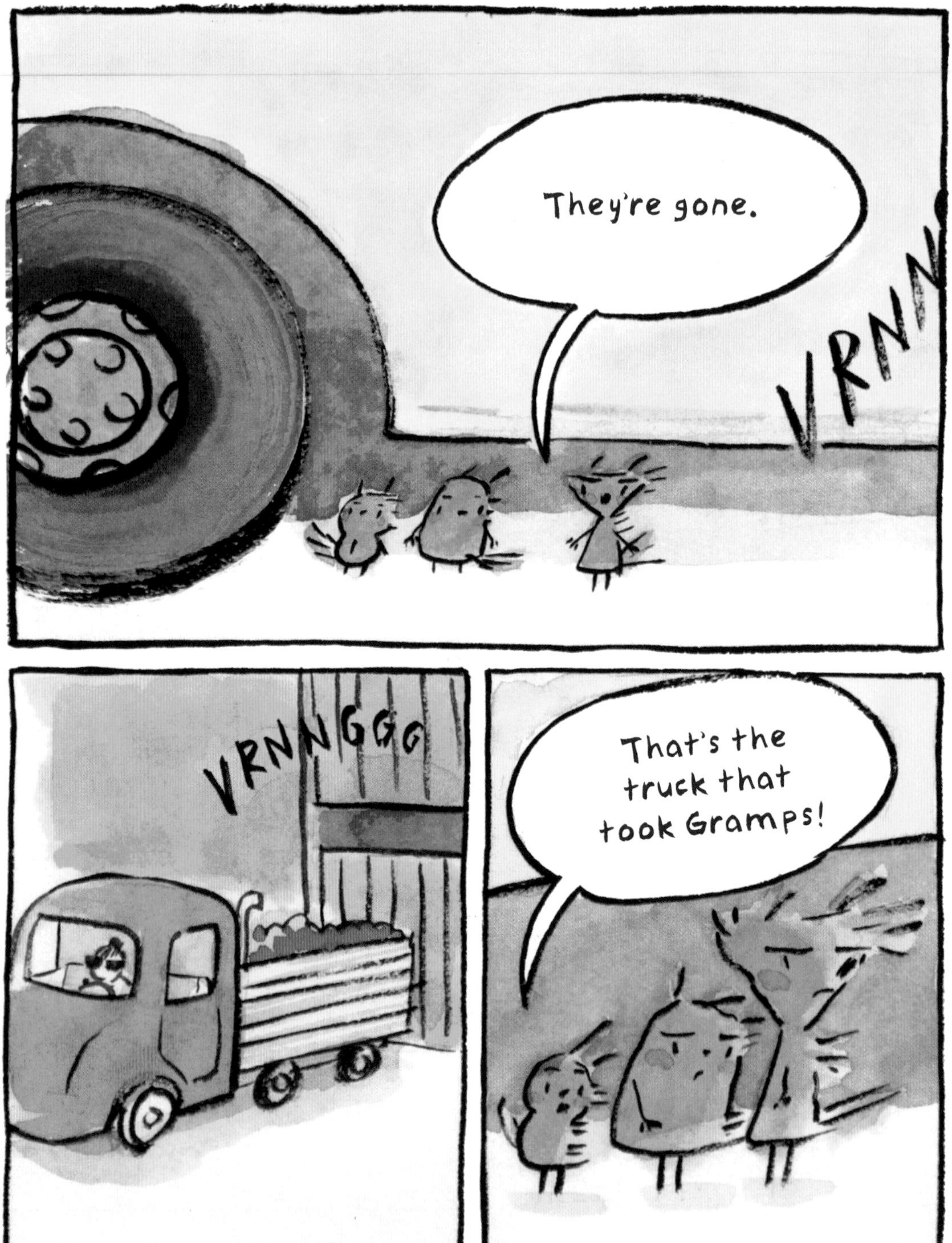
They're gone.
VRNN
VRNNGGG
That's the truck that took Gramps!

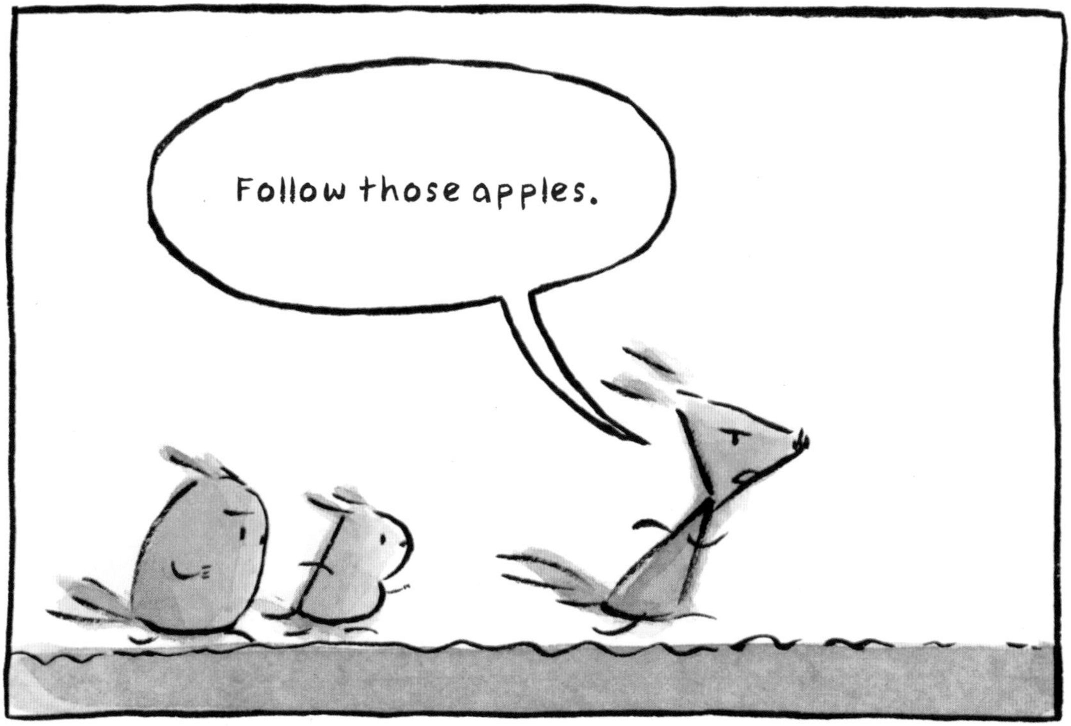
Follow those apples.

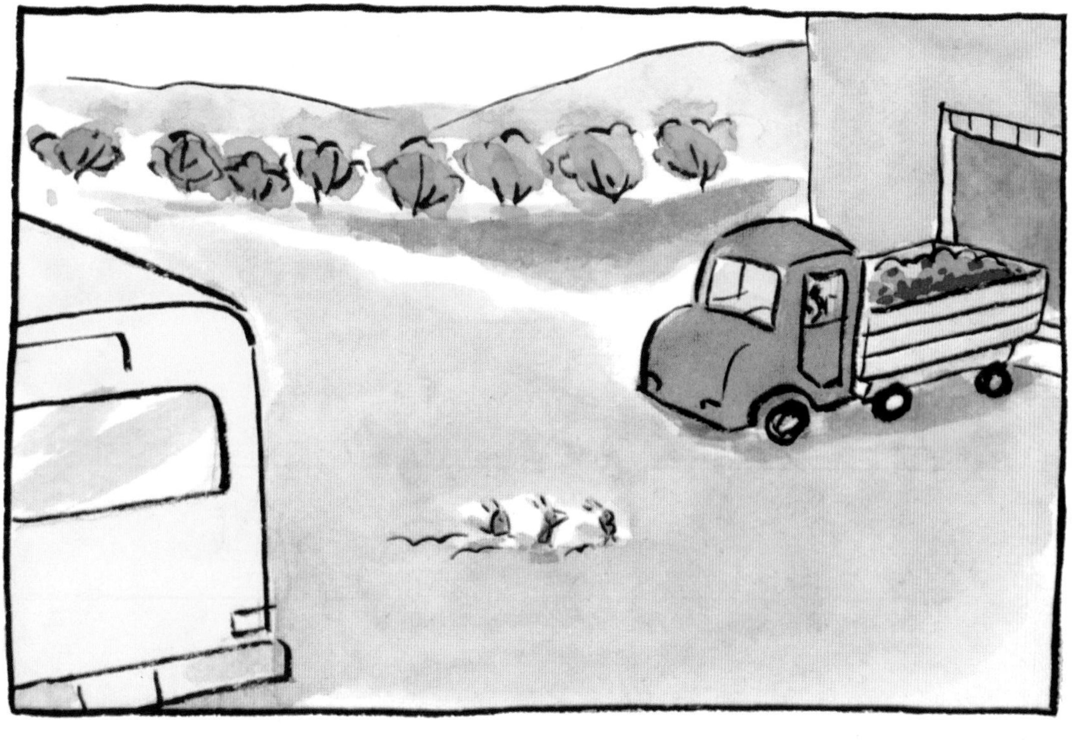

chapter 6

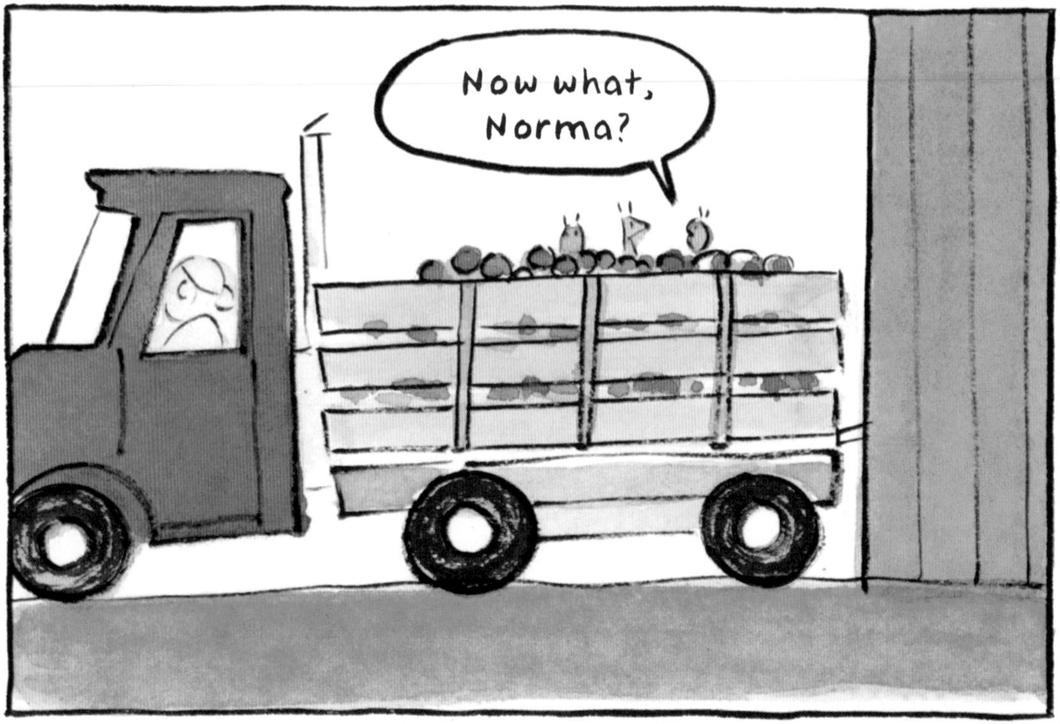
Now what, Norma?

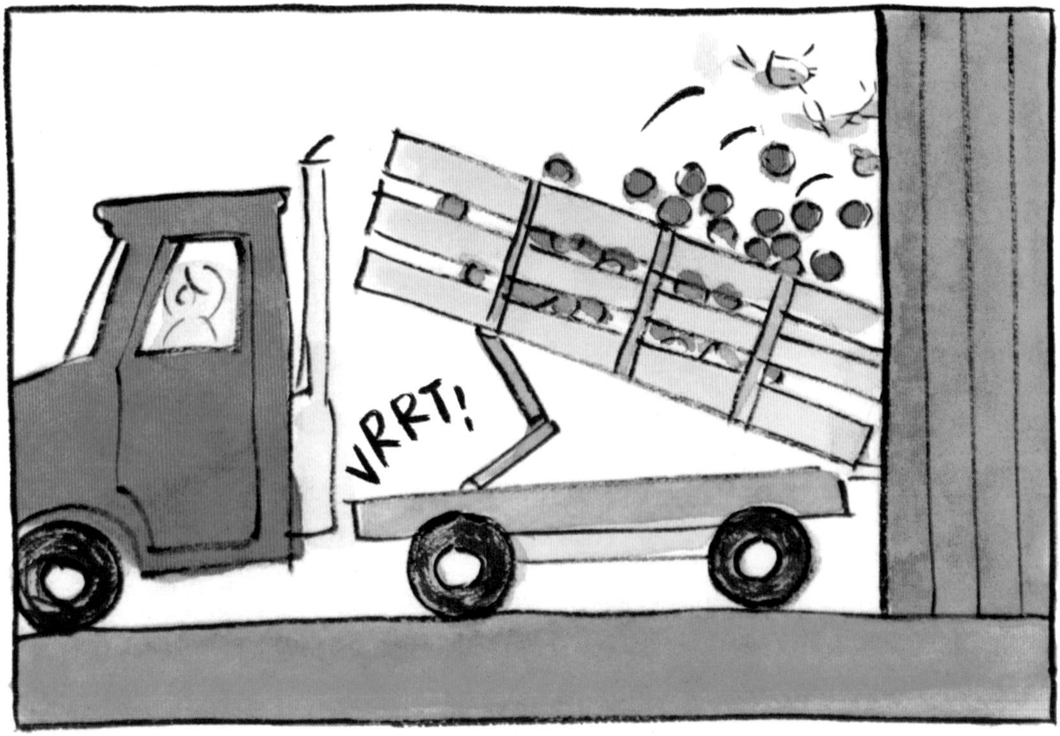
VRRT!

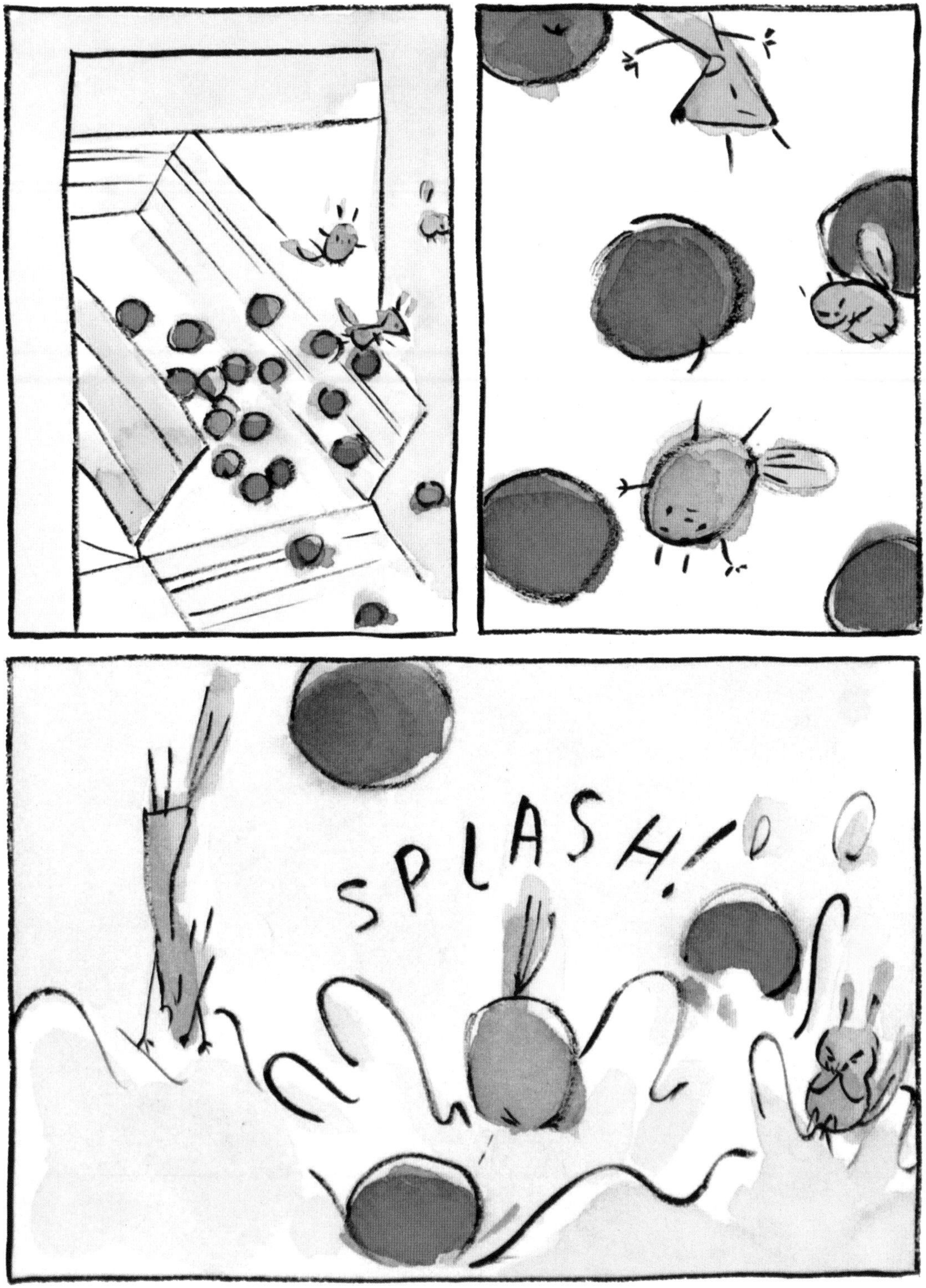
SPLASH!

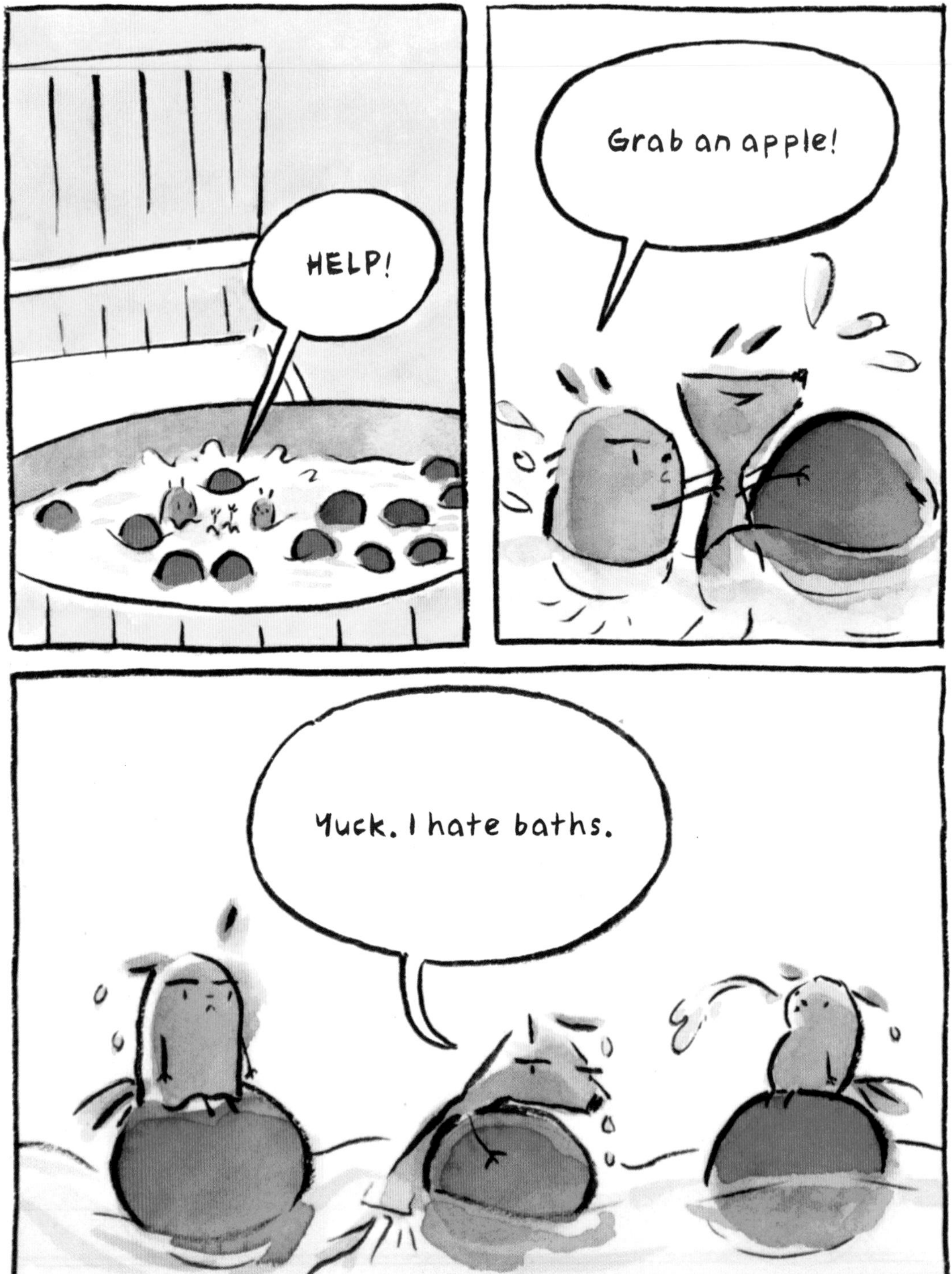
HELP!
Grab an apple!
Yuck. I hate baths.

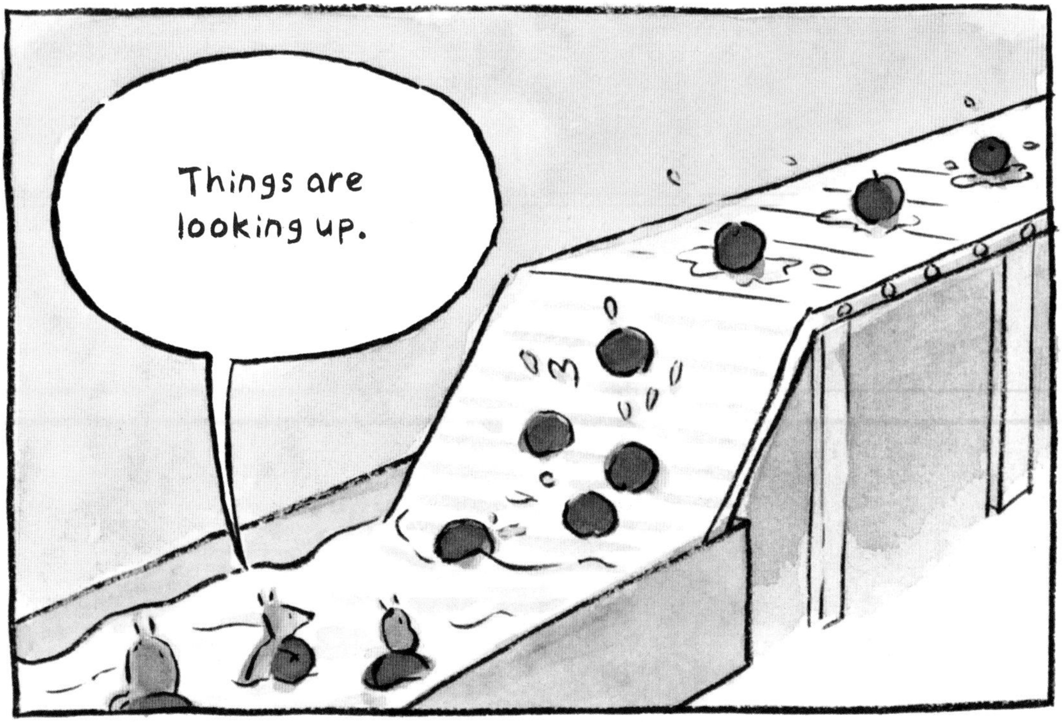
Things are looking up.

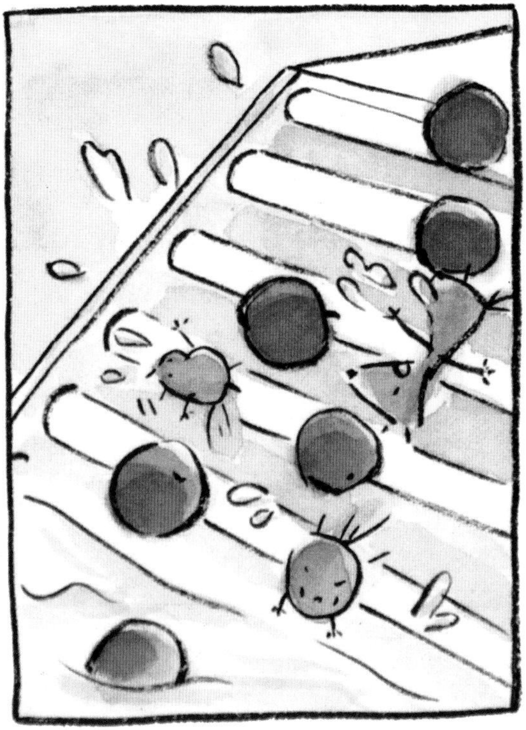

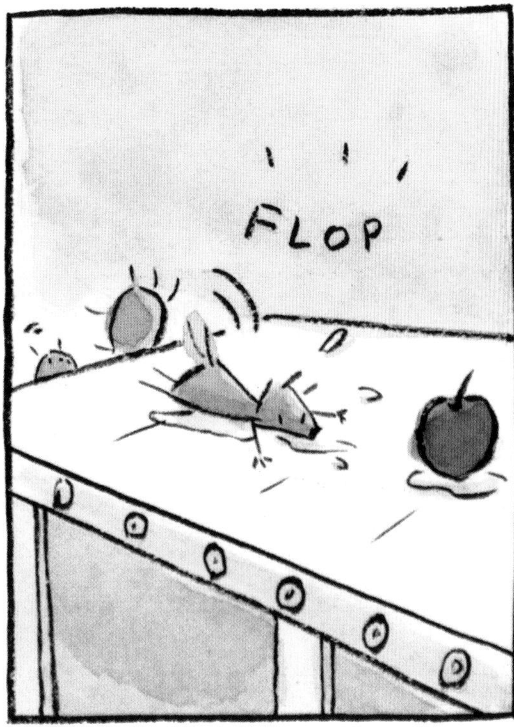
FLOP

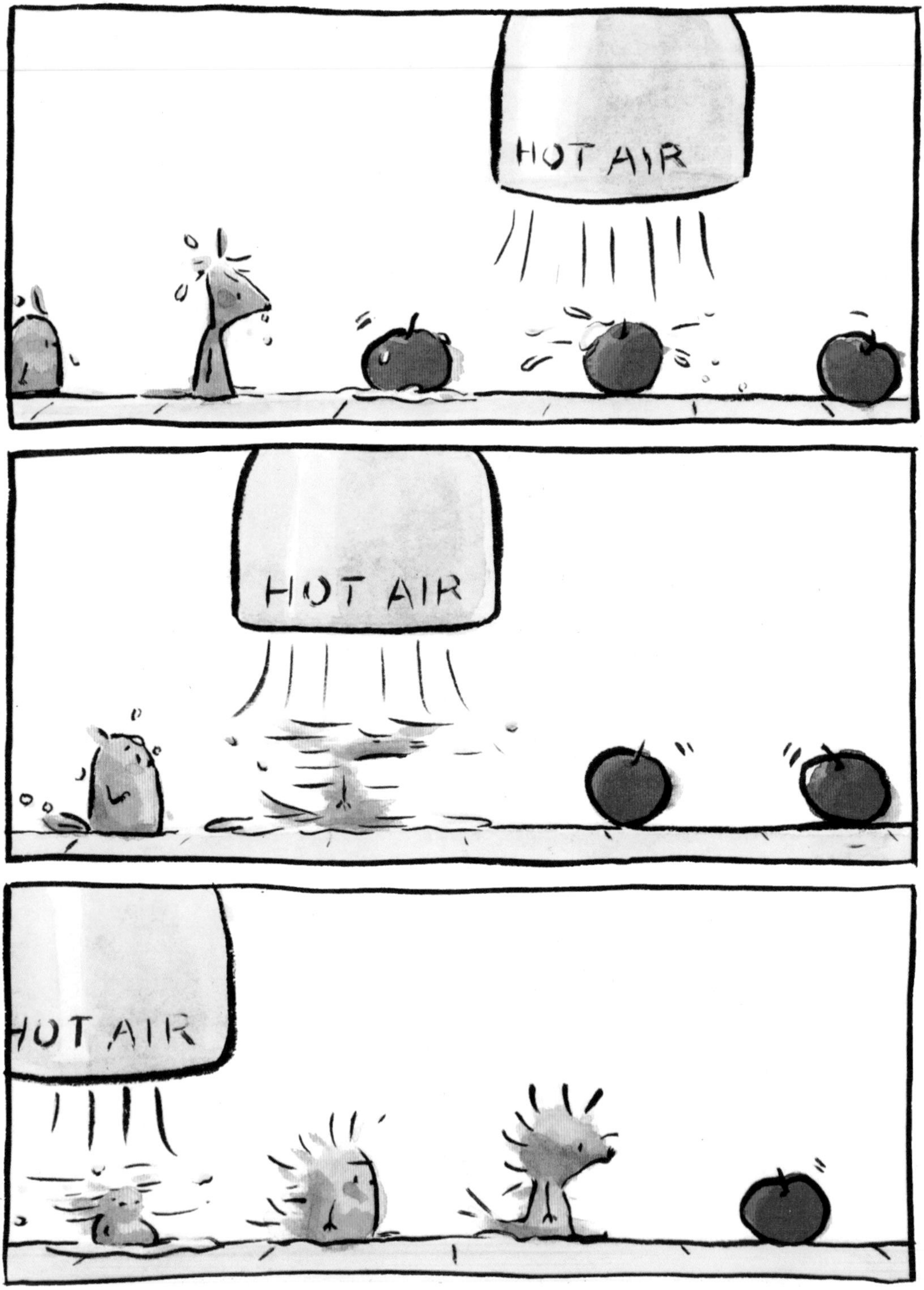
HOT AIR
HOT AIR
HOT AIR

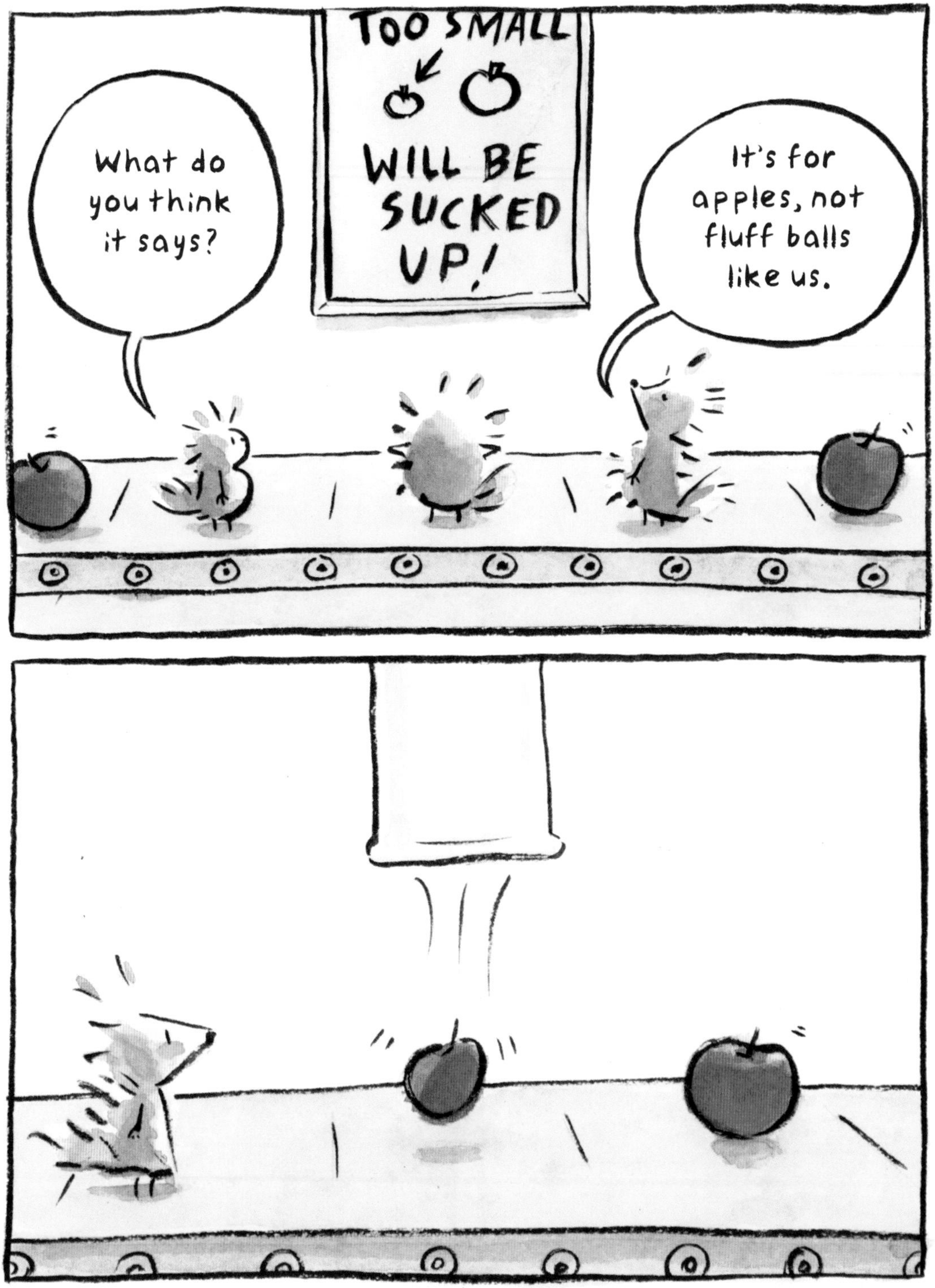
TOO SMALL
WILL BE SUCKED UP!
What do you think it says?
It's for apples, not fluff balls like us.

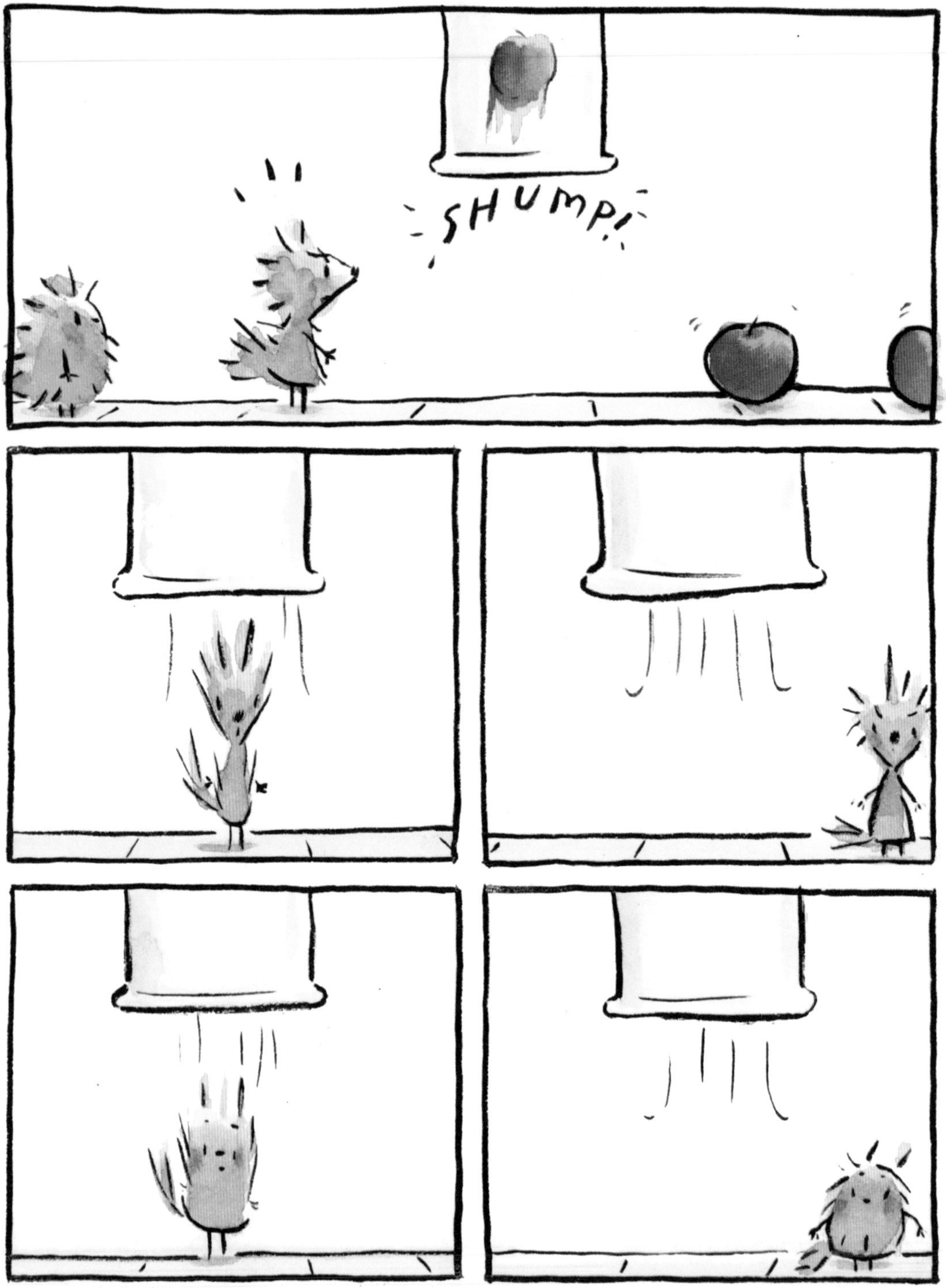
SHUMP!

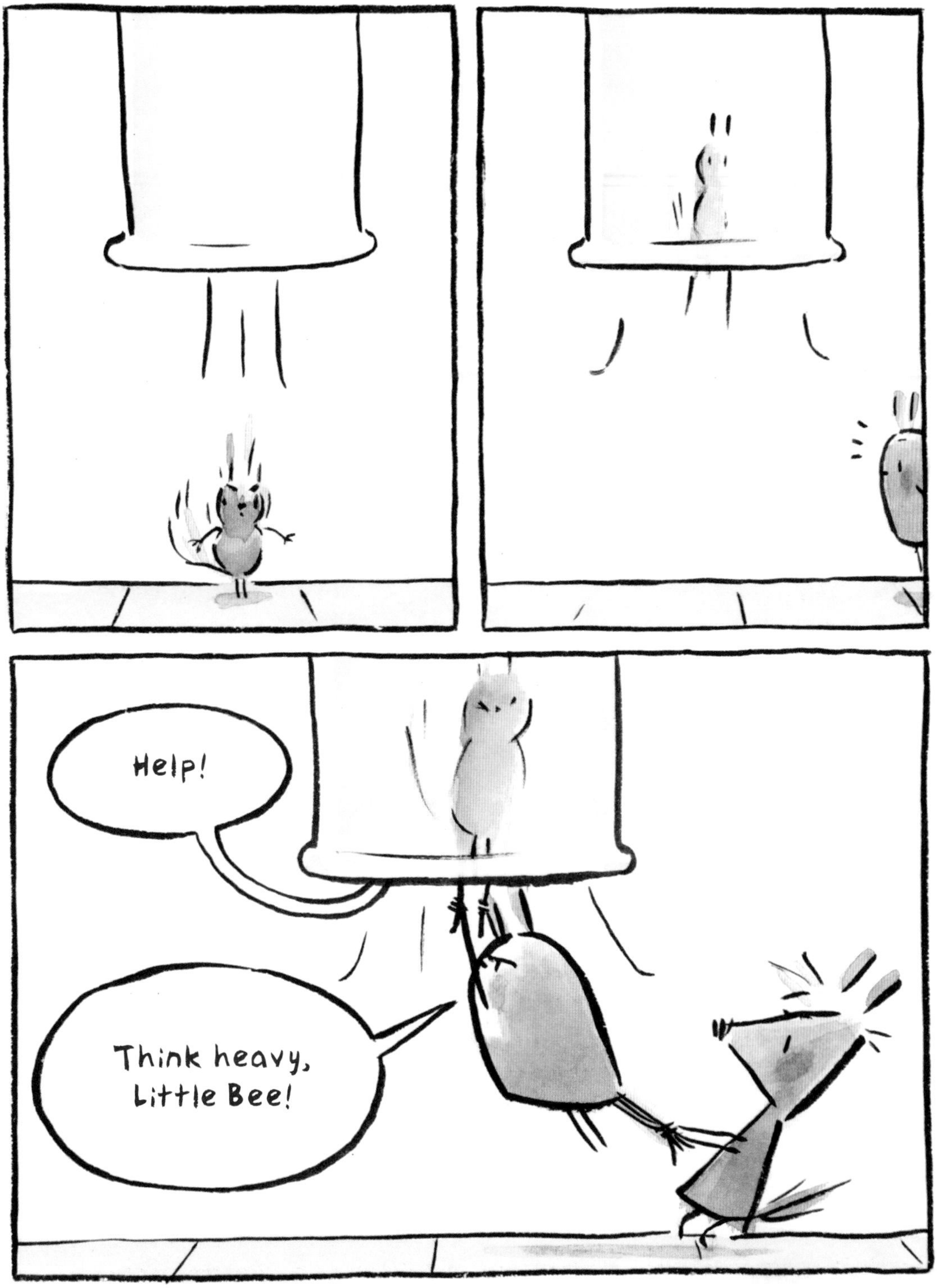
Help!
Think heavy, Little Bee!

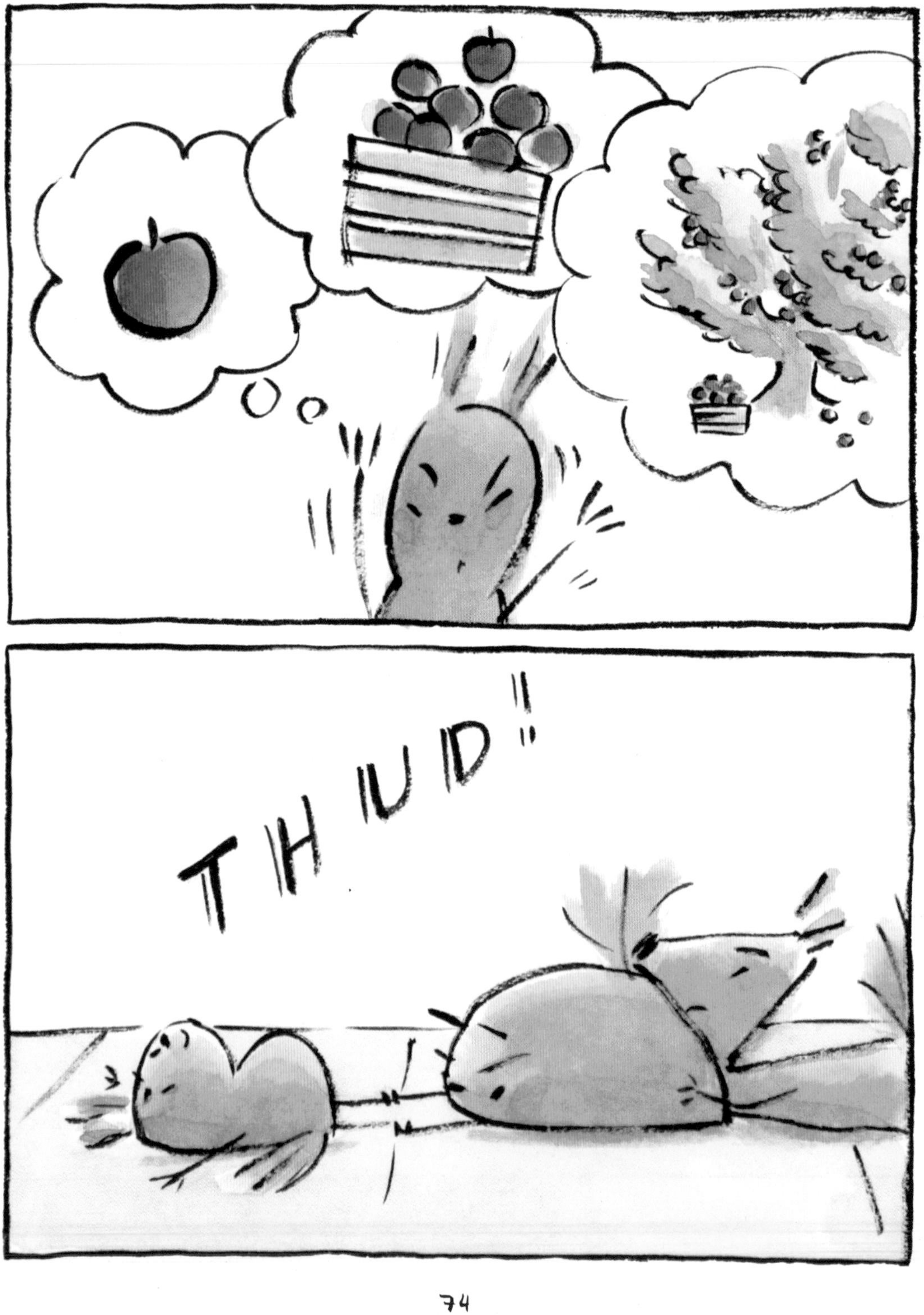
THUD!!

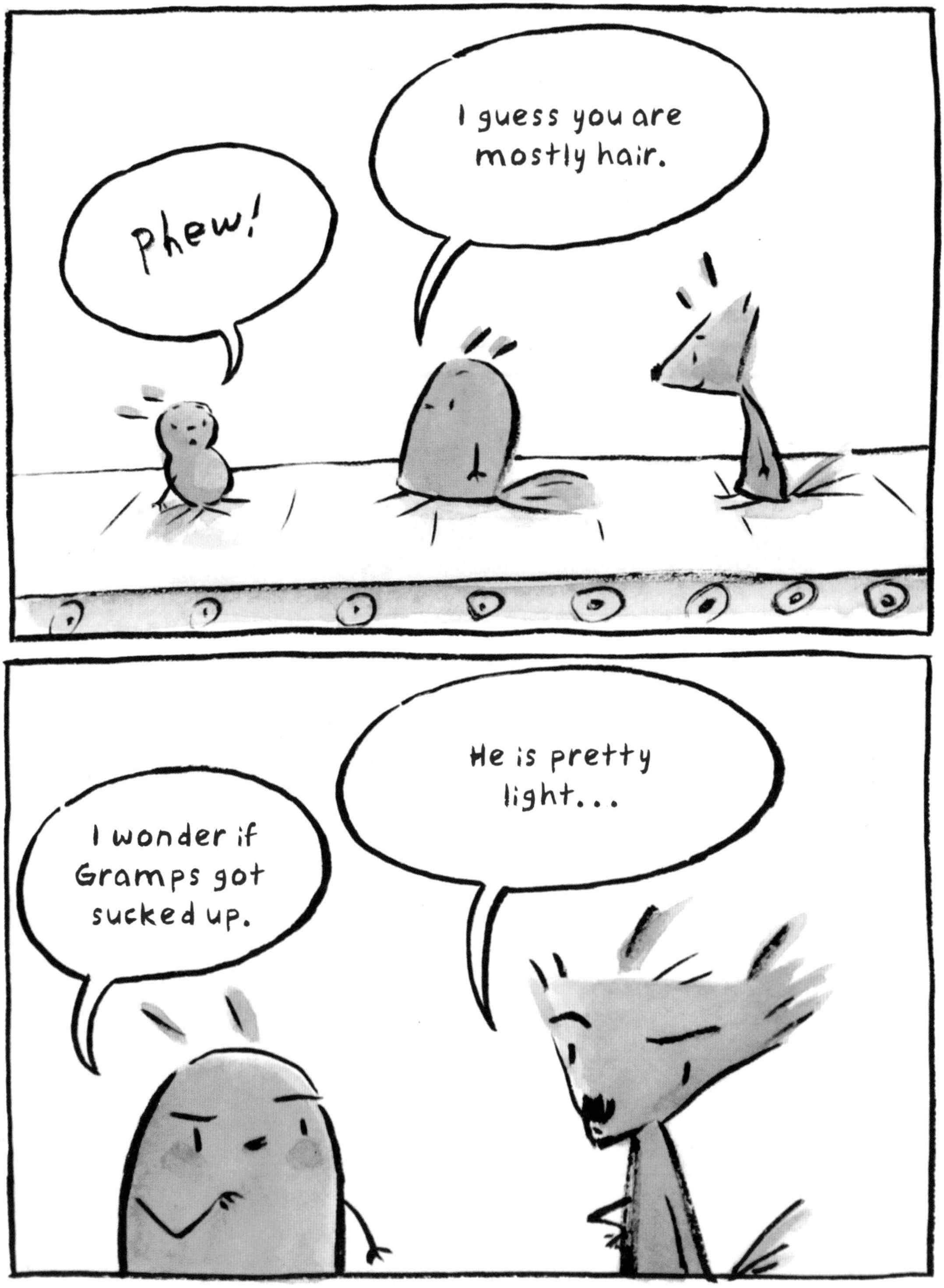
Phew!
I guess you are mostly hair.
I wonder if Gramps got sucked up.
He is pretty light...

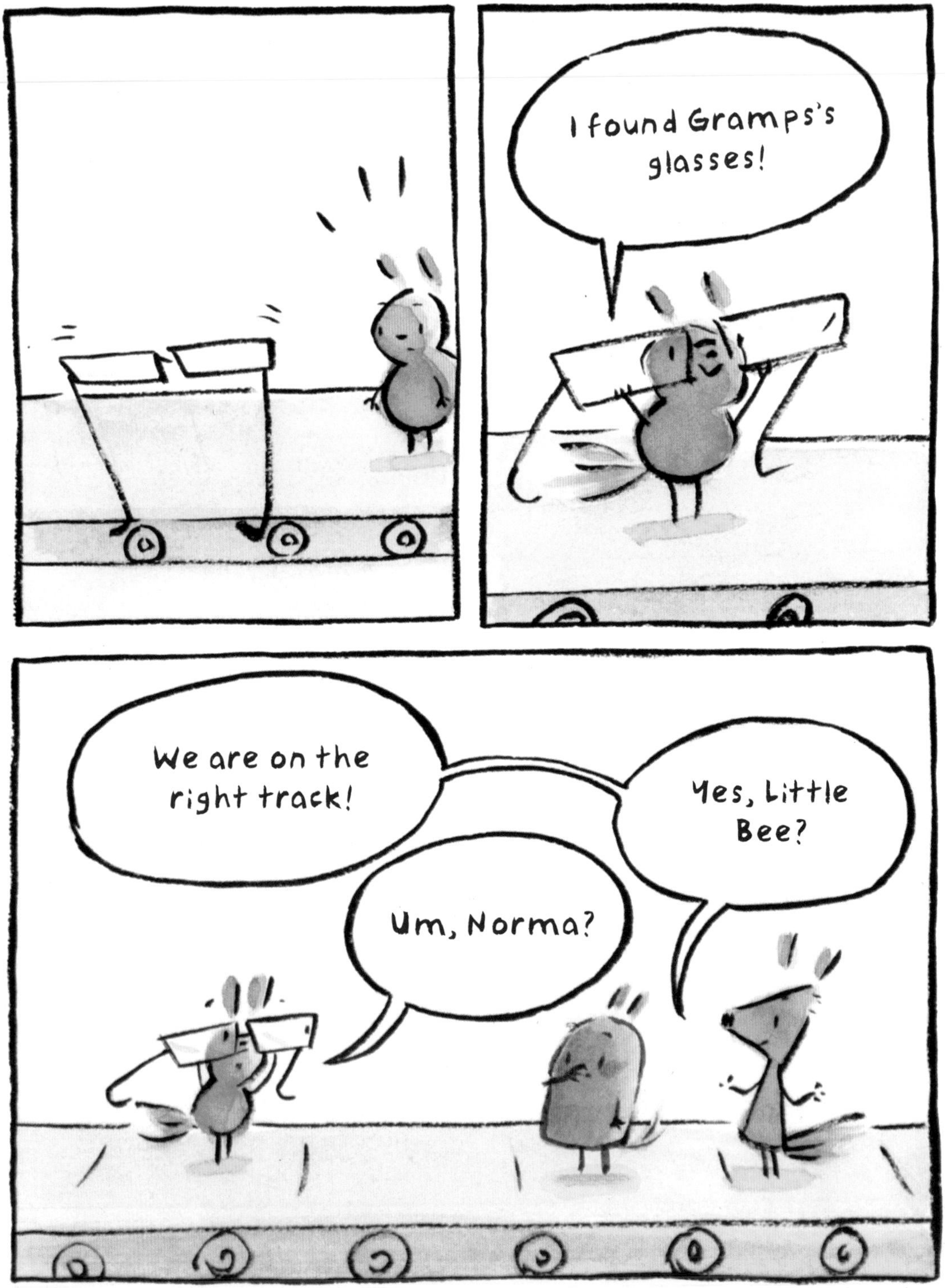
I found Gramps's glasses!
We are on the right track!
Um, Norma?
Yes, Little Bee?

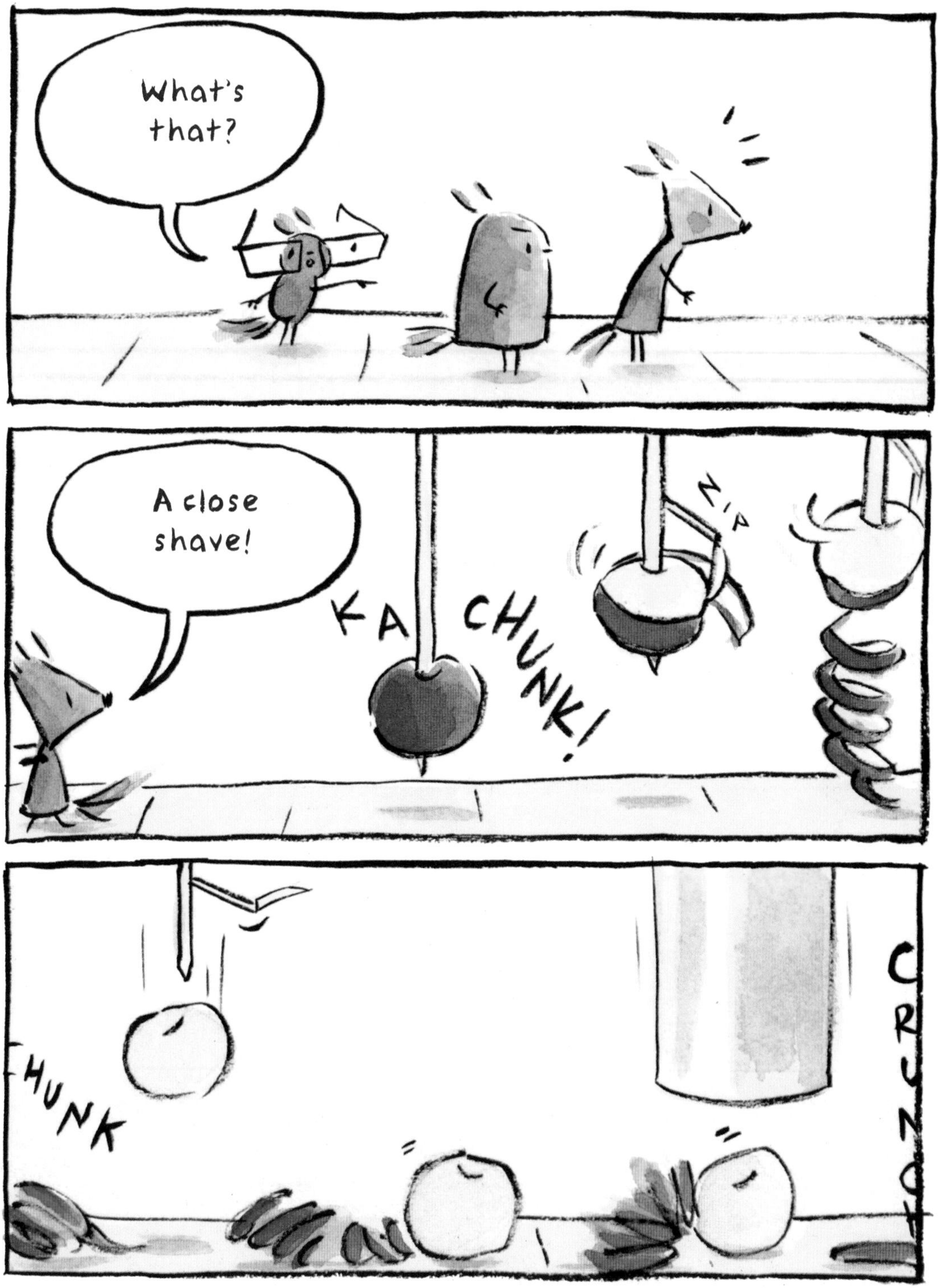
What's that?
A close shave!
KA CHUNK!
ZIP
HUNK
CRUNCH

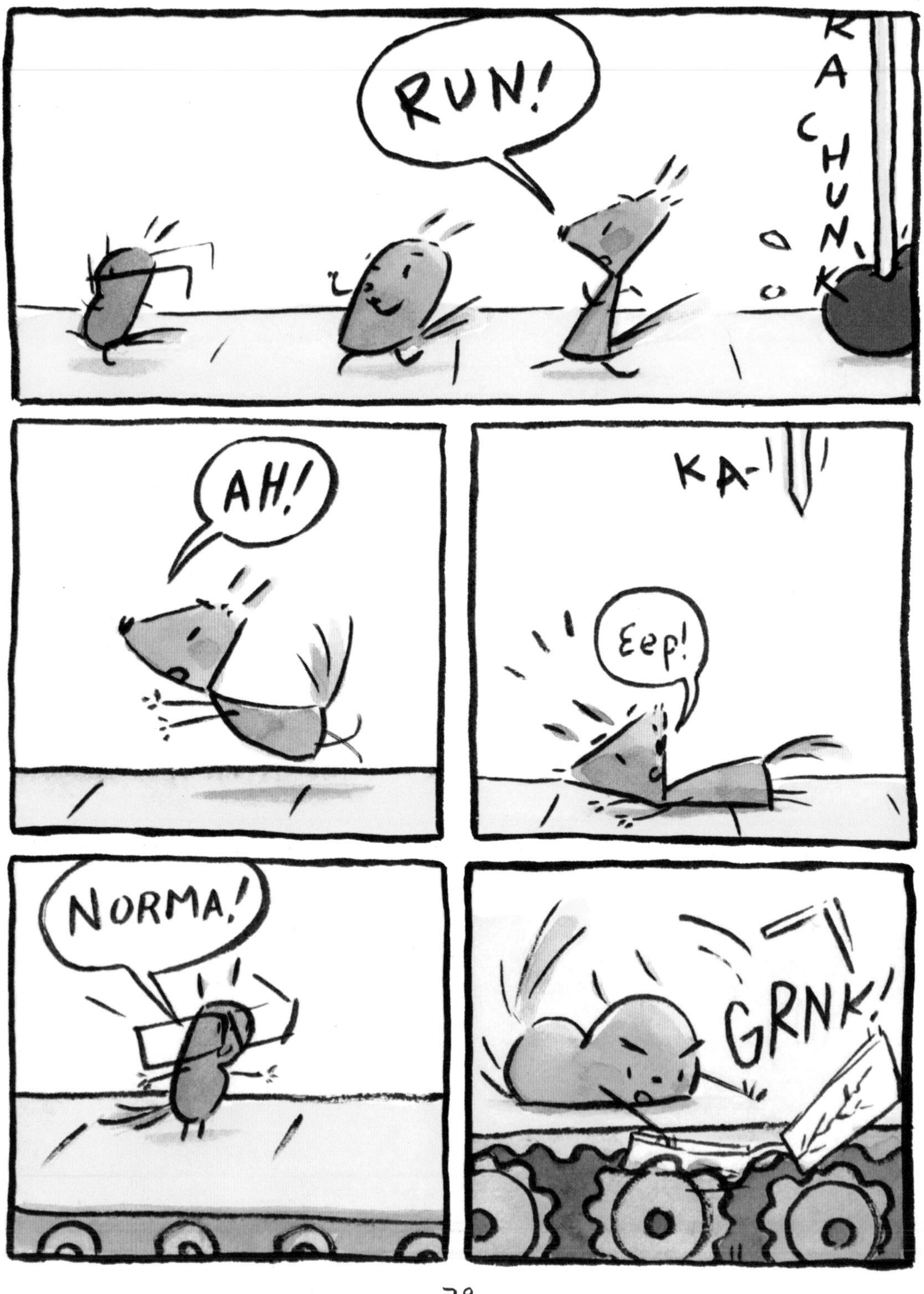
RUN!
KRACHUNK
AH!
KA-
Eep!
NORMA!
GRNK!

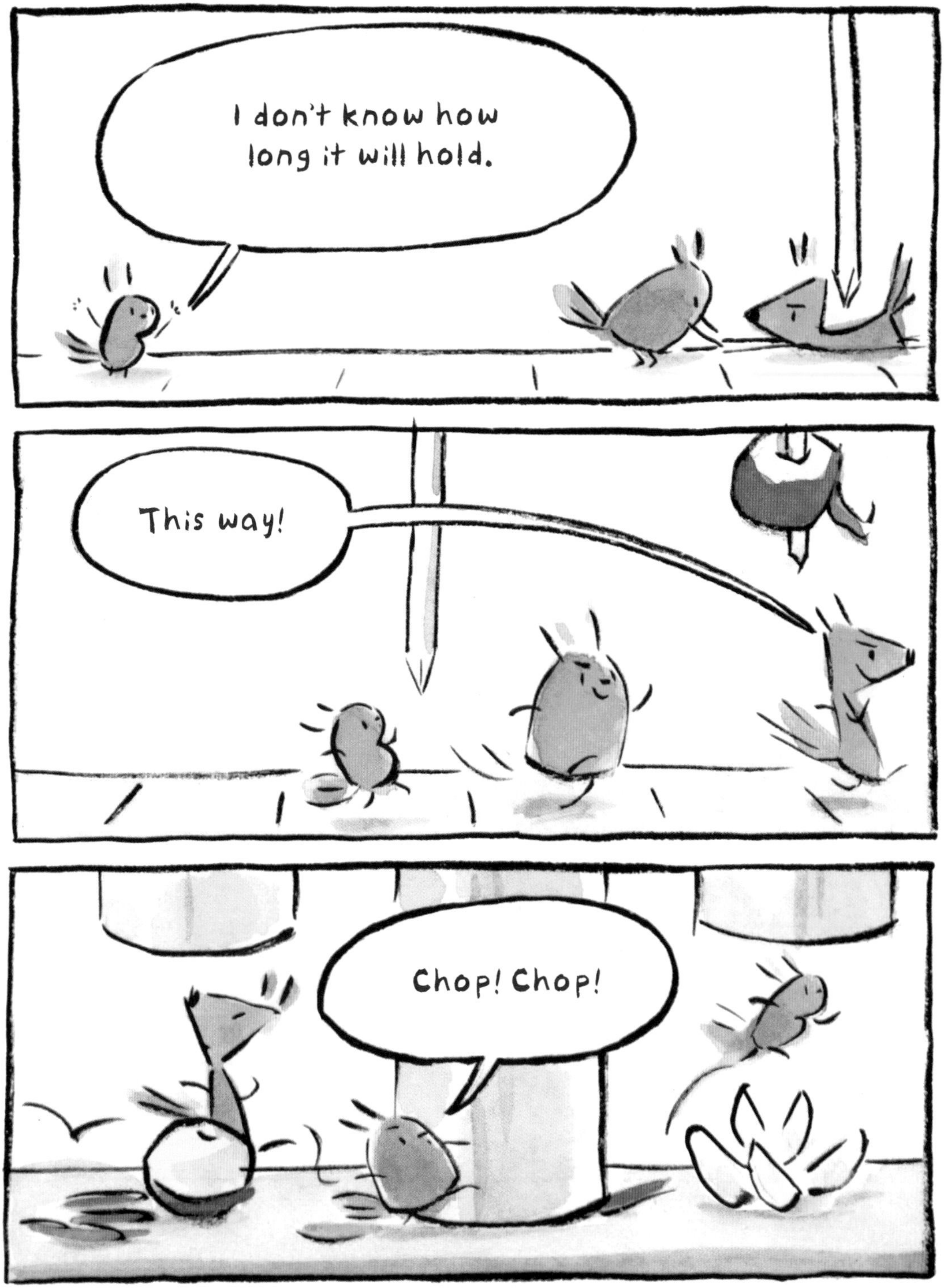
I don't know how long it will hold.
This way!
Chop! Chop!

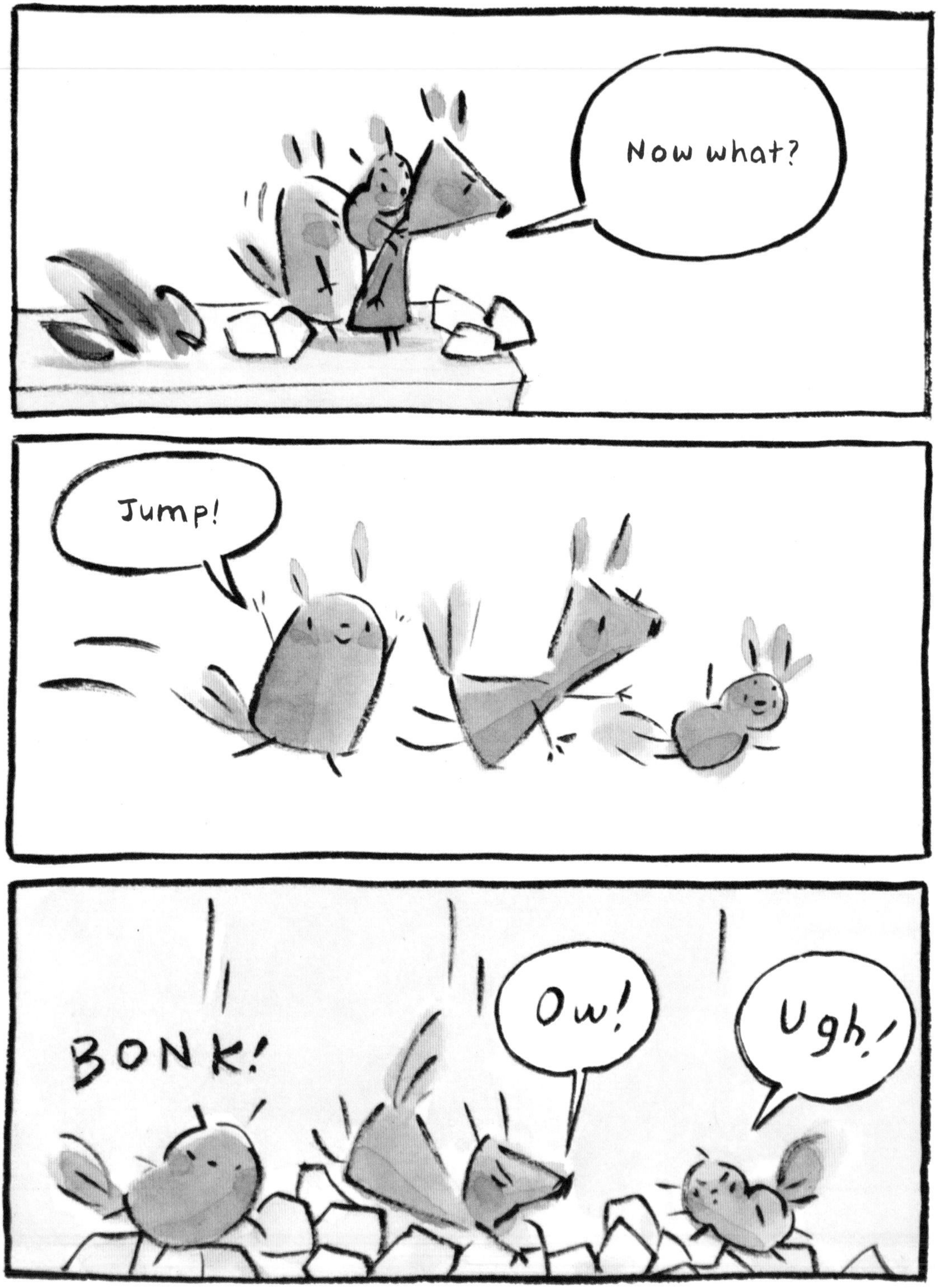
Now what?
Jump!
BONK!
Ow!
Ugh!

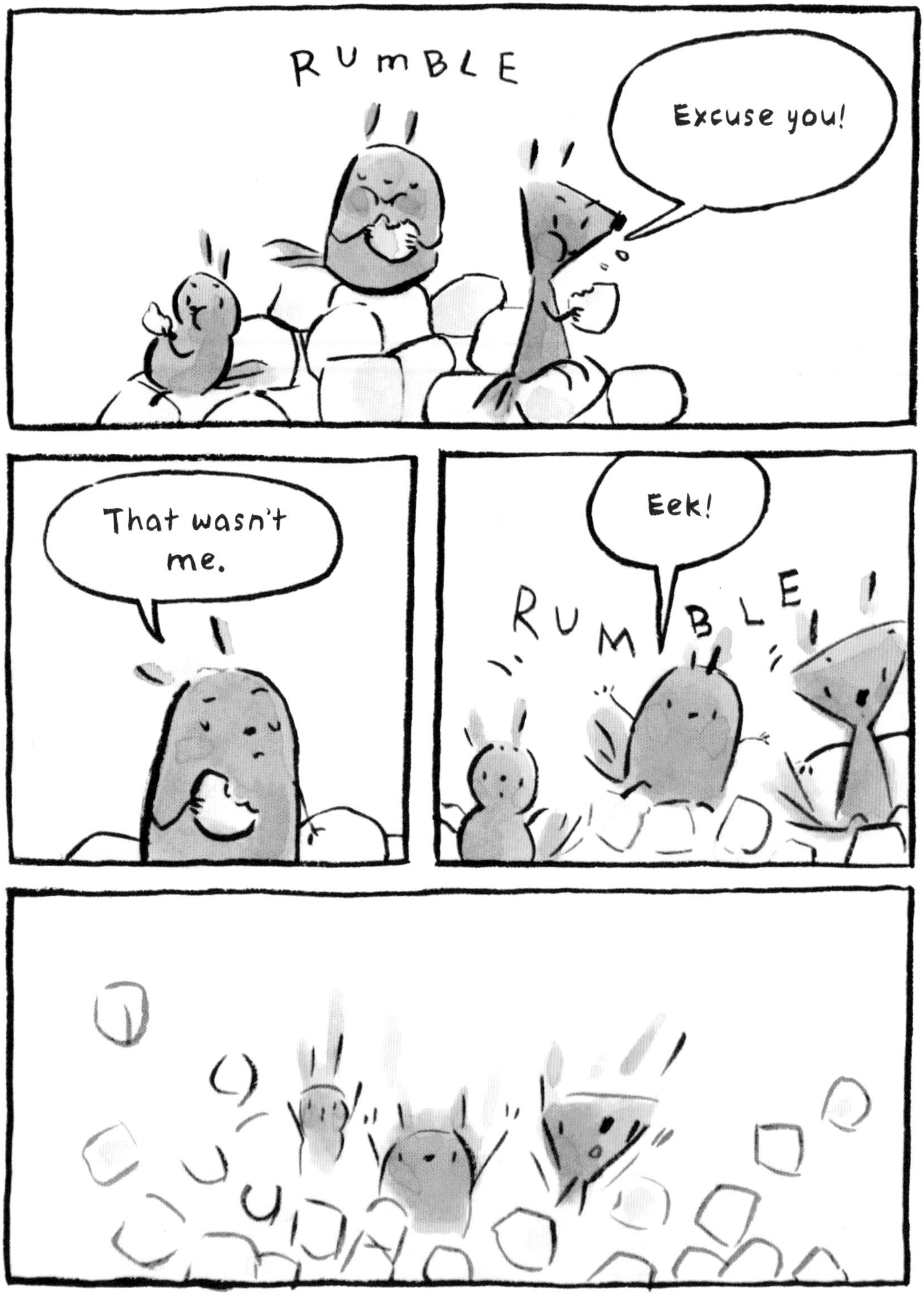
RUMBLE
Excuse you!
That wasn't me.
Eek!
RUMBLE

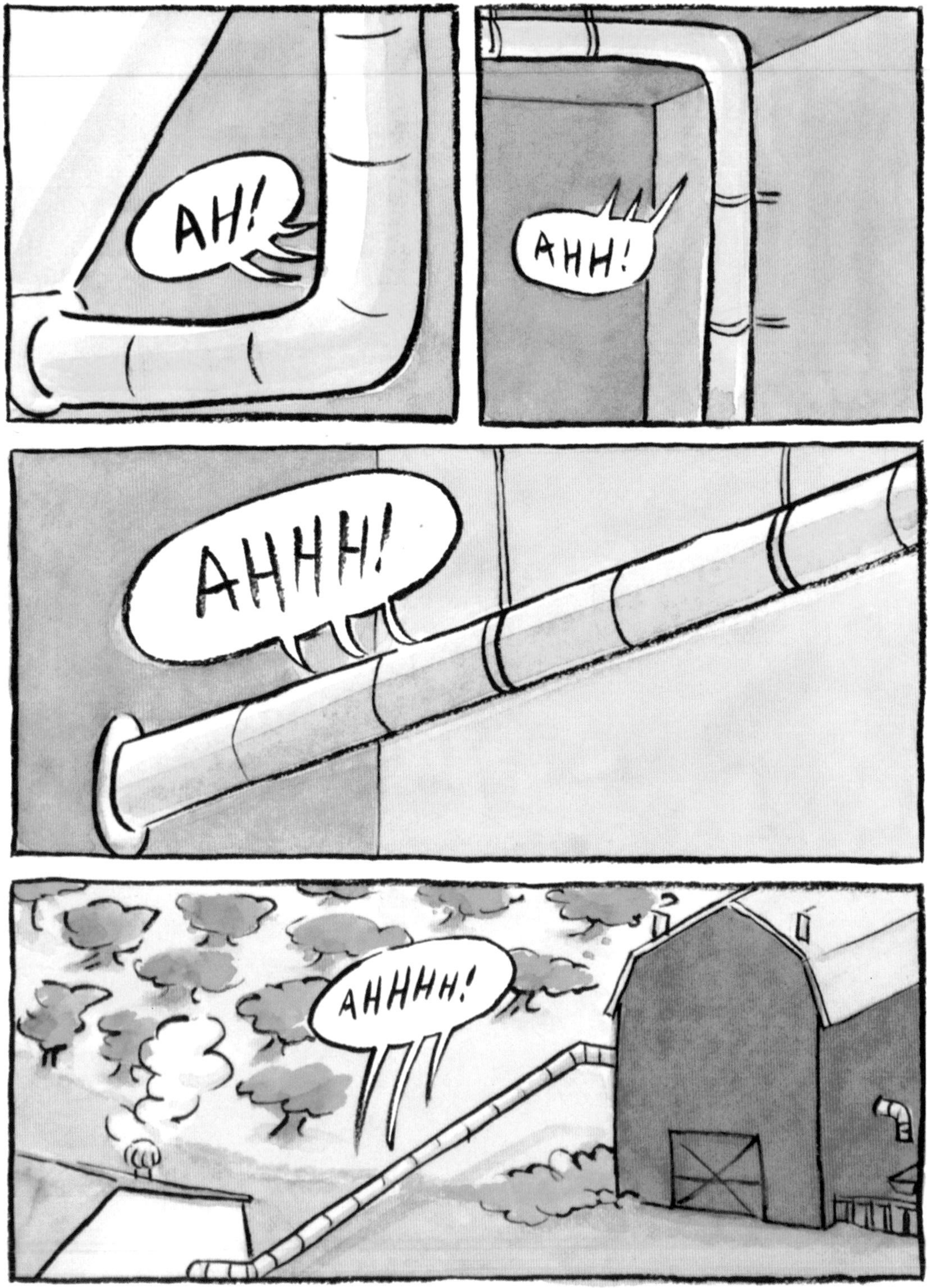
AH!
AHH!
AHHH!
AHHHH!

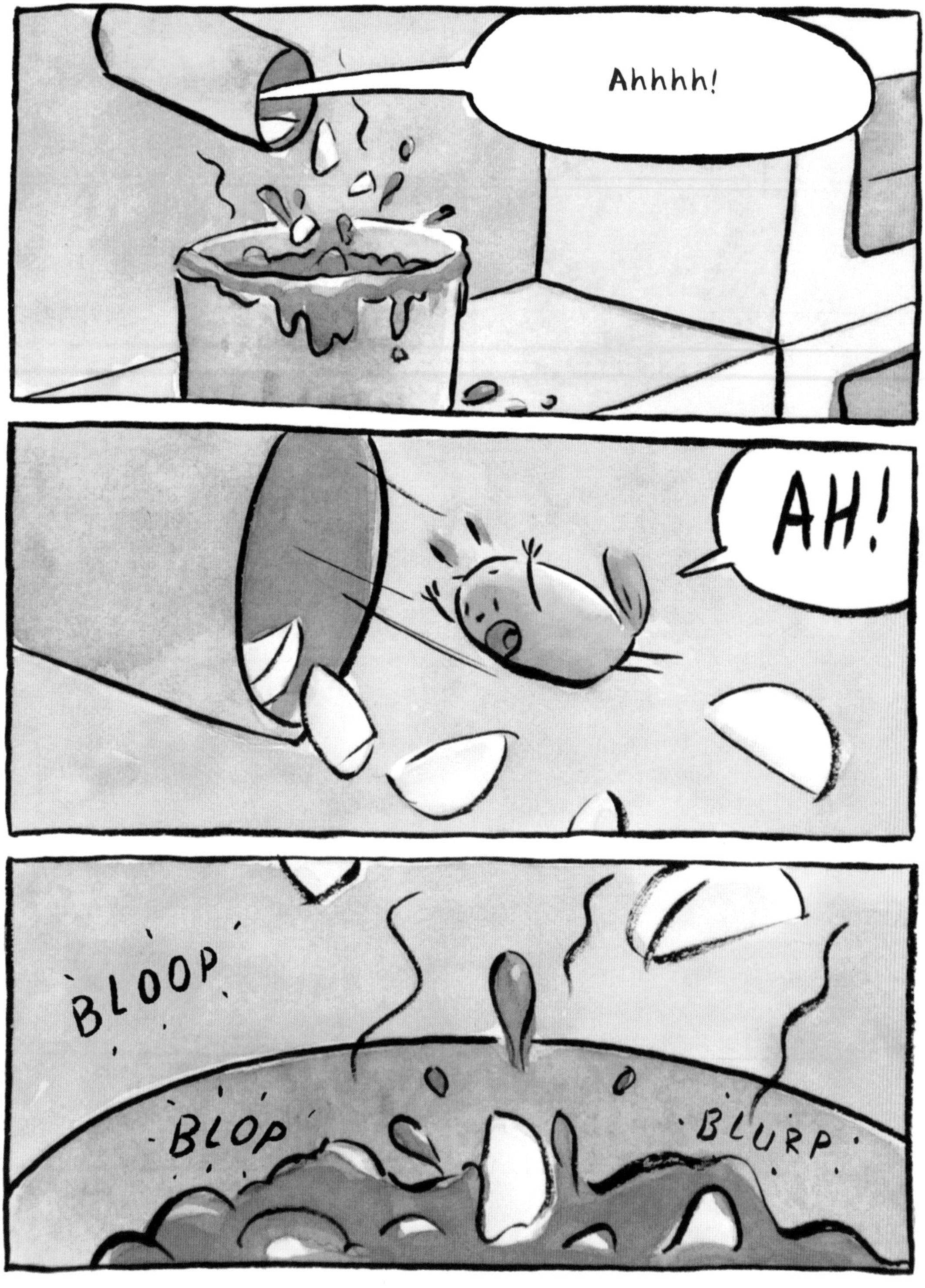
Ahhhh!
AH!
BLOOP
BLOP
BLURP

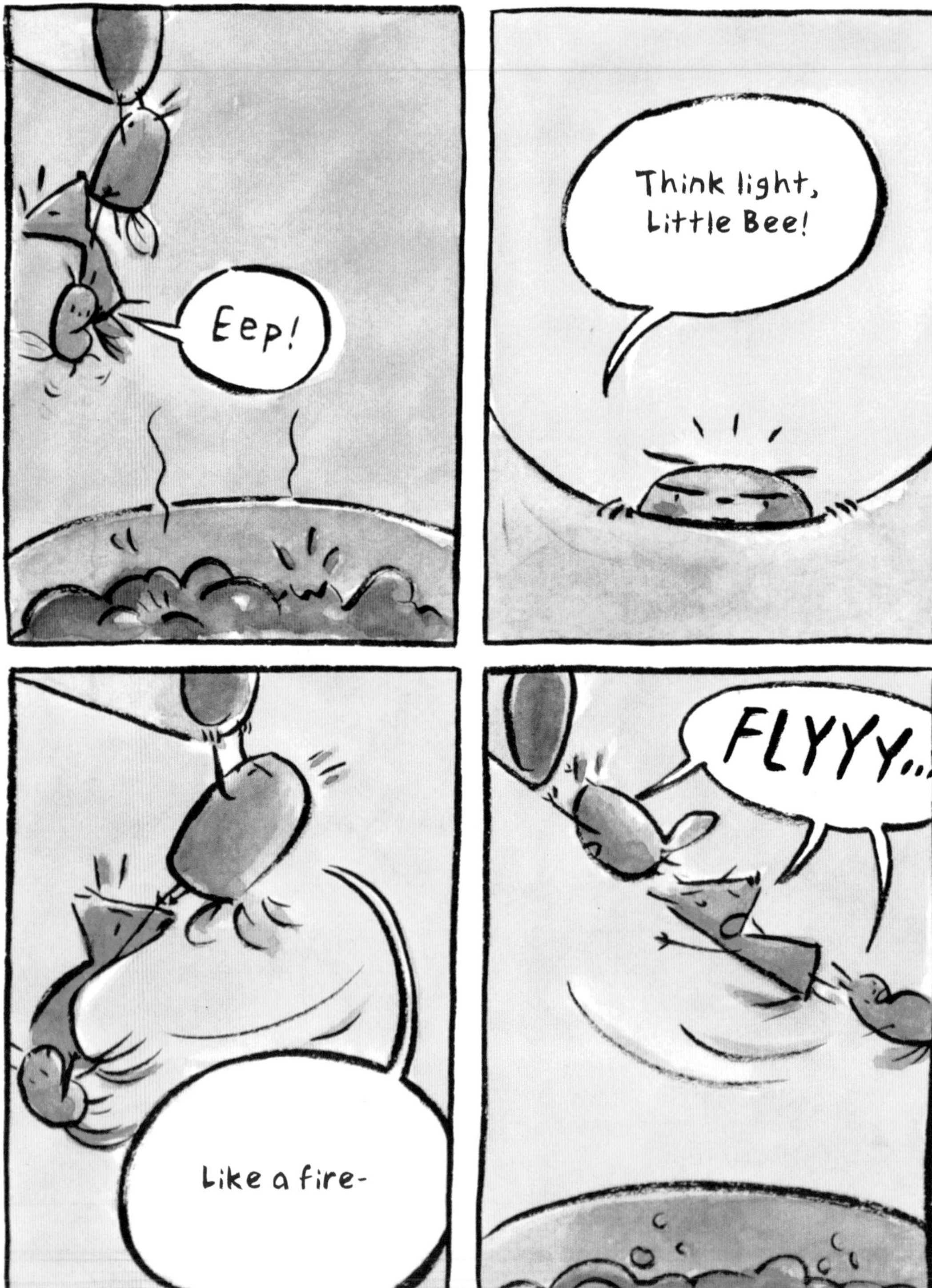
Eep!
Think light, Little Bee!
Like a fire-
FLYYY...

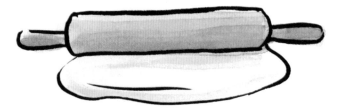

Chapter 7

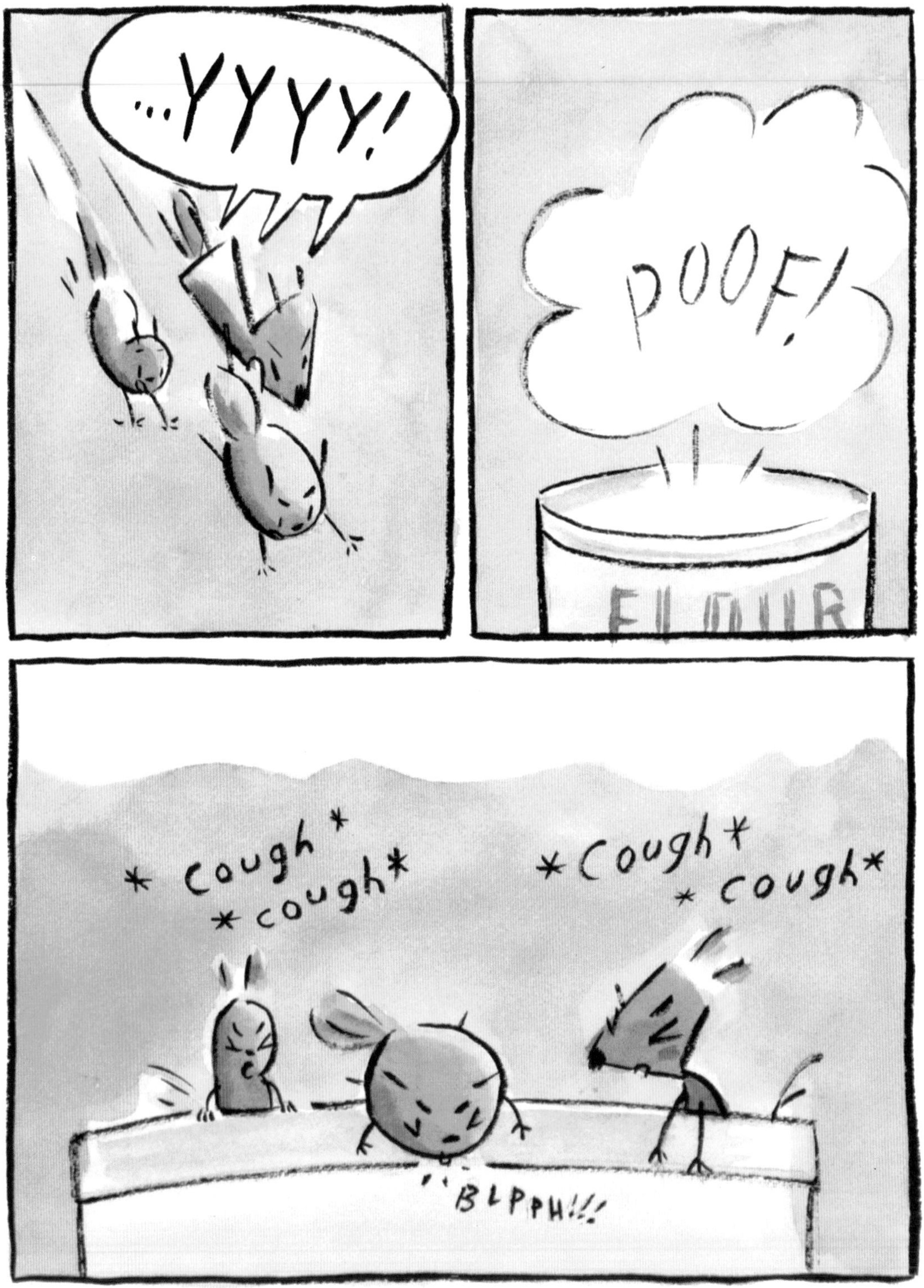
...YYYY!
POOF!
FLOUR
cough
cough
Cough
cough
BLPPH!!!

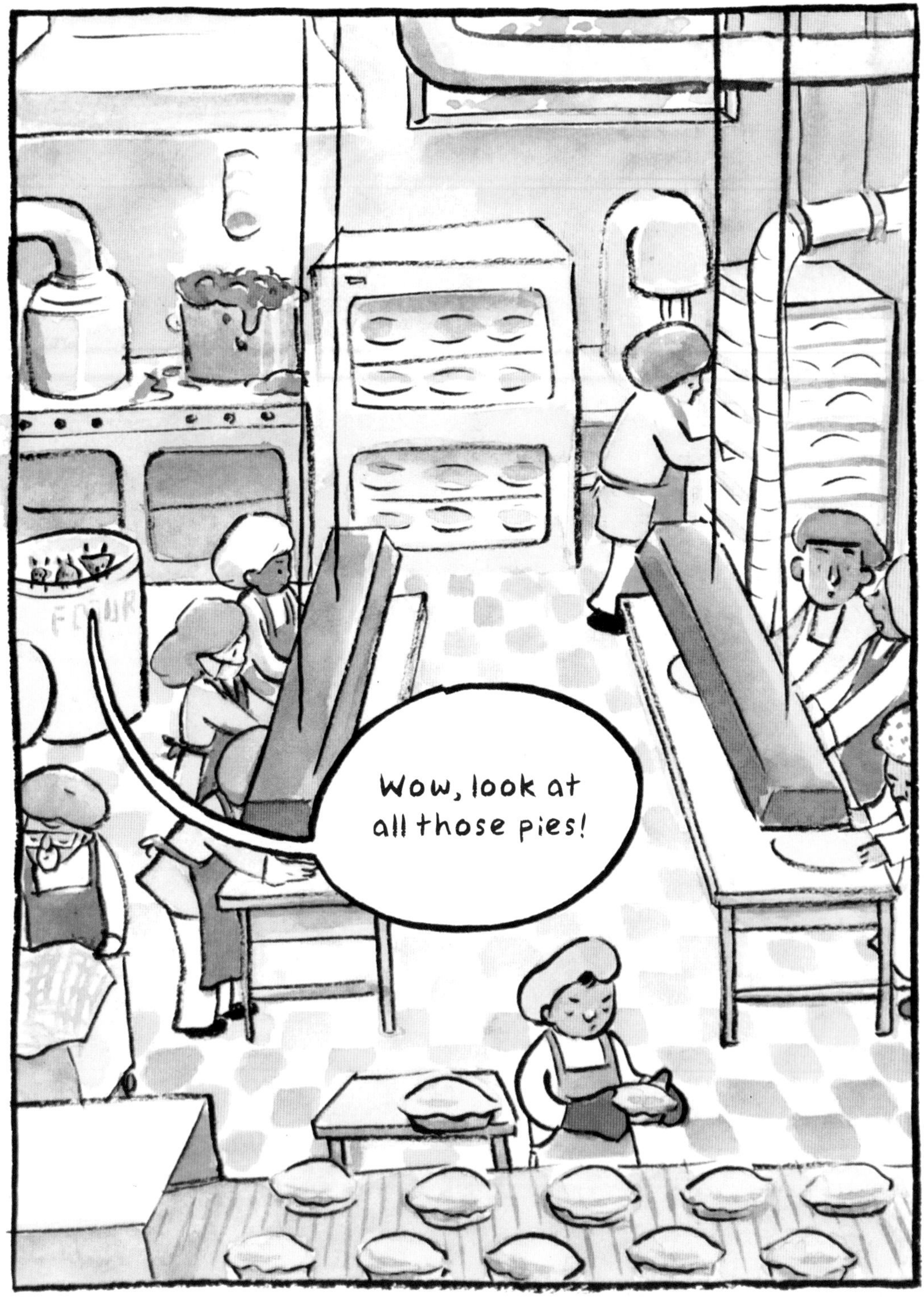
Wow, look at all those pies!
FLOUR

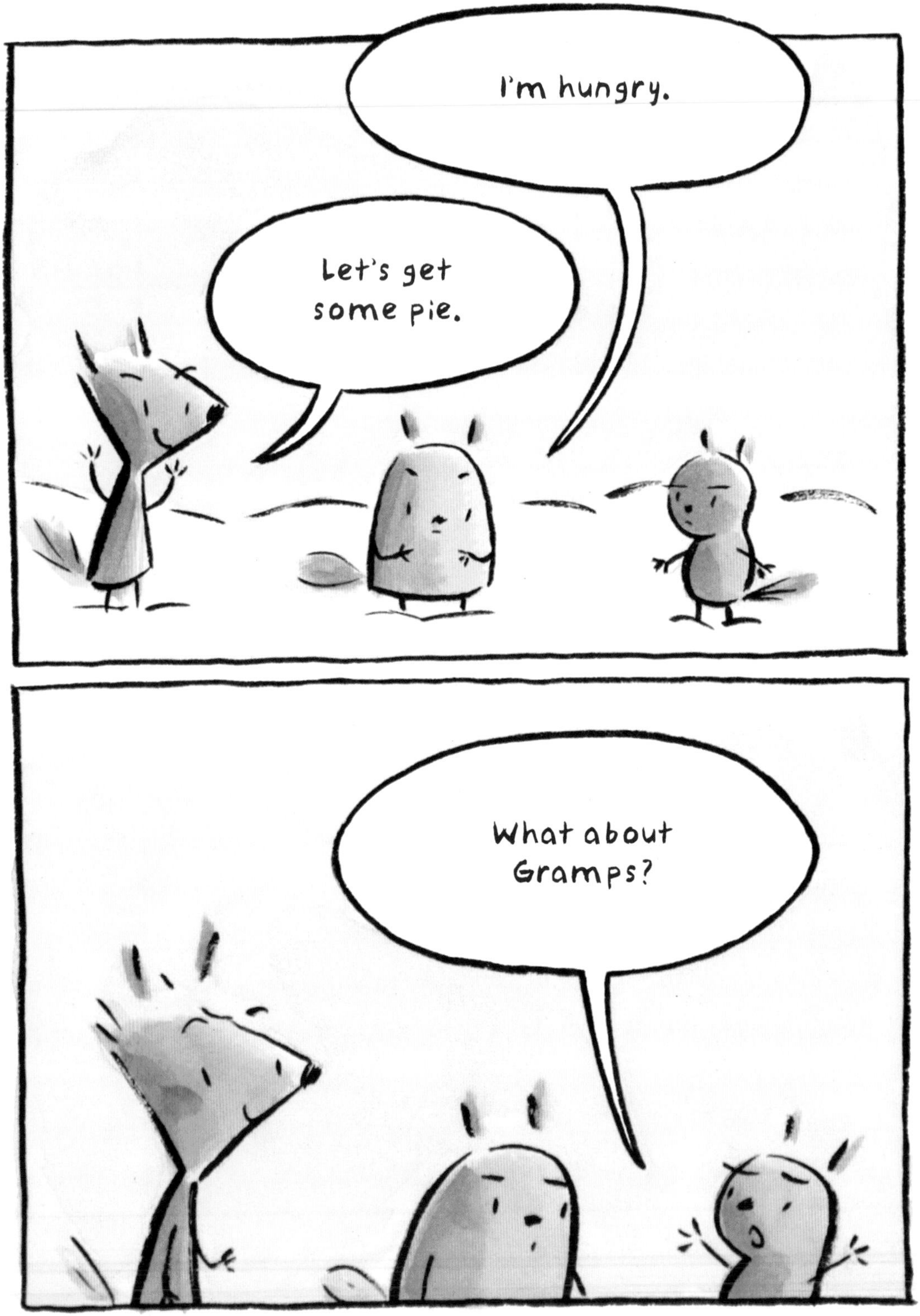
Let's get some pie.
I'm hungry.
What about Gramps?

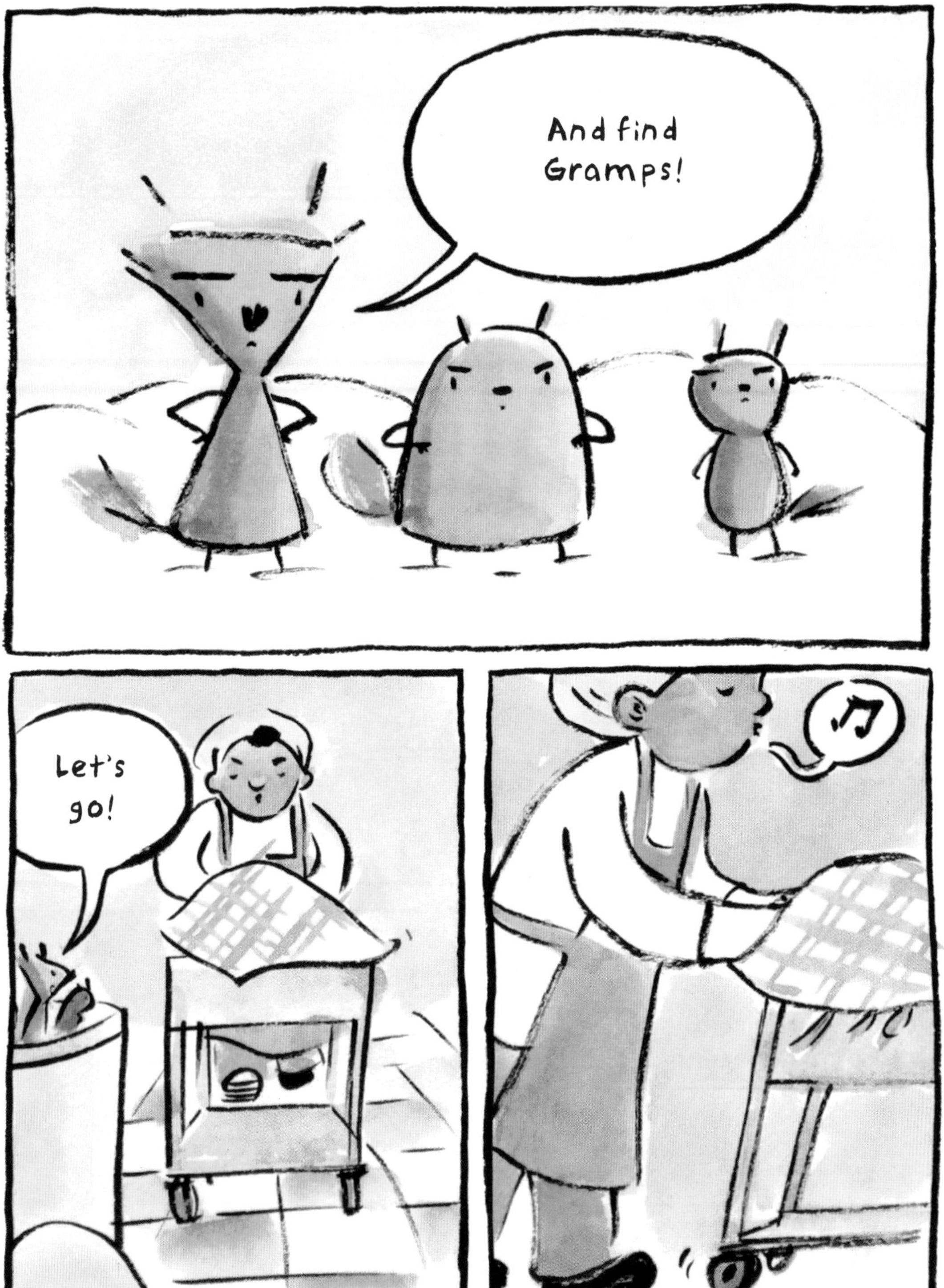
And find Gramps!
Let's go!
♫

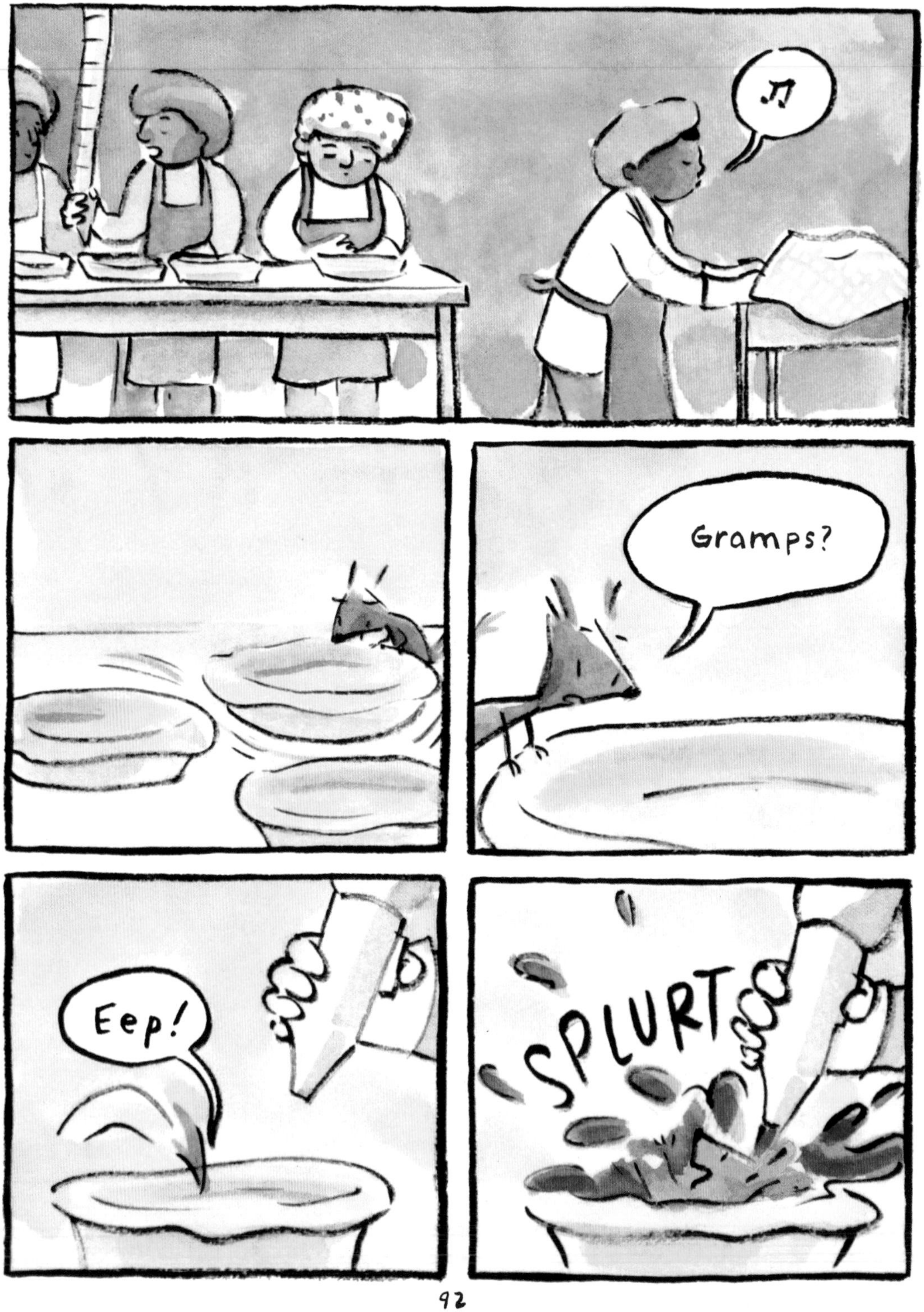
♫
Gramps?
Eep!
SPLURT

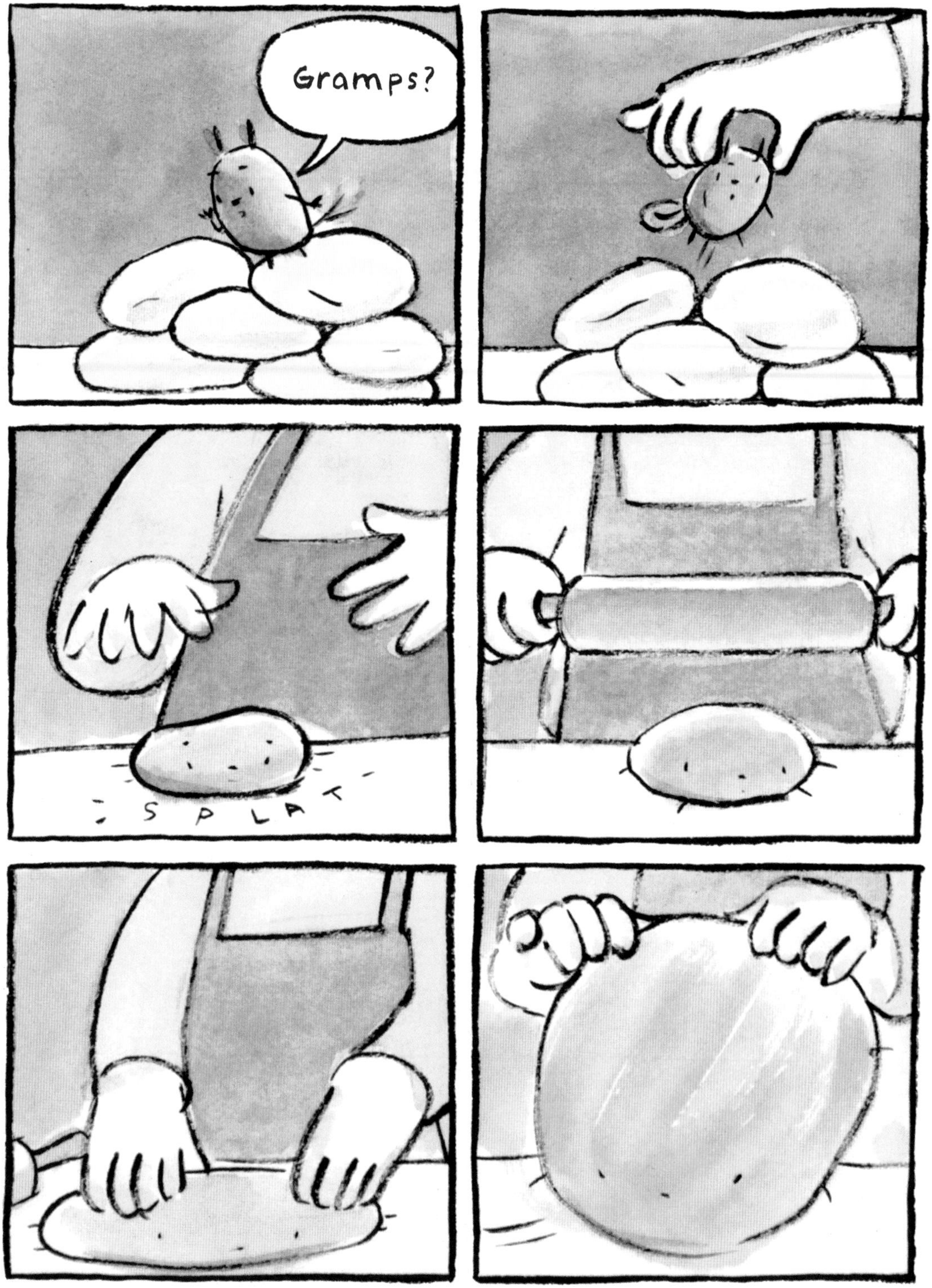
Gramps?
SPLAT

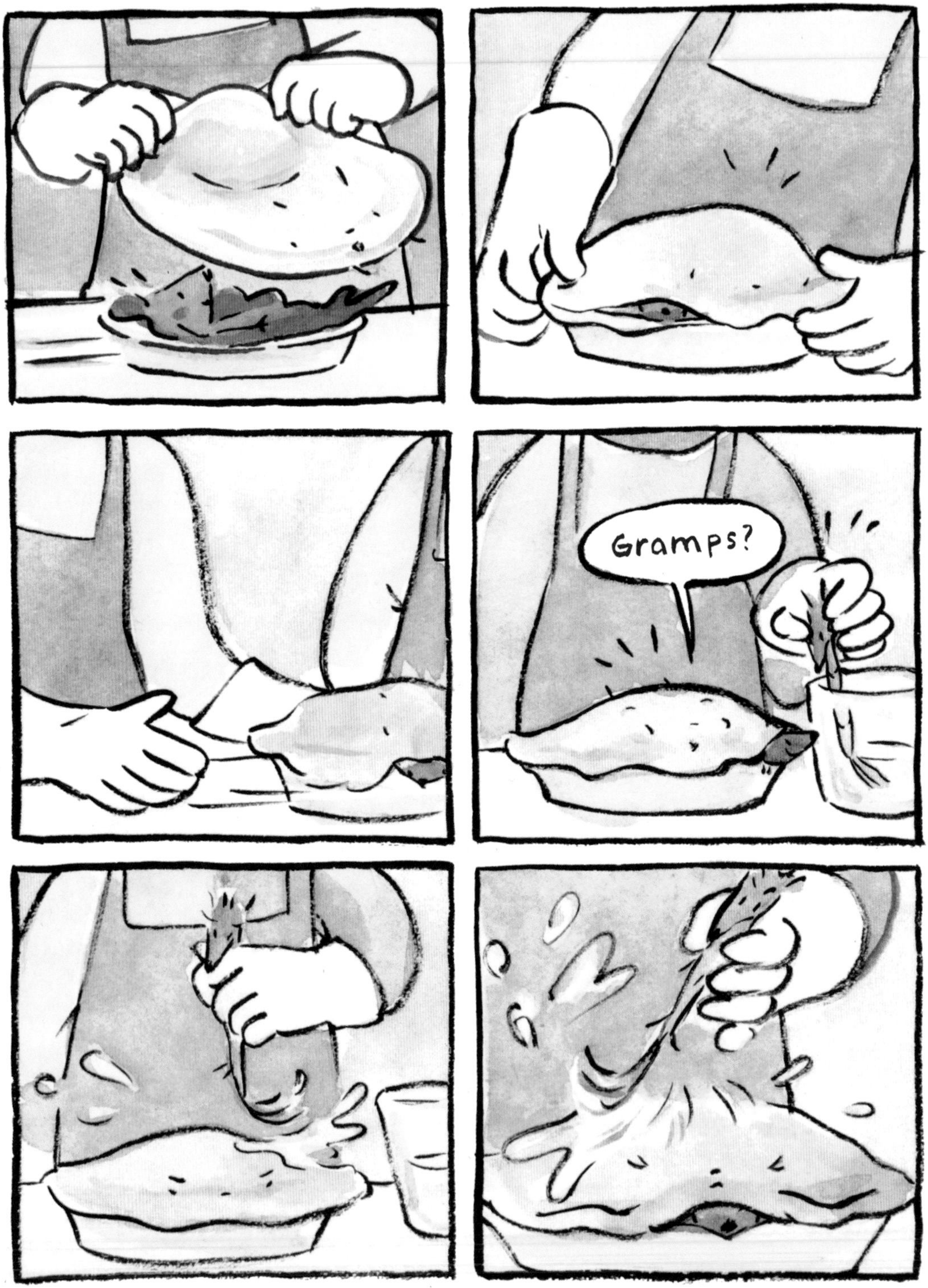
Gramps?

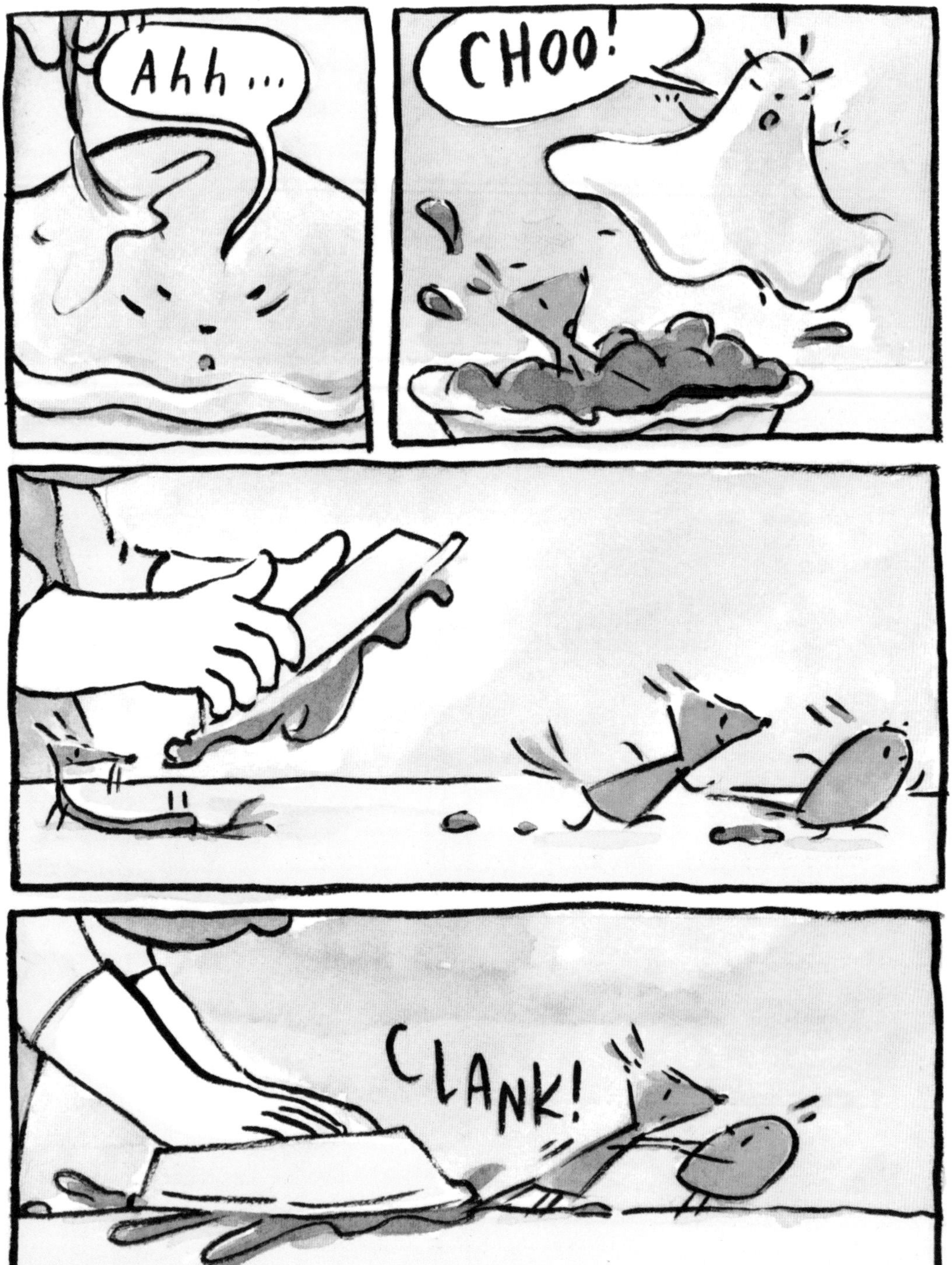
Ahh...
CHOO!
CLANK!

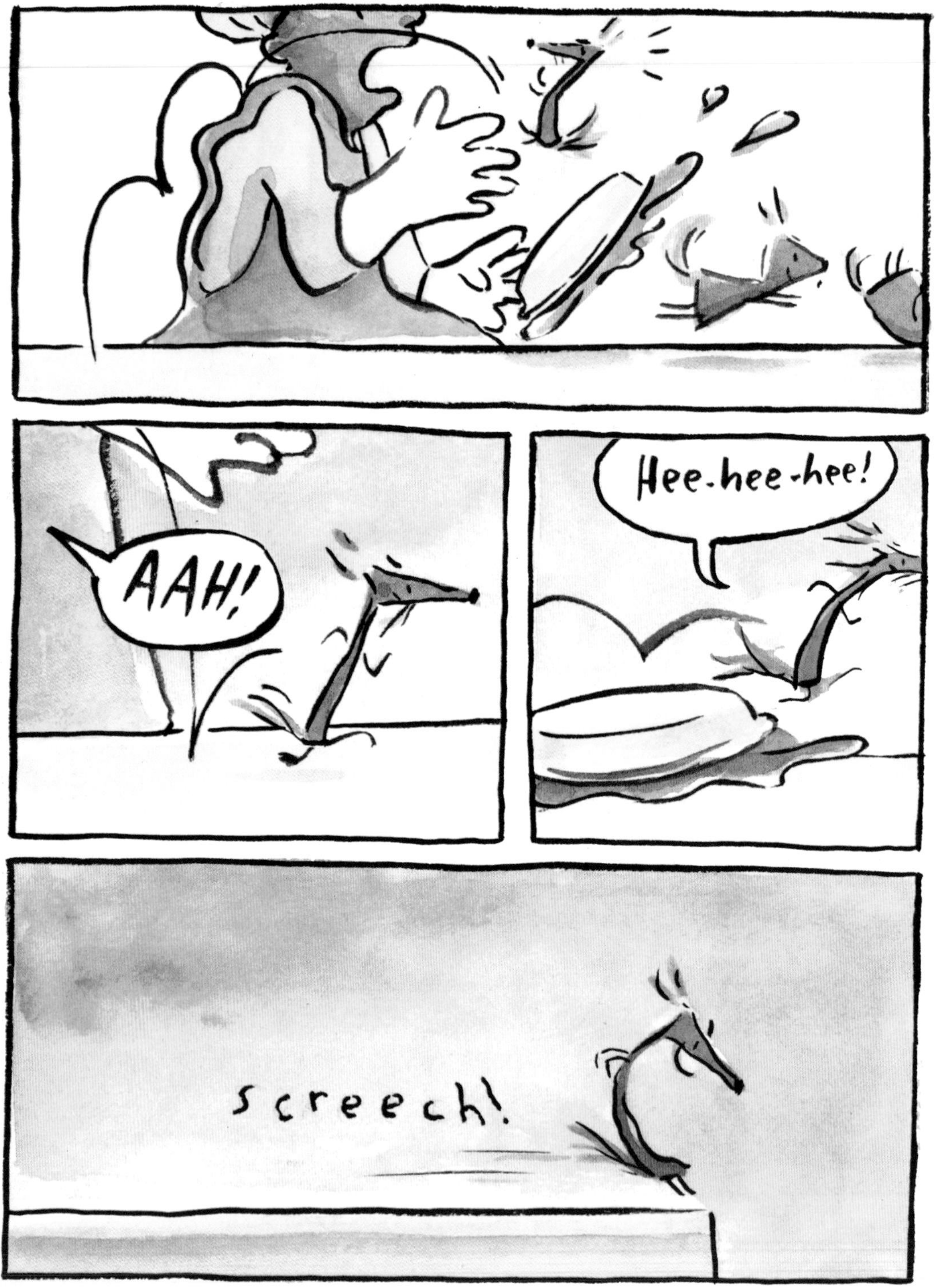
AAH!
Hee-hee-hee!
screech!

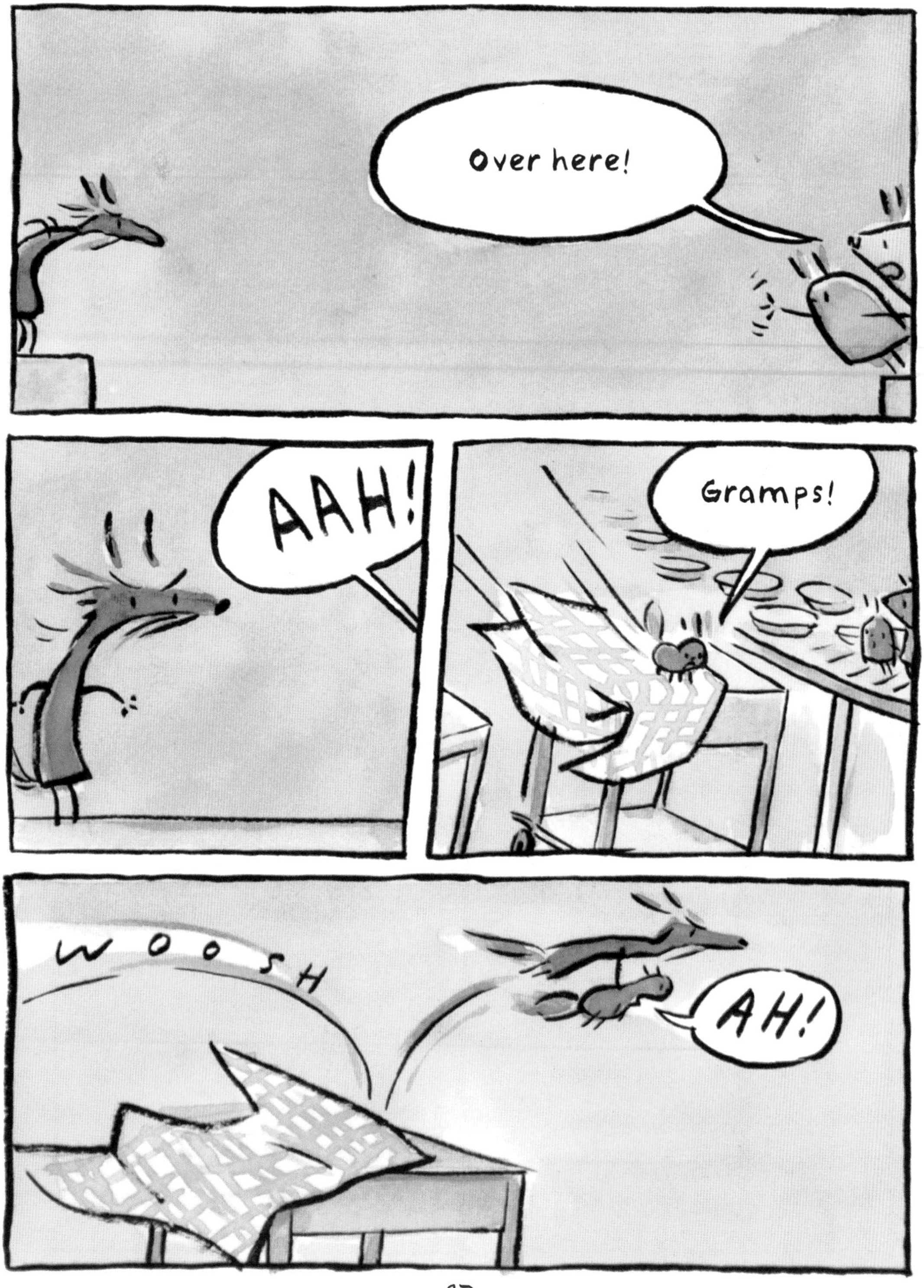
Over here!
AAH!
Gramps!
WOOSH
AH!

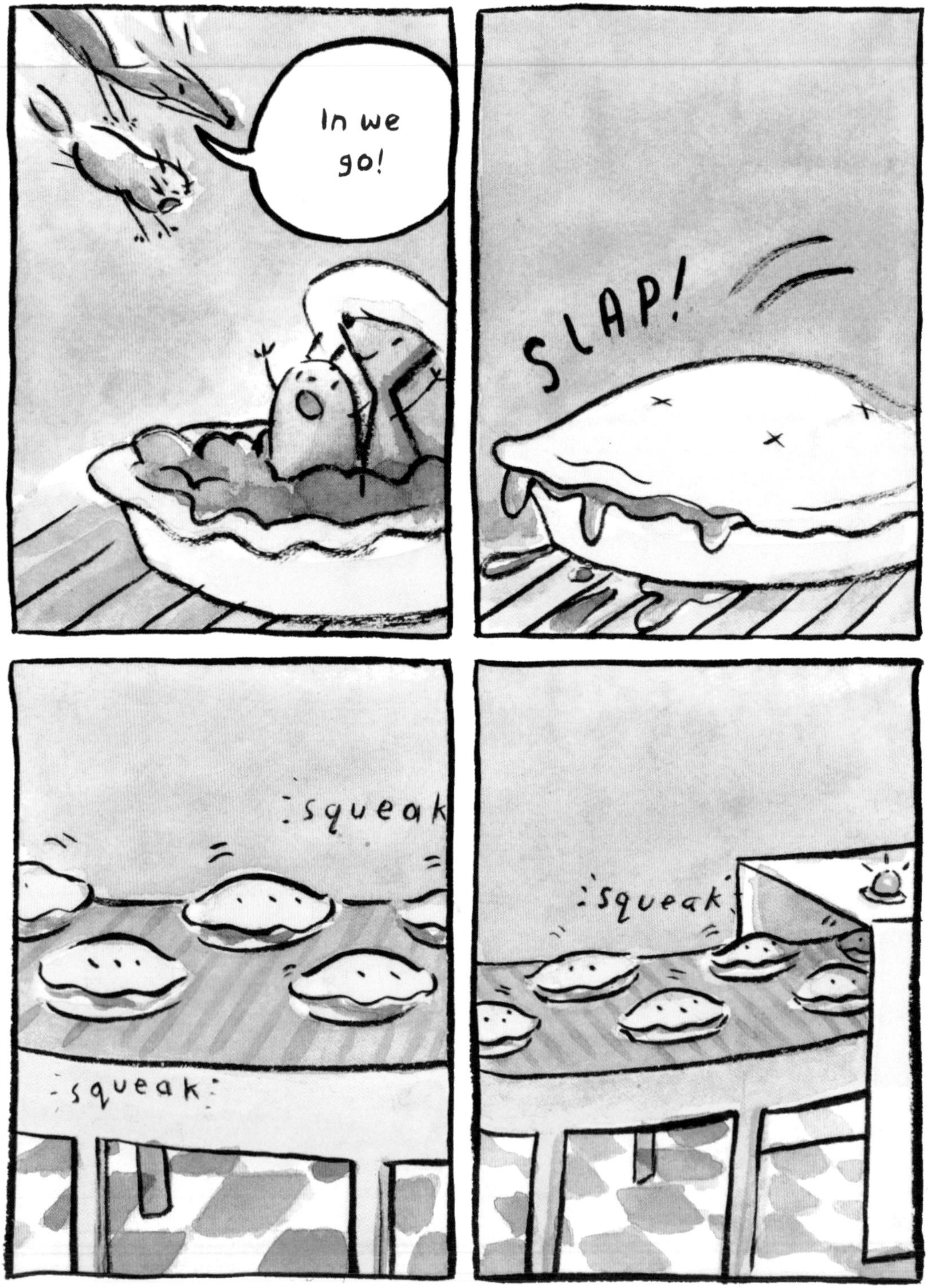
In we go!
SLAP!
squeak
squeak
squeak

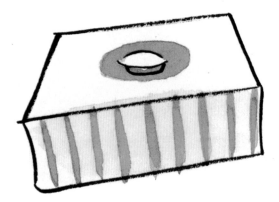

Chapter 8

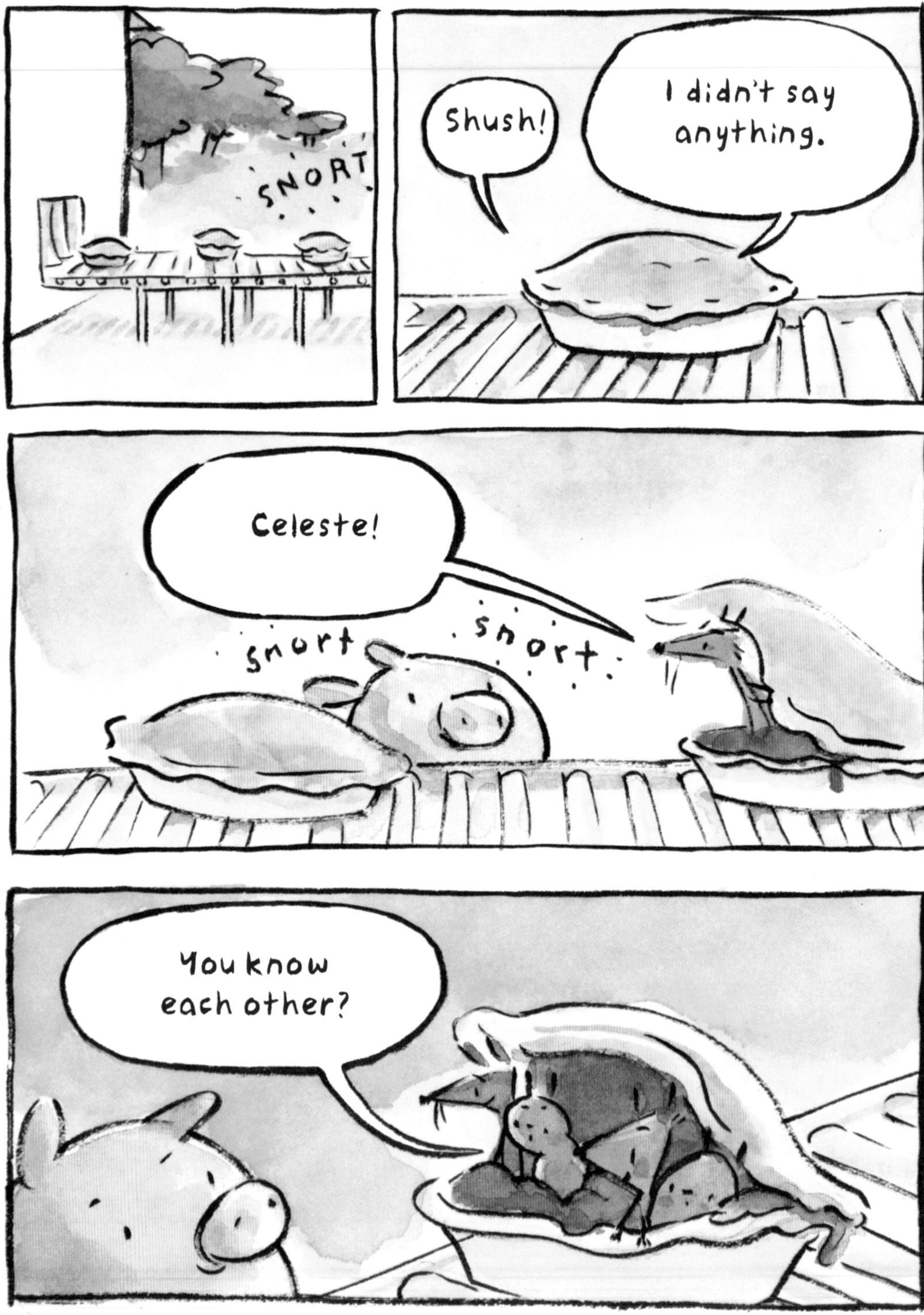
SNORT
Shush!
I didn't say anything.
Celeste!
snort
snort
You know each other?

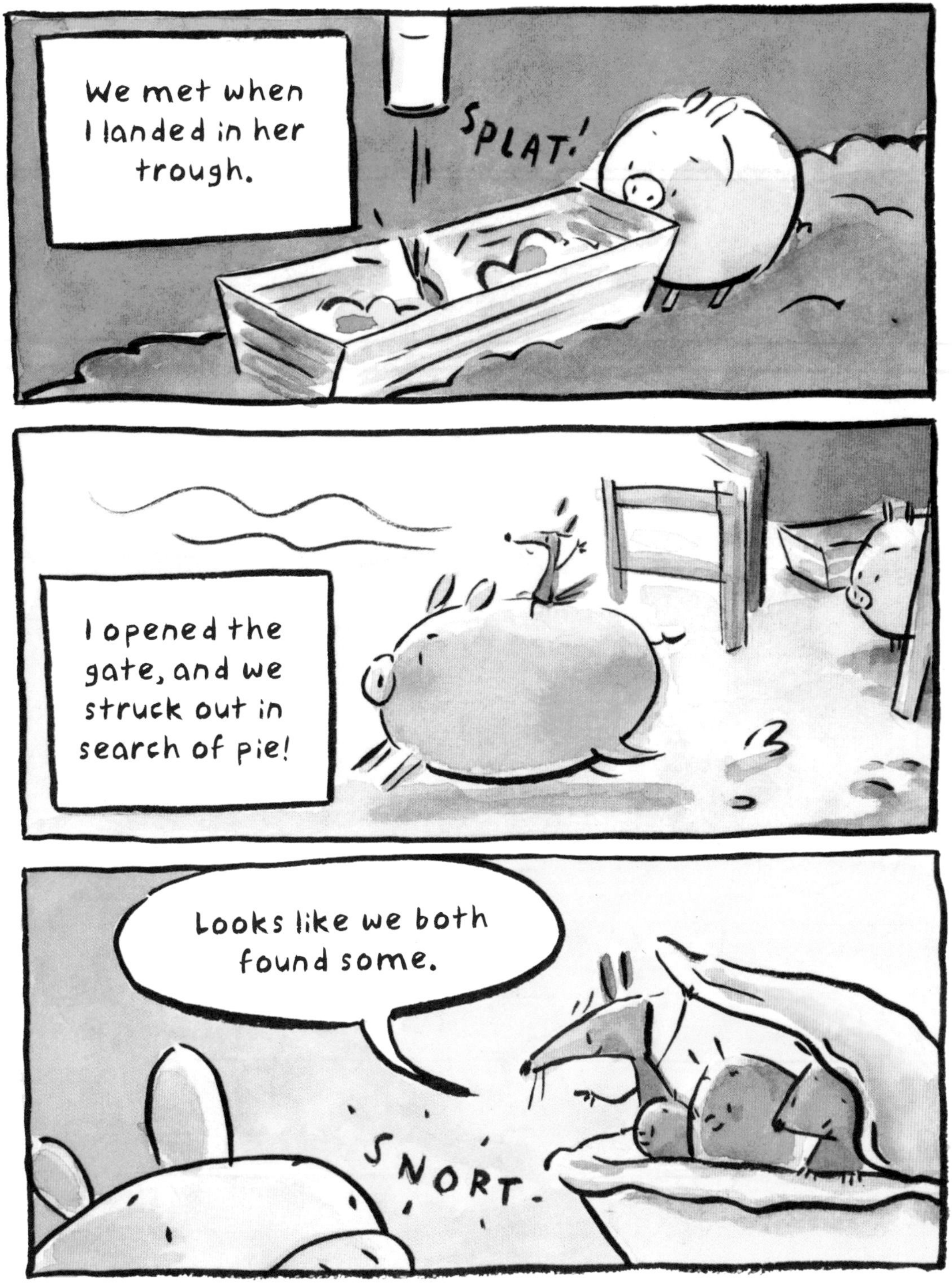

We met when I landed in her trough.
SPLAT!
I opened the gate, and we struck out in search of pie!
Looks like we both found some.
SNORT.

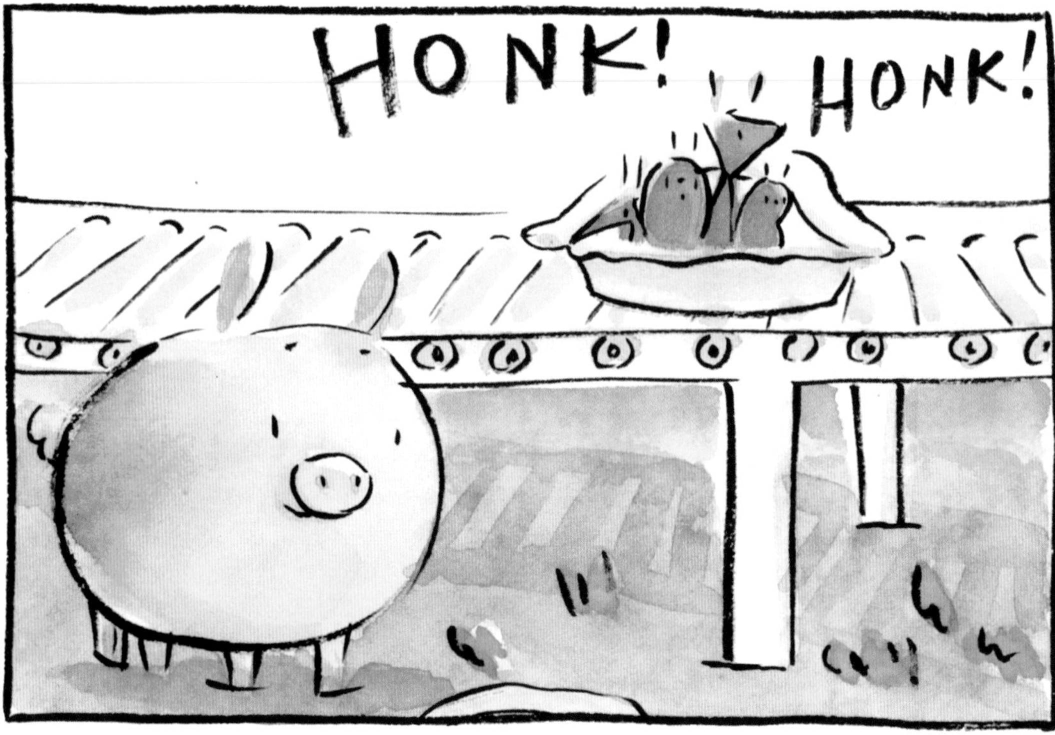
HONK! HONK!

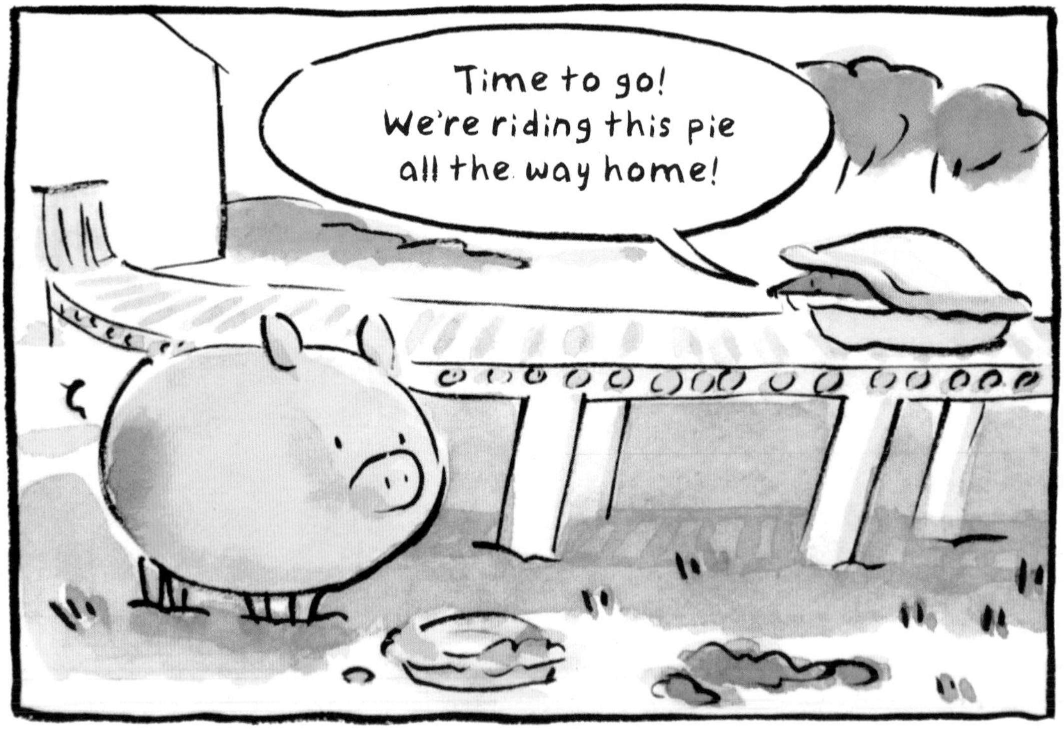
Time to go!
We're riding this pie all the way home!

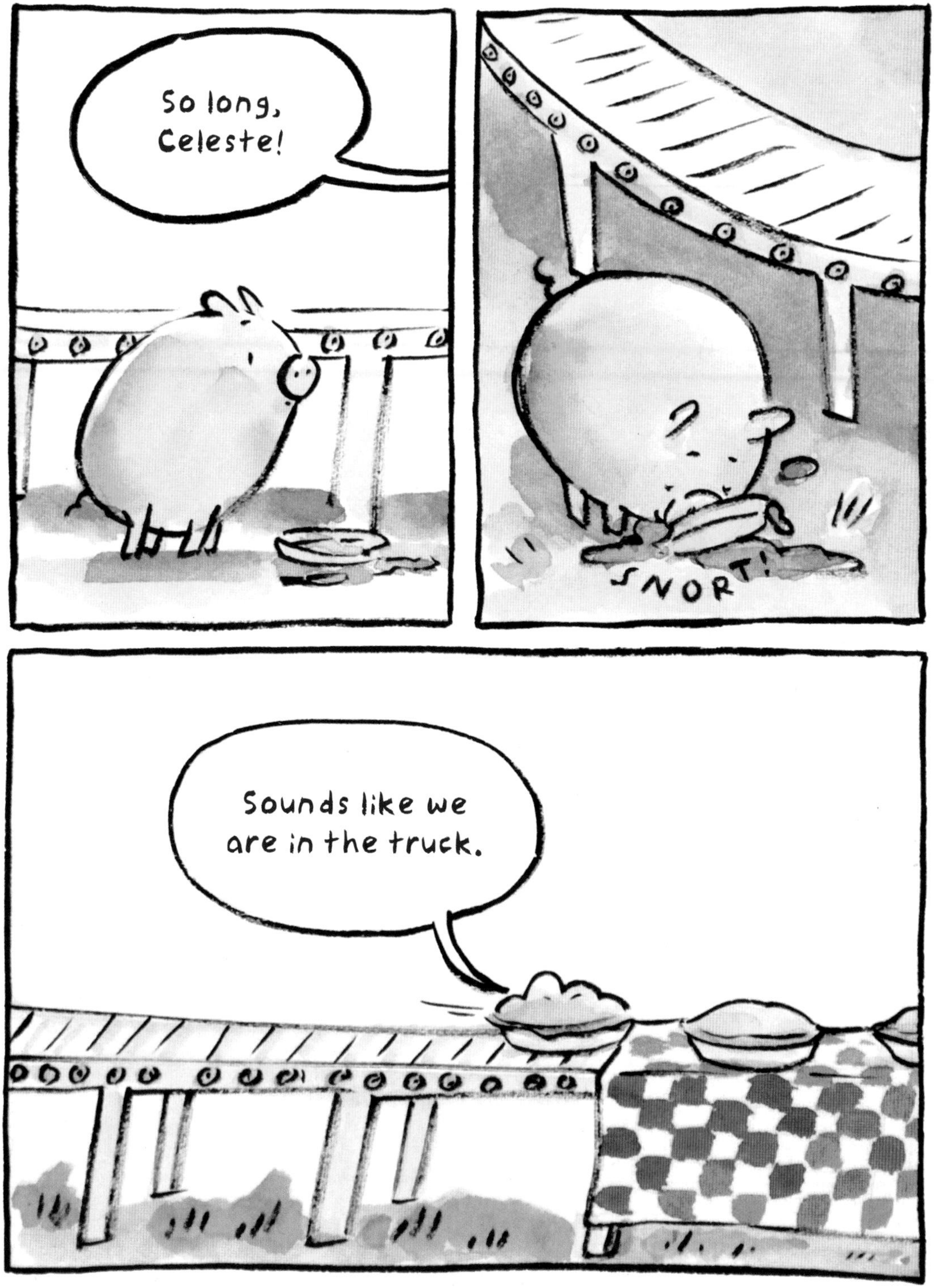
So long, Celeste!
SNORT!
Sounds like we are in the truck.

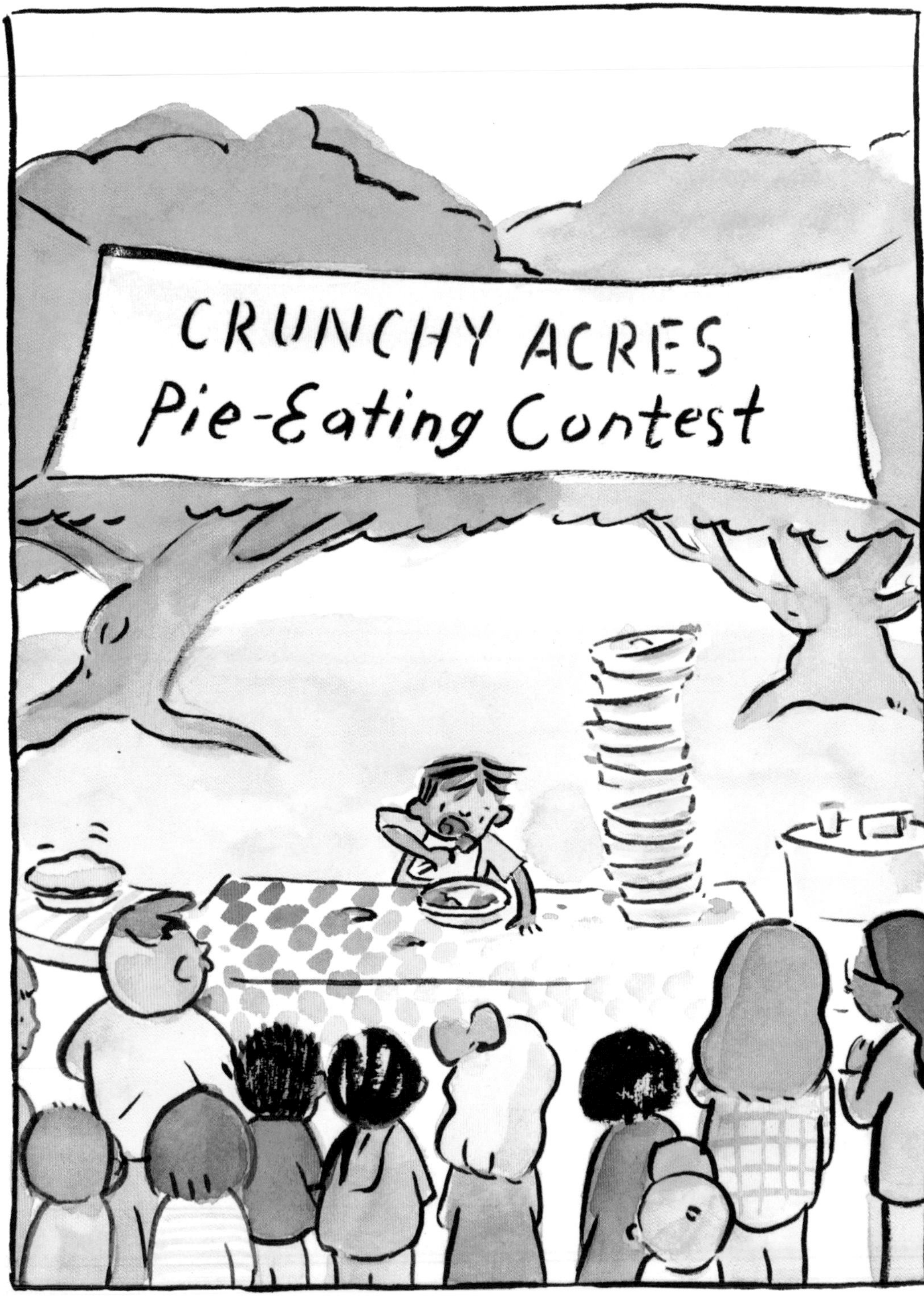
CRUNCHY ACRES
Pie-Eating Contest

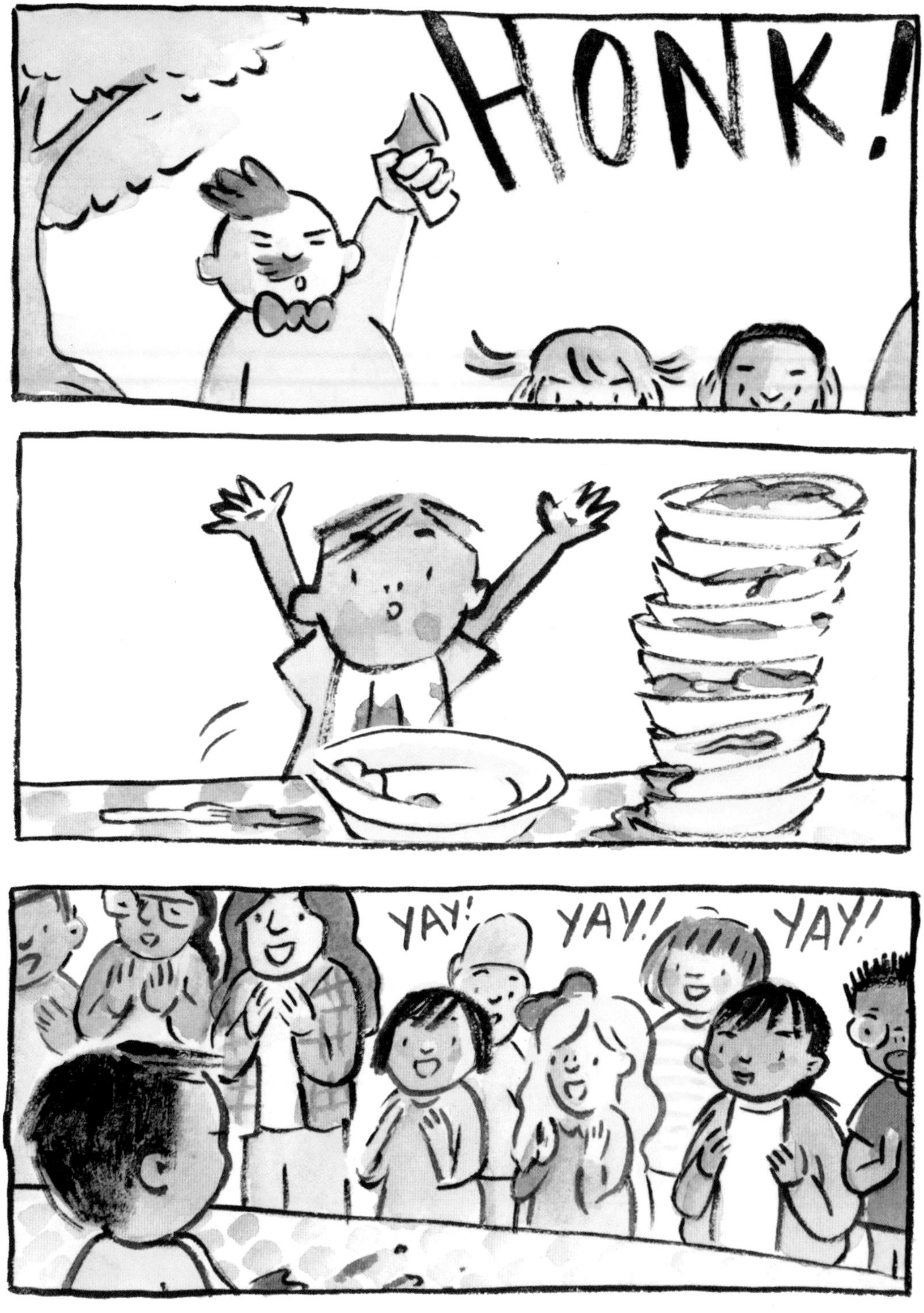
HONK!
YAY!
YAY!
YAY!

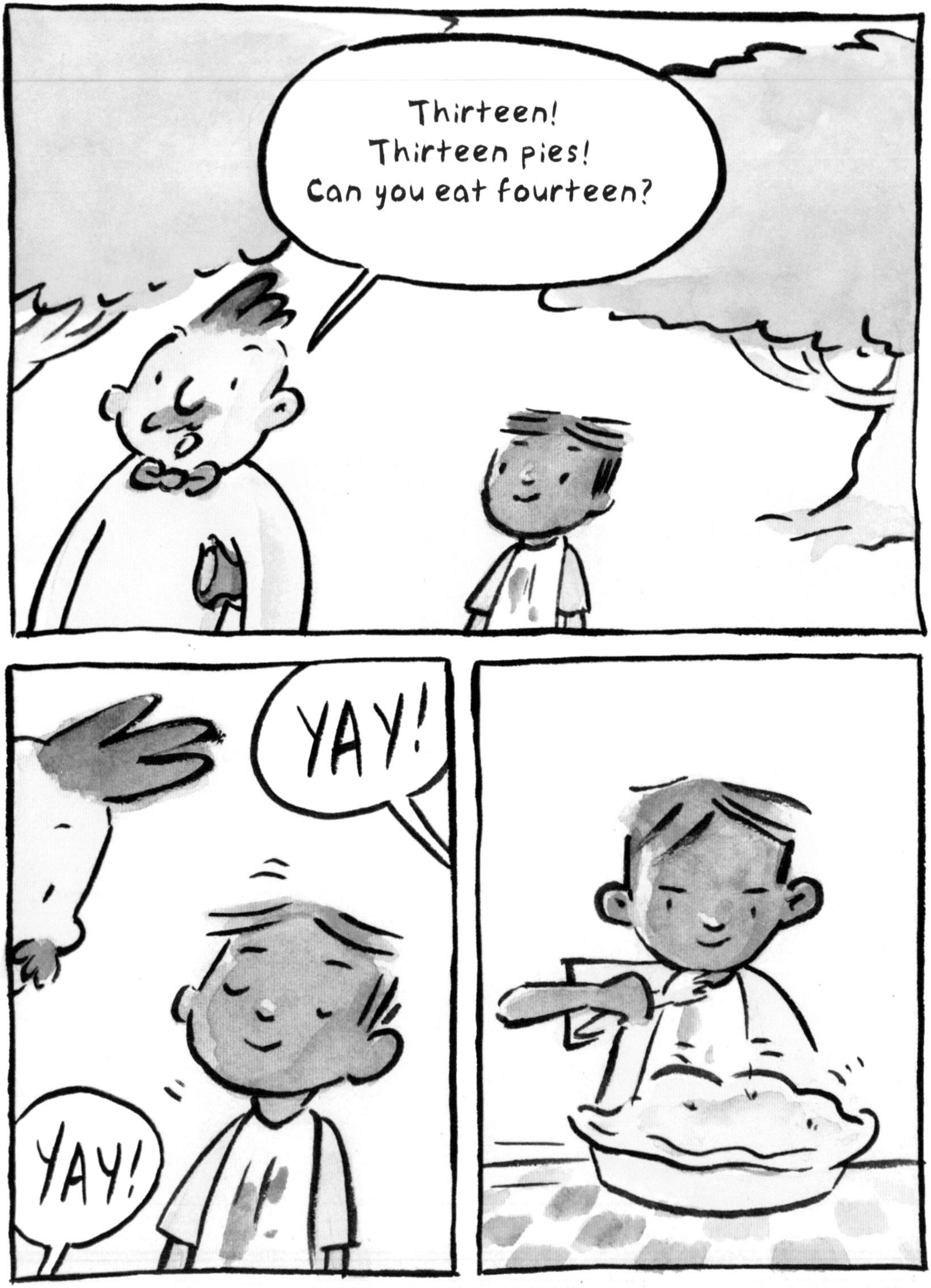

Thirteen! Thirteen pies! Can you eat fourteen?
YAY!
YAY!

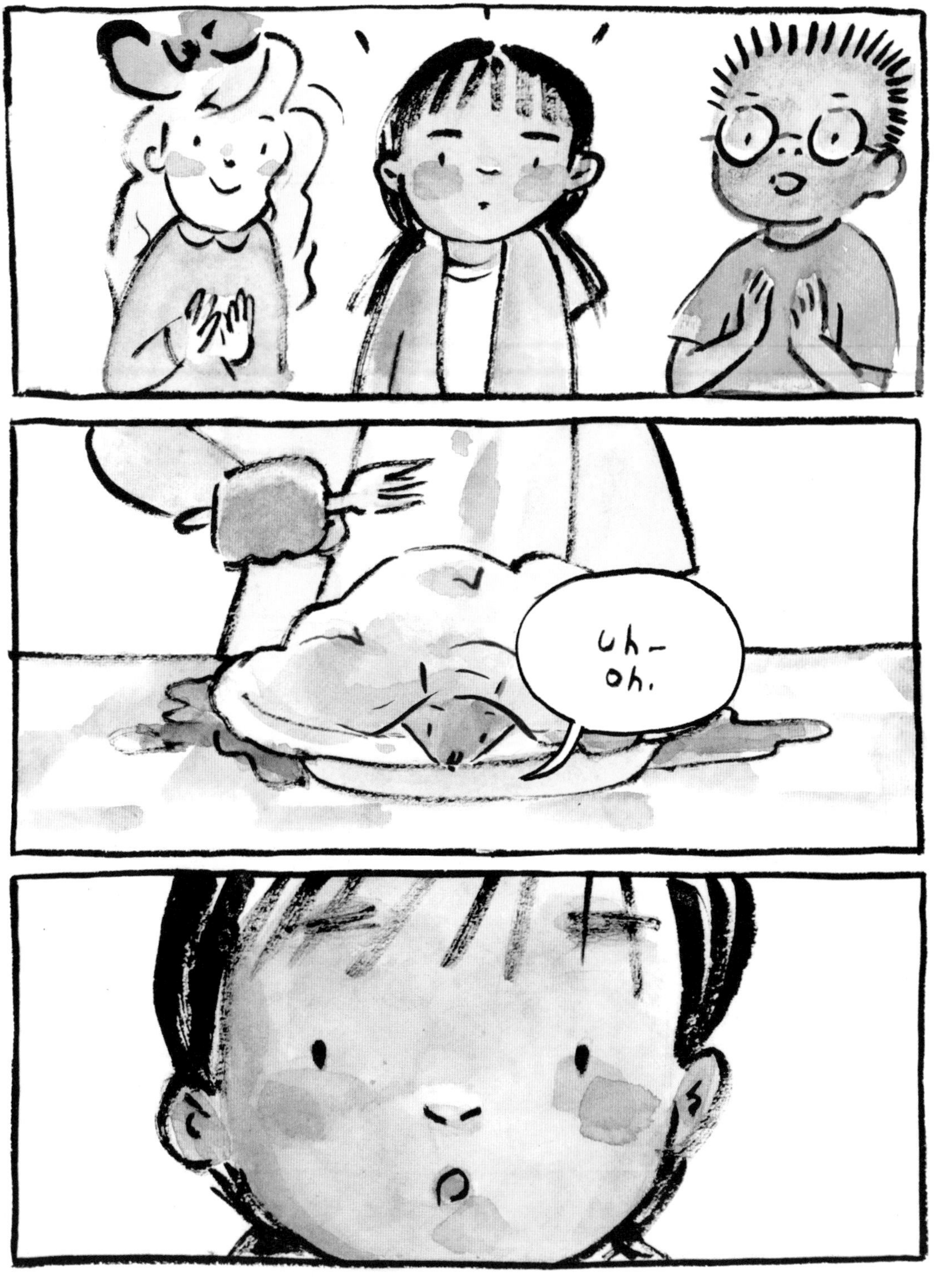
uh-
oh.

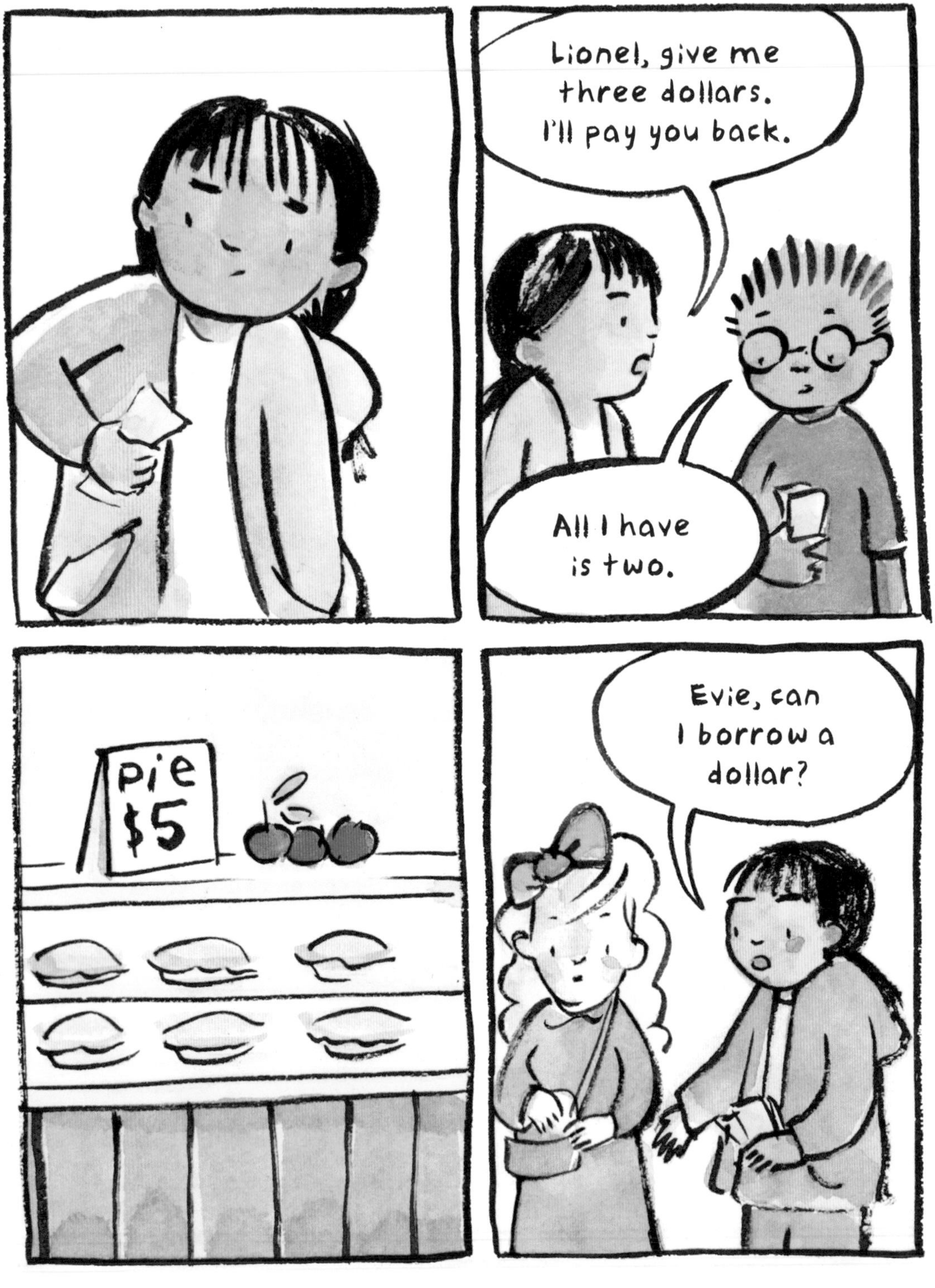
Lionel, give me three dollars. I'll pay you back.
All I have is two.
pie $5
Evie, can I borrow a dollar?

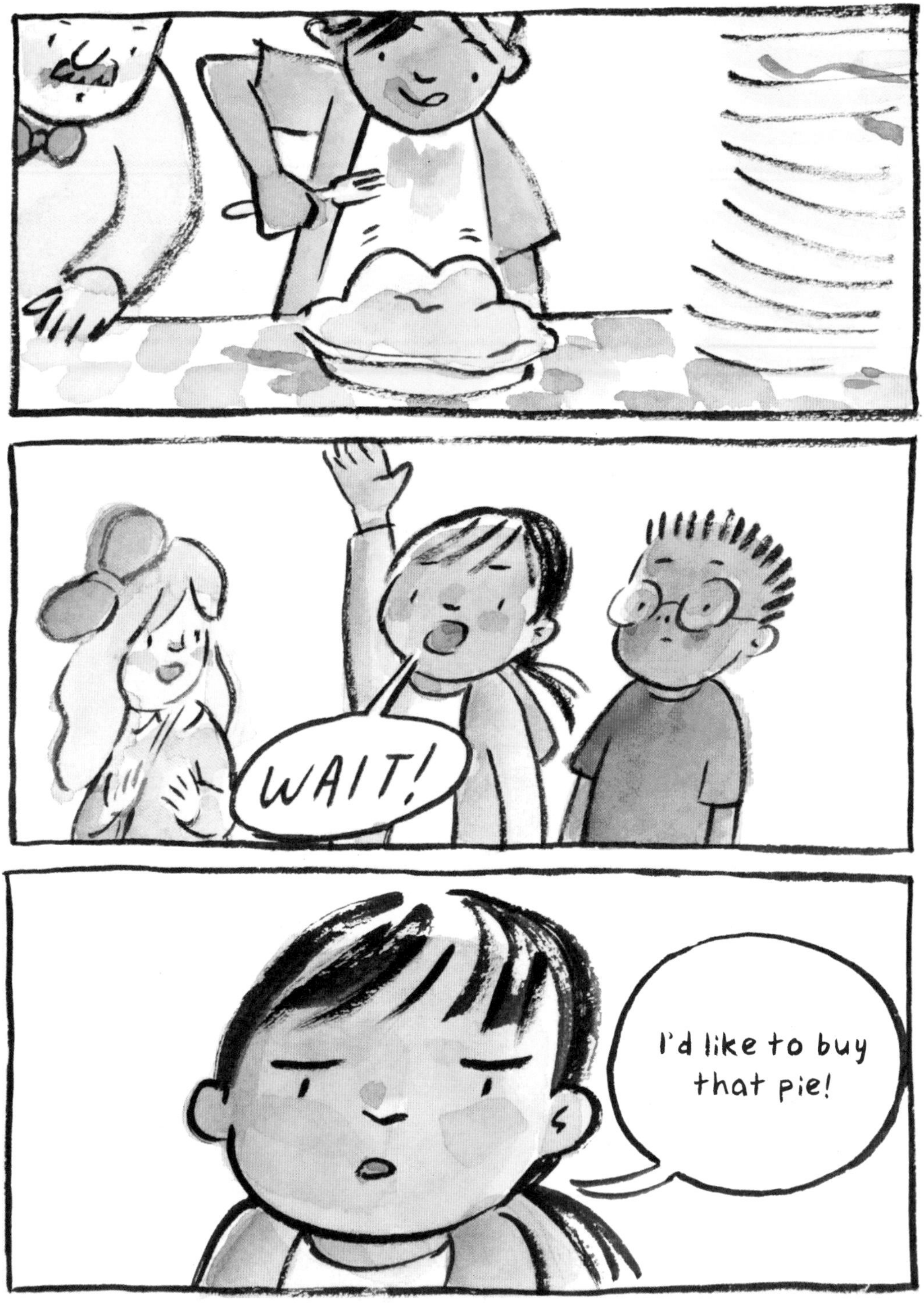
WAIT!
I'd like to buy that pie!

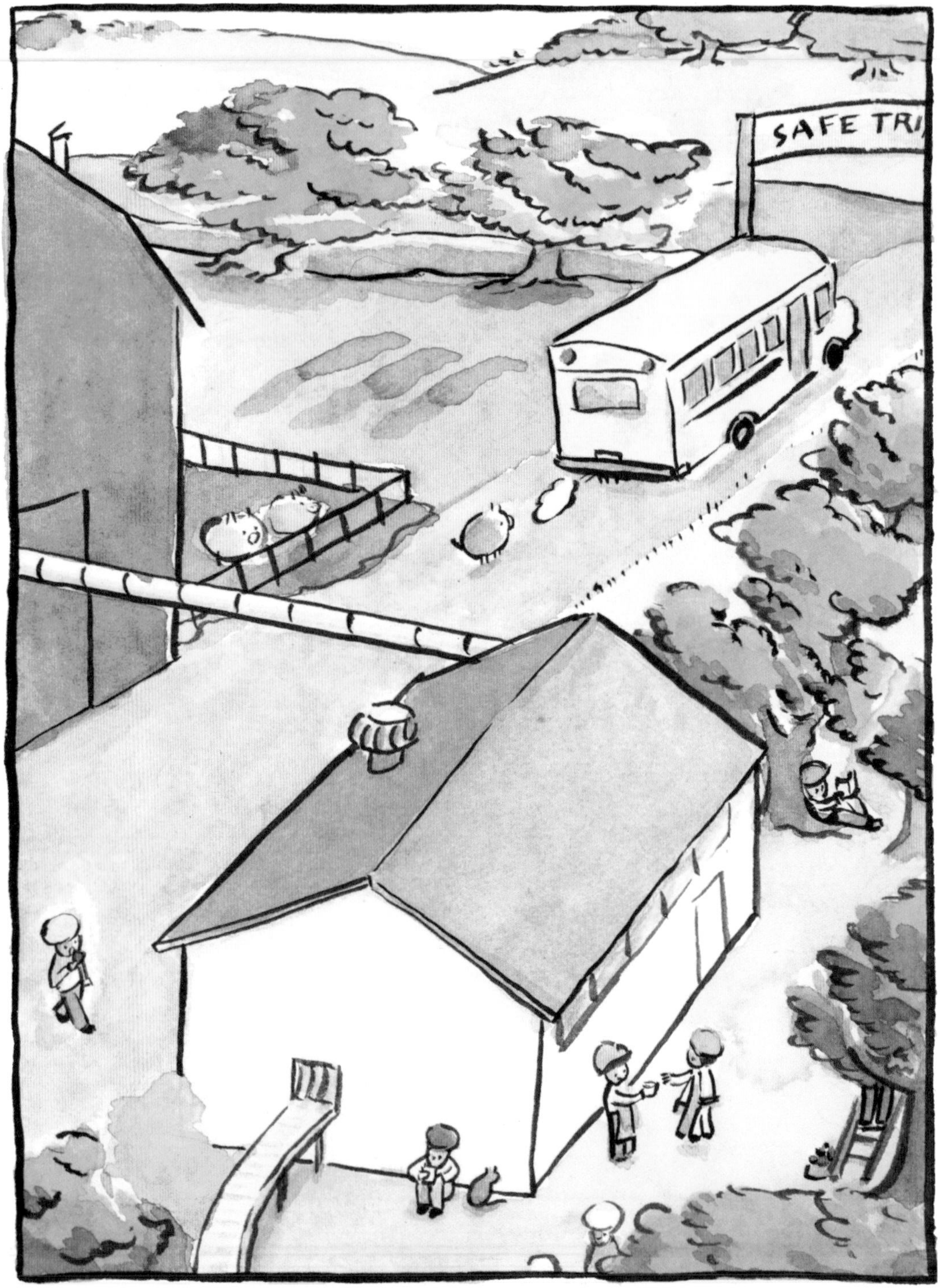
SAFE TRI

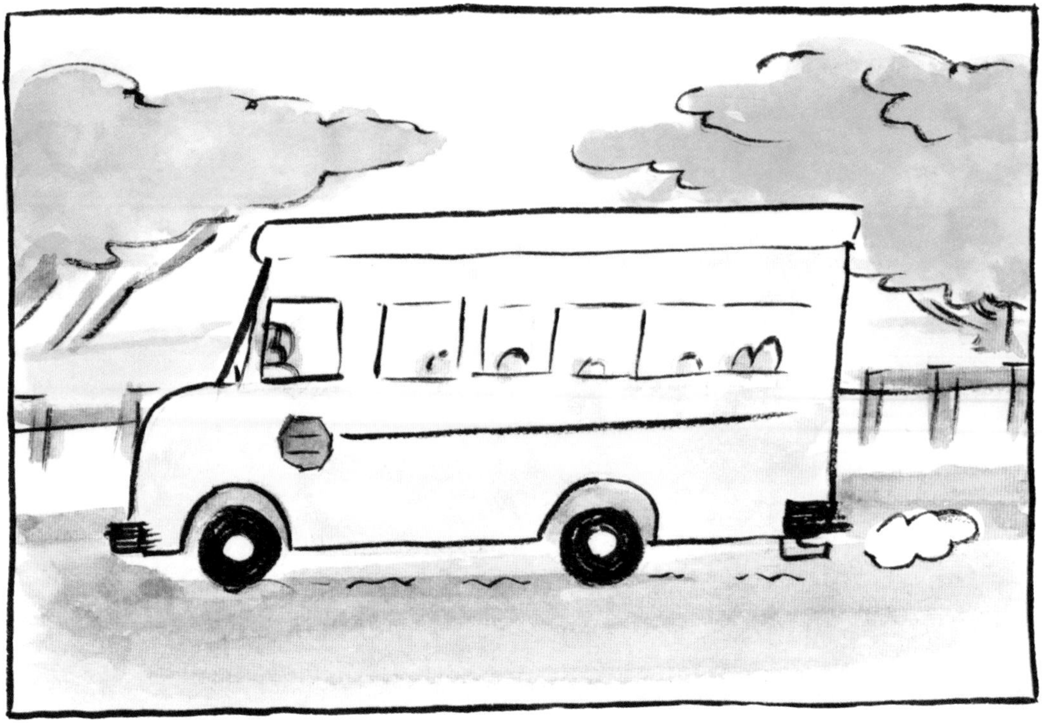

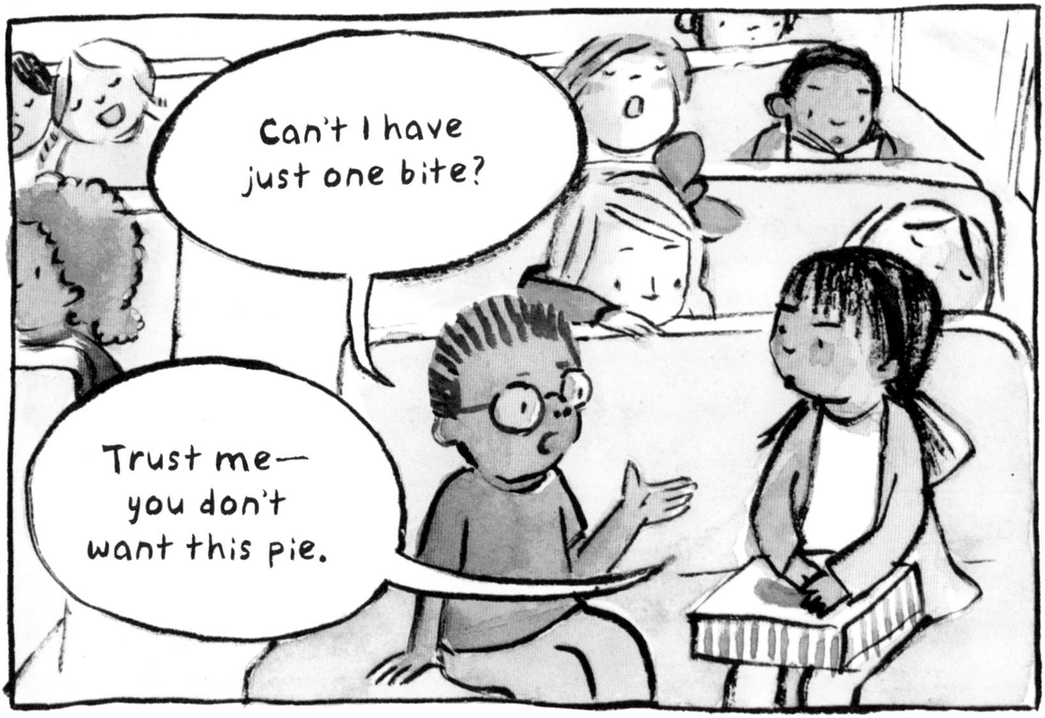
Can't I have just one bite?
Trust me— you don't want this pie.

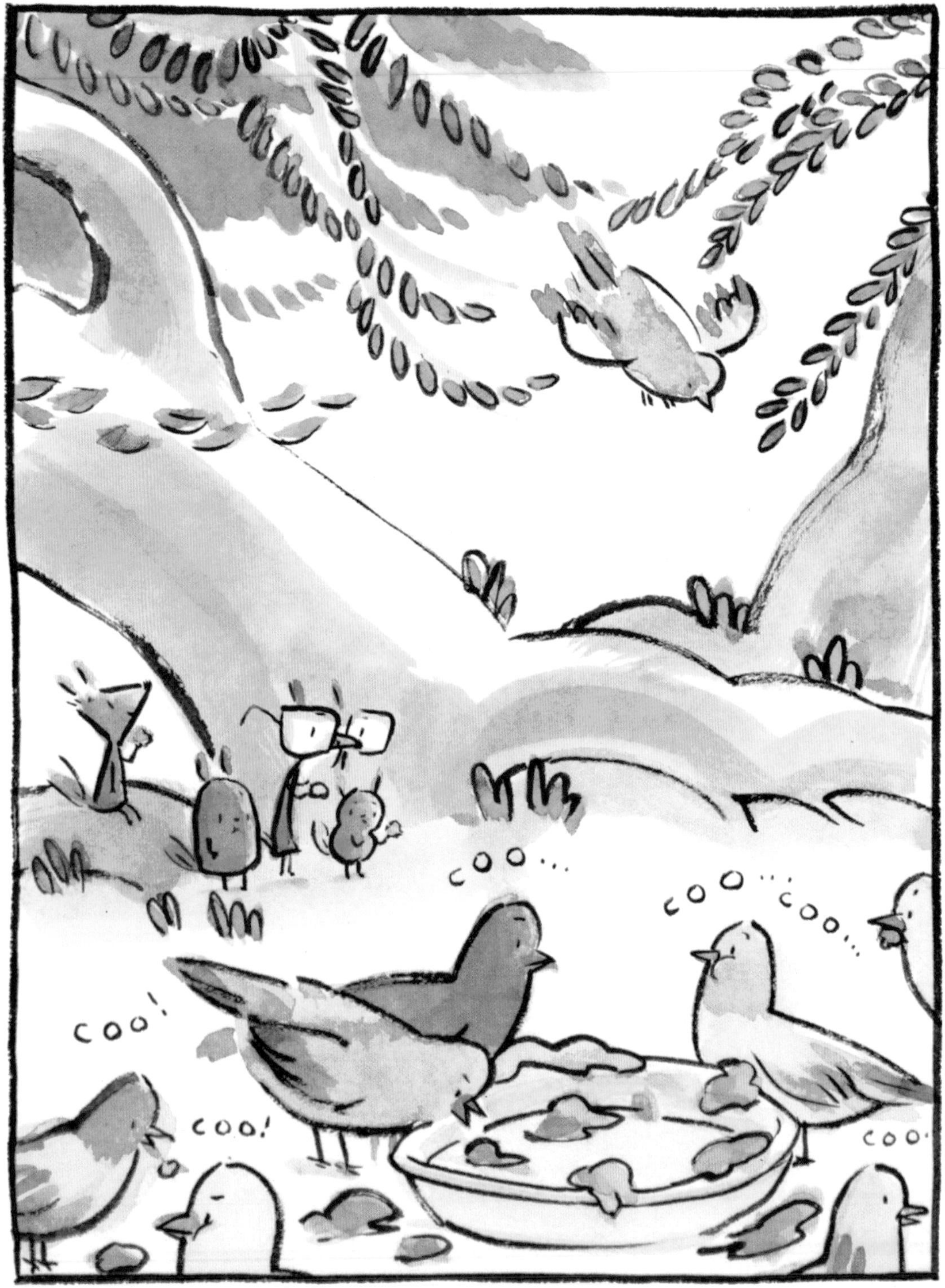
COO...
COO...
COO...
COO!
COO!
COO.

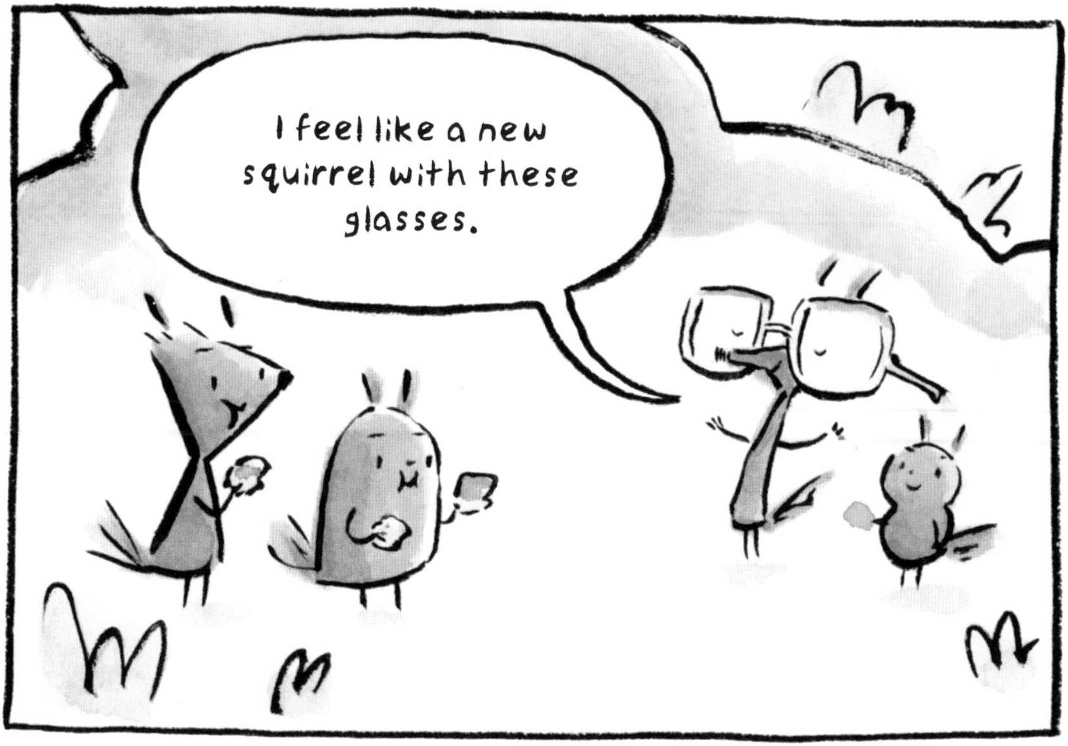
I feel like a new squirrel with these glasses.

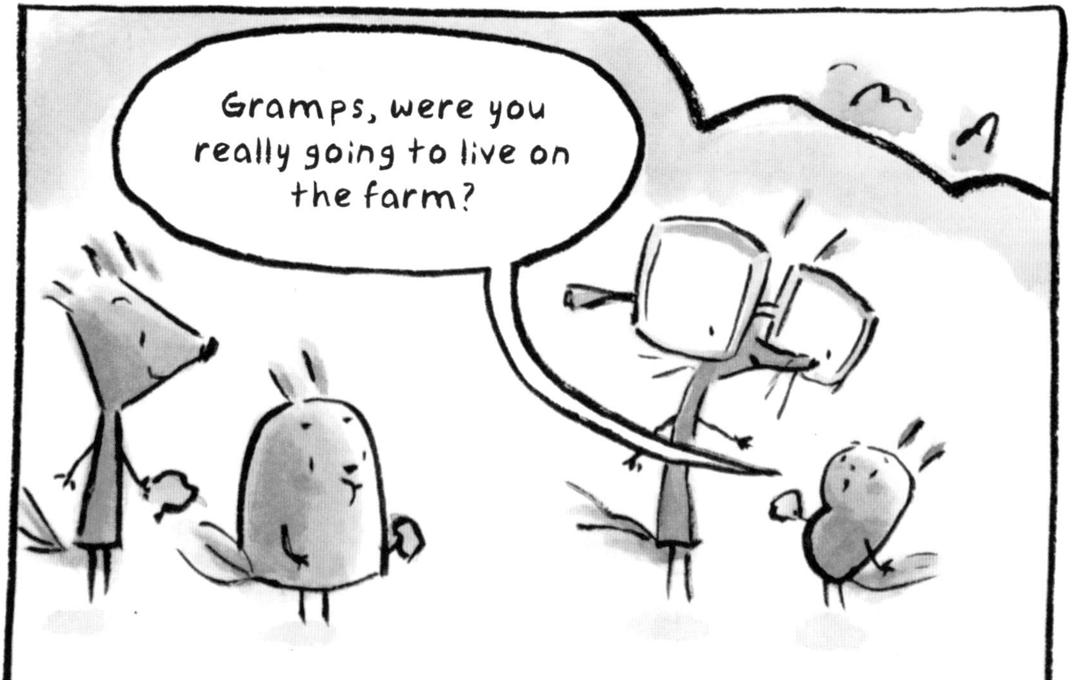
Gramps, were you really going to live on the farm?

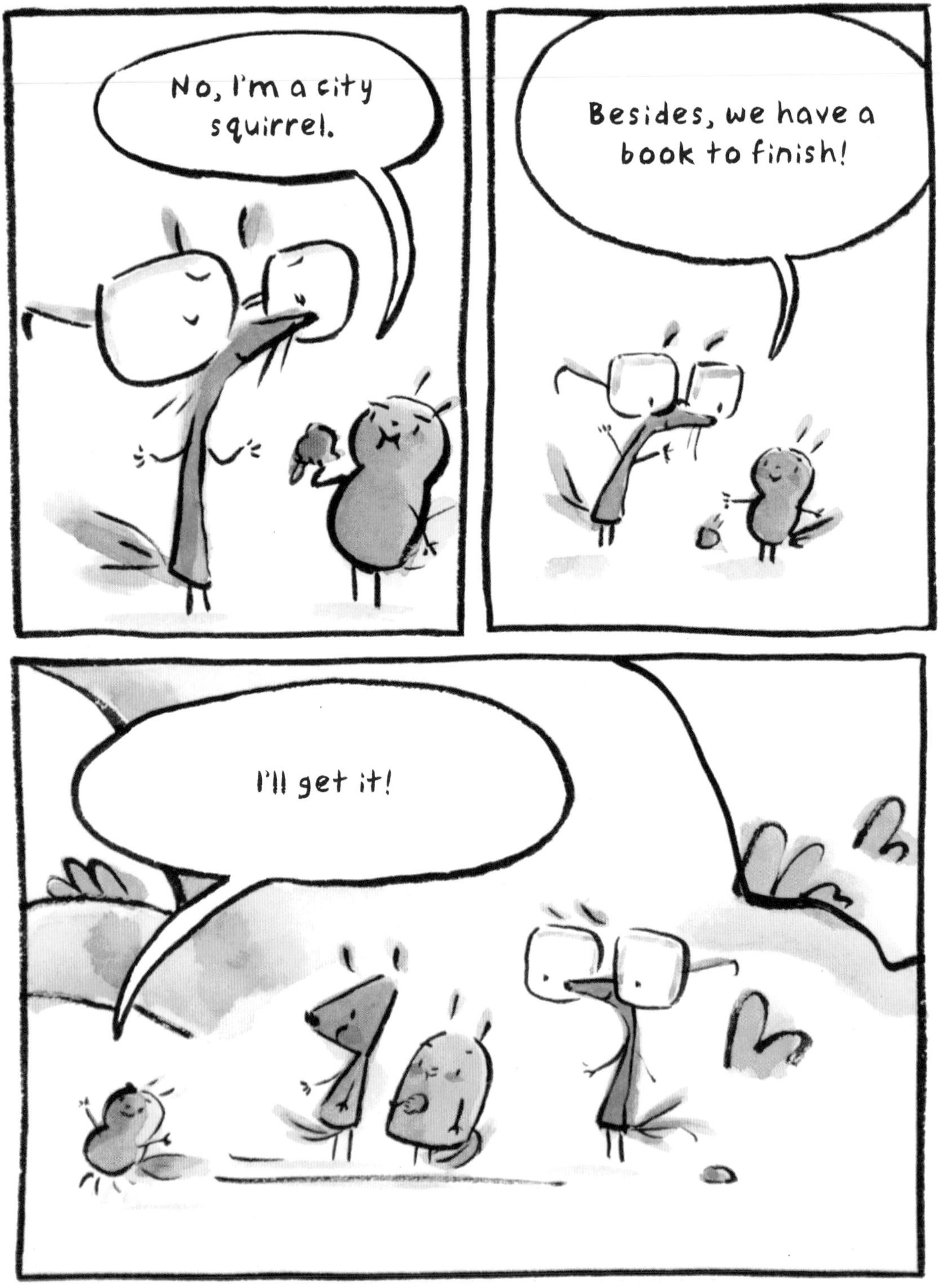
No, I'm a city squirrel.
Besides, we have a book to finish!
I'll get it!

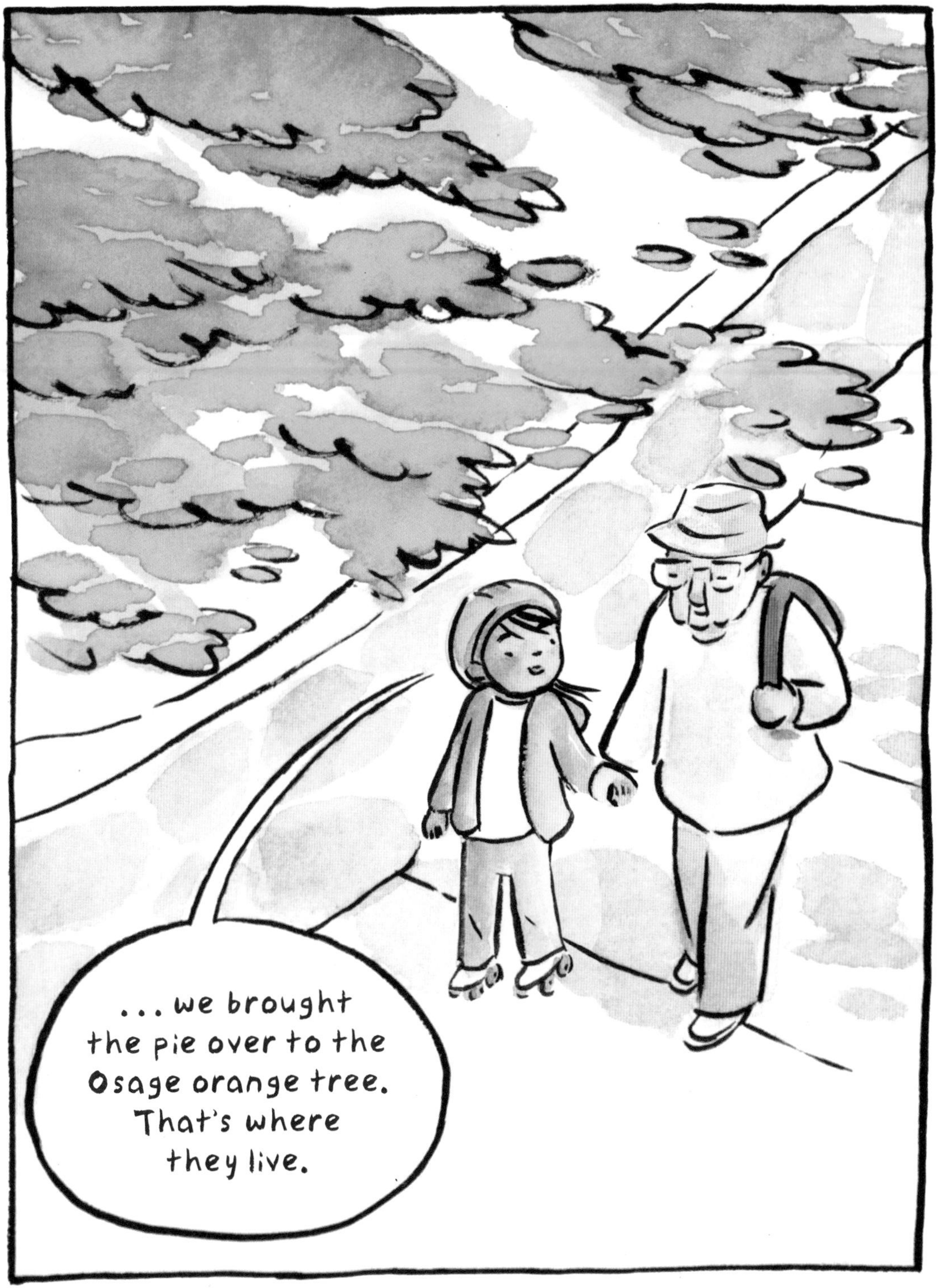
...we brought the pie over to the Osage orange tree. That's where they live.

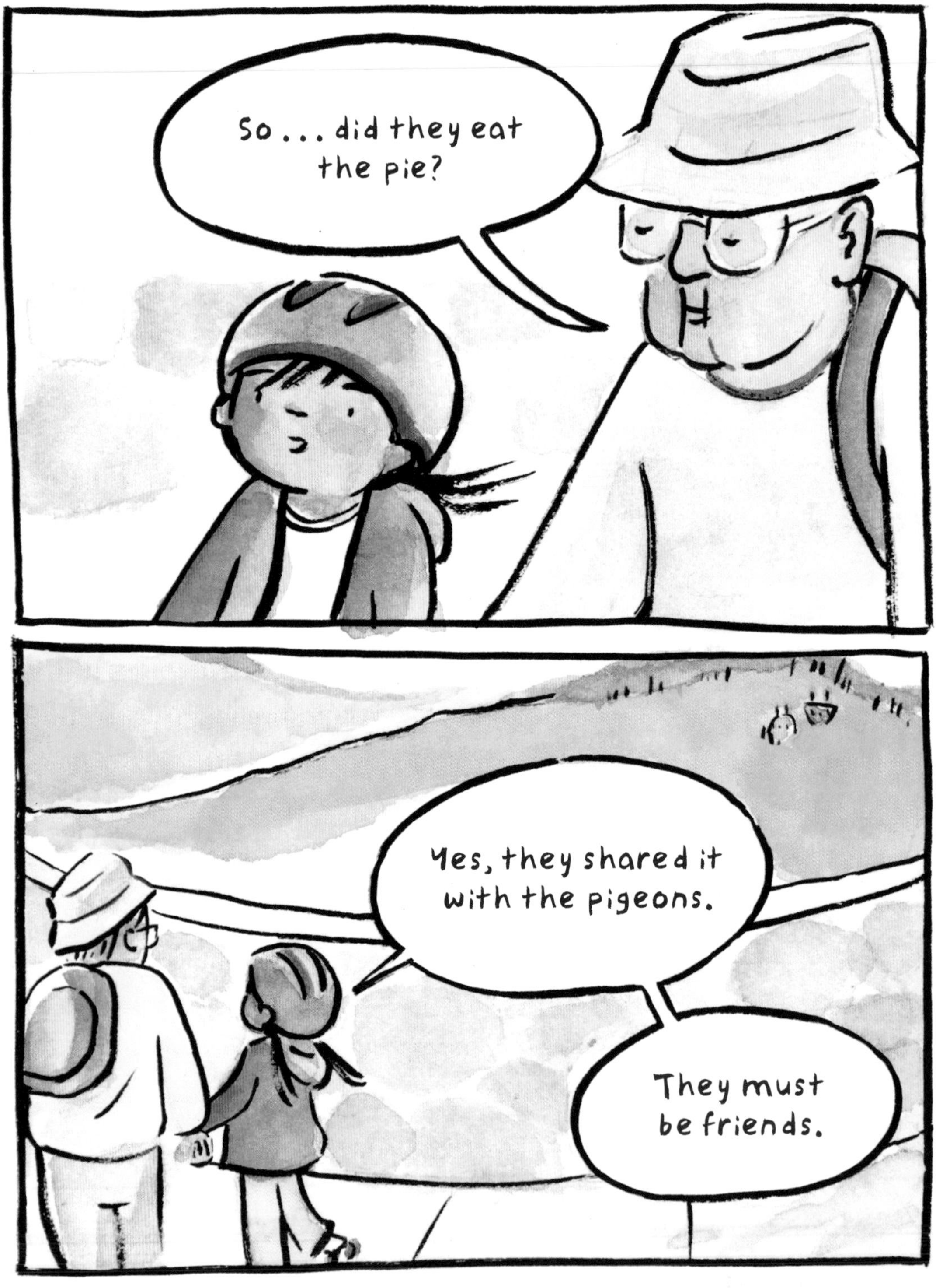
So . . . did they eat the pie?
Yes, they shared it with the pigeons.
They must be friends.

Acknowledgments

Thank you to Whitney Leopard, Patrick Crotty, Gina Gagliano, and Nicole Valdez at Random House Graphic and Erica Rand Silverman at Stimola Literary Studio.

The Norma and Belly books were inspired by the squirrels in Brooklyn's Fort Greene Park.

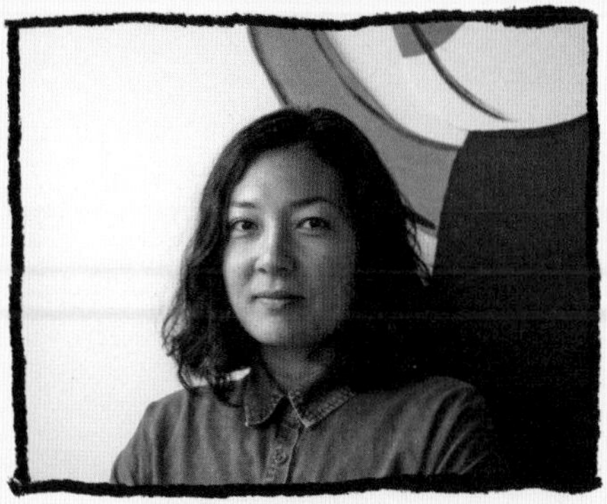

Mika Song is the author-illustrator of the picture books *Tea with Oliver* and the follow-up *Picnic with Oliver* and has illustrated several titles, including *A Friend for Henry* by Jenn Bailey, winner of a Schneider Family Book Award Honor, and *Hoʻonani: Hula Warrior* by Heather Gale. Norma and Belly is her first graphic novel series. Her books are inspired by sweetly funny outsiders.

She grew up in Manila and Honolulu and moved to New York City to attend Pratt Institute. Before picture books, she held many jobs, most successfully as an animator of children's educational content. Soon after making the leap, she received the Portfolio Award at the Society of Children's Book Writers and Illustrators Winter Conference in NYC.

She lives in New York City with her husband and daughter. She has always loved making comics.

@mikasongdraws
mikasongdraws.com